Unforgiving

Unforgiving

Patricia Haley

URBAN CHRISTIAN

www.urbanchristianonline.com

Urban Books, LLC
97 N18th Street
Wyandanch, NY 11798

ISBN 13: 978-1-60162-695-0
ISBN 10: 1-60162-695-9

First Trade Paperback Printing April 2015
Printed in the United States of America

10 9 8 7 6 5 4 3 2 1

Distributed by Kensington Publishing Corp.
Submit orders to:
Customer Service
400 Hahn Road
Westminster, MD 21157-4627
Phone: 1-800-733-3000
Fax: 1-800-659-2436

Unforgiving

by

Patricia Haley

Praise for #1 *Essence*® National Bestselling

Author Patricia Haley
and Her Inspirational Novels

"A must read . . . highly recommend this book . . . promise you will not be disappointed."
— *Urban Christian Fiction*
Today on Destined

"Haley engages one with subtle intrigue and touches of comedy. . . . An intriguing read with a subtle inspirational message woven into the story . . . Riveting."
— *Faygo's Report*

"Haley has a gold mine with this series. If I was a hat wearer, it would definitely be off to her. All I can say to her right now is, 'You go, girl!'"
— *Member of LVAAABC Book Club*

"Haley showcases how God's word can be misinterpreted with greed, lust, and selfishness."
— *RAWSISTAZ*™ *on* Chosen

"Haley shared how God does choose the most unlikely person for ministry when we think there is no way. . . . A must read . . . Highly recommended."
—*APOOO Book Club*

"Phenomenal . . . Haley did an outstanding job on each person's outlook and how, without forgiveness, no problem can truly be solved."
— *Urban Reviews*

Praise

"Haley has hit the mark yet again! I couldn't put this book down—the characters are believable and compelling."

—*Maurice M. Gray, Jr., author of*
All Things Work Together

"The story grabs the reader from the beginning, drawing you in . . . and keeping you on the edge of your seat as the plot takes unexpected twists and turns."

—*RT Book Reviews on*
Let Sleeping Dogs Lie

"The perfect blend of faith and romance."

—*Gospel Book Review*

"Haley's writing and visualization skills are to be reckoned with. . . . This story is full-bodied. . . . Great prose, excellent execution!"

—*RAWSISTAZ™ on* Still Waters

"A deeply moving novel. The characters and the story line remind us that forgiveness and unconditional love are crucial to any relationship."

—*Good Girl Book Club*

"*No Regrets* offered me a different way, a healthier way based in faith and hope, to look at trying situations."

—*Montgomery Newspapers*

Unforgiving **is also available as an eBook**

Also by **Patricia Haley**

Dedication

Unforgiving is dedicated to my special family.

No matter how vast and incredible our connections are, God has uniquely placed each of us in a specific family for a special purpose. Honestly, I won the grand prize when it comes to the family into which I was born and to the husband I married. There's no amount of money on earth that could ever replace a second with any of you. You have supported, prayed for, protected, and loved me unconditionally beyond imagination. My life is better having been connected to each of you. My soul is happy. I am blessed and count it all joy. Because of you, I have felt the most incredible love of a lifetime.
I thank God for each of you.

Soul mate and best friend Jeffrey Warnell Glass
Mother Fannie Haley Rome
In memory of my Father Fred Luck Haley
Big brother Rev. Frederick Lane Haley
In memory of my incredible and much-loved
baby brother Erick Lewis Haley
And youngest baby brother, Freddy Deon Haley

"This is how my heavenly Father will treat each of you
unless you forgive your brother or sister
from your heart."

Matthew 18:35 (NIV)

Chapter 1

How much drama and failure could one family handle before crumbling? It was a valid question for Don Mitchell, the man currently at the helm of the renowned DMI family business. He leaned against the windowsill as his back unintentionally blocked the illuminating sunshine attempting to burst into his office. He felt the warmth and yearned to soak it in, but the clutches of DMI wouldn't allow him or any other Mitchell to absorb the light fully. Plagued with tragedy, bad decisions, and an unwillingness to forgive hurts of the past, the people he loved the most were perpetually wading in a pit of despair. He folded his arms, trying to let God's grace purge him of the rising unrest in his spirit. For the first time in a long while he was confused about how to proceed.

He wrestled with his thoughts for the better part of an hour before accepting his reality. He turned to face the window, and the sunlight rushed in, bringing clarity along for the ride. Suddenly, his confusion dissipated, as if it had never existed. The answer was simple. It was time to leave DMI and Detroit. There was no question. God had called him to Detroit to help bring reconciliation to the Mitchell family. Everything hadn't turned out as he'd hoped, but then that wasn't his problem. God had called him to play a role in the process, not to be the ultimate fixer. That was God's job alone, and Don was at peace. His season at DMI had passed. He was done, and his next step was to break the news to his mother.

Don went down the hallway several doors to reach her office and found Madeline Mitchell staring into a laptop on her desk. "Mother, we need to talk." Don plopped into a chair directly in front of her.

She peered over the reading glasses perched on the tip of her nose and said, "Why do you look so serious? What's wrong now?"

Such a question in their family was sufficient to stir a hornet's nest. There was no point in rattling off a litany of wrongs, including the constant power struggle within the family. Don's mother was painfully aware of each battle, especially since she'd had ample instigation in most. Regardless, he wasn't there to rehash and toss around blame. The truth was that there was plenty to go around with not a single person deserving to be exonerated.

"I'm ready to go back to South Africa."

She took her glasses off and bit her lip. "So you're serious about leaving? You're really going to walk out of DMI and give up your CEO position?"

"Yep," Don said. "But this shouldn't be a surprise. I've told you this several times over the past couple of weeks."

"But I didn't take you seriously."

"Maybe that's the problem. No one takes me seriously when it comes to wanting something for me."

Madeline reared back and pushed her palms against the edge of the desk. "That's not true. Nobody forced you stay here."

That was debatable. For months he'd mentioned stepping down, and his mother had consistently implored him to think about what would happen to DMI if he left. "Doesn't matter. It's time for me to move on."

"Then I guess we have to appoint a replacement," she said, pulling herself closer to the desk and resting her elbows on top, with fingers clasped. "You're putting me in a tough spot, because there's no one better qualified than you to run our company. No one. You've been a savior for DMI. While you were away, that half-brother of yours practically drove us into bankruptcy, and our reputation was dumped in the toilet. After the debacle with Joel as the head, you helped us get both our finances and our image back on track."

Flattery was nice, but Don wasn't swayed. The only thing worse than not hearing God was ignoring His instruction once he had heard from Him. Don knew God had released him from DMI, and the others had to accept it too. They'd either reconcile or kill each other in the process. Either way, he wasn't staying around to find out which one they chose.

"You're talking about me being great for DMI. What about you?" he asked Madeline.

"What about me?" she asked as her eyebrows shrugged.

"You started this company with Dad. Why don't you take over as CEO?"

"Are you out of your mind? I'm sixty-six years old. I have served my time in hell and on the mountaintop. Don't get me wrong. I love DMI and what your father and I have built here. You know this is my fifth child, but it has never been my desire to be at the helm—never. I enjoy standing behind the leader and moving stuff out of the way so that person can run this place with a strong hand," she said shaking her tight fist in the air. "That's what I do, and I've done it well." Her shoulders relaxed. "Just like you, it's time for me to press on toward the next chapter in my life."

Don wasn't sure exactly what that meant, given that she hadn't shown interest in anything outside of her children and DMI. "I guess that leaves Tamara." Don knew his mother would always put him and his sister ahead of Joel, the lone son resulting from his father's past marital indiscretion.

Madeline's heart wept as she longed to have her estranged daughter run the family business, but she was too much of a businesswoman to squander their success by letting emotions rule her decisions. Madeline rested her forehead against her interlocked fingers and closed her eyelids. "We know she's not ready. Let's face it. She's doing well as a junior-level assistant, but that's miles from your corner office on executive row."

"I agree, but you know she might not understand," Don replied.

"Who knows? But we can't worry about her reaction right now. We have to move forward before you leave me high and dry."

"Never that." Don chuckled. "Then if it's not you and it's not Tamara, my replacement has to be Abigail. She's already the executive vice president. It's not much of a stretch to make her the new CEO." Madeline was eager to interrupt, but Don didn't give her a chance. "Let me finish."

She nodded for him to proceed.

"Abigail has been loyal to this family. She worked as an assistant for Dad, an executive under Joel, and as a right hand for me. She's put up with a lot of hurt from Joel and from me too. She's been in the trenches with us, and most importantly, I trust her. She deserves this shot."

Madeline was itching to jump in with a rebuttal. "I don't question her loyalty. I can also appreciate her disappointment about not landing a Mitchell man, but what did Abigail expect? You might not act like brothers, but you do share a bloodline. Falling in love with two brothers is taboo and destined not to end well. She can only blame herself for the fallout and her wounded feelings. She shouldn't be upset about both you and Joel having chosen other women, leaving her out in the cold." Madeline shut her eyelids as her head bobbed from side to side. "I get how awful that might be for her. I really feel badly for her too, but I'm not about to give her the golden key because I feel sorry for her. Maybe you and Joel feel like you owe her something, but I don't."

"Come on, Mother. You can't mean that."

"Humph. You think I don't? Abigail has done a great job and has been compensated handsomely. As an executive vice president, she's making over four hundred thousand, plus a very generous twenty-five percent annual bonus and plenty of other benefits and perks."

"This isn't about money."

"You're right. It's about family, legacy, and birthright." Madeline gently glided the palm of her hand across the top of her head, pressing down any loose hairs. "This company was built to stay in the family. That is nonnegotiable for me, which is why there's only one choice." She cleared her throat. "I know you think I'm crazy, but Joel is my choice."

"You can't be serious."

"He's gutsy, and I like that," Madeline said.

"You mean more like reckless."

"I told you last month he'd come to me and apologized for his actions in the past. As much as I'd like to discount his little visit, I can't. I'm a pretty good judge of character, and I'm telling you he was sincere."

Don wanted to be impartial and felt like he was. He could easily have reverted to nursing his childhood wounds of rejection, which were due to playing second fiddle to his father's second family, with baby boy Joel seemingly getting the best Dave Mitchell had to offer. He could allow the hurt to justify his vote against Joel at this critical point in the DMI succession plan. Yet he didn't have a need for revenge. It wasn't in his heart. His lack of support for Joel was based purely on merit and a gut feeling. Don wasn't as easily convinced of Joel's turn from the dark side as his mother appeared to be. It was true that Don championed reconciliation and forgiveness in the family, but he operated with wisdom too. Joel had made devastating business decisions, like bargaining away two divisions, secretly signing on a ton of debt, and merging DMI with an Eastern religion–oriented company that had conflicting priorities and beliefs. Forgiveness was great and necessary, but it didn't mean that consequences were instantly wiped away. Clearly, some situations were irreversible. Don was sure of it. Joel had created several such situations, making it difficult for Don to see him as a viable candidate for the helm of DMI.

"Let's face it. He has the experience and the pedigree. Besides, we can't overlook the fact that he led DMI through the largest growth spurt we've ever had when he took over four years ago," Madeline added.

"Abigail was here during the growth spurt too."

"But she wasn't the leader. Joel was." Madeline stared at Don. "I like Abigail. You know I do. I appreciate her intellect and her loyalty, but if my children aren't in the lead role, I'm going with the next best candidate, and that's Joel. It's not even a close race between the two of them. He's a Mitchell, and she isn't. It's that simple."

"I'm blown away that you trust him this much, with everything that happened on his watch."

"I haven't forgotten, but as you've told me too many times, everyone deserves another chance. In Joel's case, it's the third, fourth, or fifth," she said while laughing.

"True, but still I'm going with Abigail."

"Then, my son, we'll have to agree to disagree."

"So what are we going to do?" Don asked with his gaze locked with his mother's.

"Take it to a vote with the board of directors."

"You sure you want to go there? Because I have two votes," Don uttered.

"Whose?"

"Mine and, most likely, Tamara's. You know how she believes in empowering women. I'm sure her vote will go to Abigail."

"I don't want to burst your bubble, but Tamara votes only for herself," Madeline said.

"You're probably right, but I'm not worried. I'll get my votes."

"You can best believe, I'll get mine. I'll go as far as getting his mother on my side, if absolutely necessary."

"What can Sherry do? She doesn't have a vote on the board," Don stated.

"True, but never underestimate the power of a mother. If I've taught you anything over the years, you should know that much." Silence fell over the office. Then Madeline extended a hand to Don. "May the best person win."

Don stood and leaned across the desk to shake his mother's hand, imagining the many things that could go wrong. The surge of solace he was claiming at that moment rested on the notion that God had a plan for him and the other Mitchells. He *had* to; otherwise going to battle against Madeline Mitchell was suicide. "Who's going to tell Tamara that we're not recommending her?"

"Hmm. Now, that's a good question," Madeline responded. "For now it can wait, because I'm going to call Joel and get his candidacy rolling. You might want to do the same with Abigail."

Don agreed and headed for the door.

"Hang on. This might be a bumpy ride," she added.

"Isn't the saying 'What doesn't kill us makes us stronger'?"

Madeline grinned in response. Don left, realizing that Armageddon had been launched in the Mitchell dynasty. Whether they'd survive or fall was a big question, and only time would tell what the answer to that question was.

Los Angeles Public Library
Lake View Terrace Branch
10/17/2016   2:17:17 PM

- PATRON RECEIPT -
CHARGES

1 Item Number 3724...
Title Unforgiving /
Due Date 11/7/2016

Your library card gives you...
online courses. Start learning...
http://www.lapl.org/learn

To Renew www.lapl.org or 888-577-5275

-Please retain this slip as your receipt

Chapter 2

Joel entered the master bedroom, where his wife, Zarah, was lounging in a chair situated not too far from the bed. "Can I get you anything?" he asked.

"No, not for me. I am good," she said, sipping a cup of tea with milk.

"You sure? Because I have to run out for a little while. Madeline called and wants me to stop by the office." She hadn't given details, but in his desperate desire to get back into DMI, Joel was answering whenever Madeline beckoned. If she wanted to see him in the office, then he was going with no questions asked. But Zarah had become his priority too, at least until the baby was born.

Admittedly, he hadn't always shown a willingness to hang around home. Only a few months ago he'd been desperate to end his marriage. Zarah did not feel the same way, and he vividly recalled asking for a divorce as gently as he could. Joel had encouraged her to go back home to India, while he had planned on sitting the separation out with a close friend in Chicago. A few weeks into the separation, they found out Zarah was pregnant. Joel was making strides in the marriage, but he couldn't block out what he perceived as devastating news on that fateful day when she made the announcement about the baby. The unexpected pregnancy had left him confused and grasping for answers. On the one hand, he felt guilty for wanting a divorce. On the other, he felt trapped. Nothing felt right about their relationship. He didn't want to be heartless, but diving back into a loveless marriage wasn't the answer, not even for the unborn child. That was his immediate reaction to the crushing news. After Zarah suffered a near miscarriage about a month ago, he was forced to do some deep soul-searching. His compassion and his sense of obligation kicked in, rendering him unable to leave Zarah in the midst of her high-risk pregnancy.

He stroked her forehead and let tranquility fill the bedroom. He would make sure she was comfortable before he headed out of the house. "If you'd like, I can get your assistant to come and spend a few hours with you. I won't be gone longer than that."

"No, please go. I will be fine. And I am not alone. The housekeeper and the cook are both here. I will call them if I need help."

Joel bent down on his knees in front of her. "Okay, if you're sure." He gently laid his palm across her slightly bulging belly and peered into her eyes. "Call me if you need anything, and I mean *anything*."

"I will," she said, laying her hand on top of his.

Joel didn't pull his hand away. He'd come a long way toward earnestly supporting the mother of his unborn child. Maybe it was crisis affection, the kind of emotion that came about when two people suffered a traumatic situation and bonded. He didn't really know, and he wasn't going to get caught up in overthinking his decision. His devotion to Zarah was too fragile to withstand intense introspection.

"I'll see you later," he told her.

Five minutes after Joel left, Zarah rang up her sister-in-law. They hadn't spoken since Zarah's hospitalization last month, and she was eager to talk with her friend.

Tamara answered after several rings.

"I'm so glad to reach you," Zarah told her.

"I've been worried sick about you," Tamara said, and her concern gave Zarah strength.

"I'm much better, and the baby is keeping well."

"Thank goodness. Where is that husband of yours? Is he taking care of you like he should, or did he run back to Chicago already to be with his so-called friend?"

Zarah ignored the comment about Joel being with another woman during his random trips to Chicago. He was still her husband, and she'd taken their vows seriously from the moment they were married. She could have told Tamara that it was engrained in her culture for the woman to honor her marriage no matter how difficult it became, and that she would hold fast to that behalf. Zarah couldn't utter that statement, however, because it wasn't her reason for wanting to be with Joel. In truth, her adoration for Joel extended beyond tradition and culture. He was in her soul, and she loved him unconditionally. She intended to be the only one for him, and as far as she was concerned, no other woman existed in his past or present.

"He's been very good to me. Joel will be gone for a few hours. Can you come over for a visit?"

"I'm on my way."

Zarah adored her sister-in-law and had clung to her during those trying months when Joel didn't seem to care. Being in the States, and away from her family in India, had made the situation especially devastating for Zarah. Tamara had been a lifesaver. She'd helped Zarah in the past, but Joel was her future. Zarah longed to have them both in her life, although it didn't seem possible most of the time.

Roughly thirty minutes passed before Tamara arrived at the house and was ushered into the master bedroom upstairs by the housekeeper. Zarah's continence lit up as they embraced. Tamara took a seat in the chair near Zarah's with only a small coffee table separating them. Sitting on the edge of her seat, Tamara reached for Zarah's hand and sandwiched it.

"You look good. Are you and the baby seriously okay?"

"Yes, we are both good," Zarah said, nodding. "I am to stay in bed mostly, but I'm good. For my baby, I will do anything."

"Thank goodness," Tamara said, letting Zarah's hand go and easing back in the chair. "You had me worried. I didn't know if you or the baby was going to survive. You had me scared," she said, grabbing Zarah's hand again and then quickly releasing it. "So what's going on with that husband of yours?"

"He's been wonderful."

"He better be or else."

"I don't want to speak badly about my husband. He's done well by me. I'm happy, and this is going to work for us. I know it in my heart."

Tamara flailed her hands in the air. "Fine. If you want to stay committed to a guy like him, I'm still going to be your friend. I don't understand what you see in him, but that's your call. I'll leave it alone."

Zarah was relieved.

"Since you're happy and in love, are you giving up on running your father's company?" Tamara asked.

"I don't know. I haven't the energy to think about business."

Tamara didn't want to push too much, but she'd worked too hard over the past couple of months at getting Zarah to crawl from Joel's shadow and take control of her professional destiny. Zarah had groveled for Joel's affection and attention repeatedly without success. "We've made huge progress with getting your name out there as a legitimate businesswoman. Nobody, especially Joel, thought you'd be interested in running your father's multimillion-dollar company. You've stunned a lot of people. After you have the baby and take a maternity leave, we can get back to work."

"I'm not sure what I'll do once the baby is here. Being a mother is most important."

Tamara wasn't about to let her efforts be lost. Zarah had to take her rightful place running the small empire she'd inherited as part of her father's massive estate. She owned half of Harmonious Energy, and DMI had the rest. She also owned the West Coast division of DMI, because Joel had willingly given it to Zarah's father as part of the DMI and Harmonious Energy merger. Tamara laughed, thinking about the irony of it all. A piece of the empire Joel had squandered away in a greedy business deal was being handed over to Tamara without his knowledge. The real kicker was that the wife he'd acquired in the exact same deal was the person who was actually partnering with Tamara behind his back.

The notion of beating Joel at his own game of deceit and trickery was electrifying. That was why Zarah couldn't slip back into the role of a docile wife who let her opportunistic husband run her life. Tamara needed Zarah to continue gaining strength and notoriety in the corporate arena. Her livelihood depended on it. She was so close to getting Zarah to sell her the West Coast division that nothing was going to derail Tamara's plan.

Unfortunately, there was a list of contenders who wanted the division, and on that list were Joel, Don, and her mother. She couldn't let them win, not this time. Yet Zarah's risky pregnancy was a factor Tamara couldn't ignore. She didn't feel right pressing for a professional favor at this very second, but her chance would come. Soon she'd seal the deal with Zarah and close this chapter of unrest.

Tamara could taste the freedom as she salivated over the gravity of her idea. Buying the division was her single best opportunity to distance herself from the Mitchell family. The two thousand miles between Detroit and Southern California were about the right amount of distance to keep her sane. A mile less and her family was bound to drive her crazy.

"There's no need to rush toward an answer right now. You need to rest and have a healthy baby, and then let's figure out where to go from there. Who knows? By then Joel might return to his old ways," Tamara said, snapping her fingers in the air while sneering. "Because I highly doubt that the new and improved Joel is going to stay in Detroit long enough to keep up this family-man role. Where is he, anyway?" Tamara asked, leaning forward.

"He went to the office to see your mother."

"For what? You know those two don't get along," Tamara said.

"I'm not sure, but he seemed very pleased to get her call."

The two ladies chatted for another ten minutes or so. Tamara was distracted the entire time. What could Madeline want with Joel? Tamara's curiosity got the best of her.

"I better go. Joel will be back any minute, and it's best that I'm gone."

"Yes, you are right, but one day I hope we can all sit together and have a cup of tea."

Tamara didn't see that happening. As far as she was concerned, Joel was the enemy. Being the son conceived by his father's mistress wasn't why she felt disdain toward Joel. Her contempt rested squarely on his actions. He represented everything she hated: he was a man who used his power to manipulate and control any woman weak and naive enough to care about him. There were many

Joels in the world. She gritted her teeth, hating each one, including her older brother, Andre. She still hadn't gotten over the fact that he had raped her in their family's house when she was seventeen. She hadn't gotten over her last boyfriend, Remo, either. Tamara despised how his abuse and his controlling ways had her moving from city to city. She didn't like having to live with the constant fear of him finding her. There was no place for men like Joel, Andre, and Remo in her world.

Tamara knew Zarah would be waiting a long time for a family get-together with her and Joel. Hell might not have to freeze over completely, but there would at least have to be some frost there before she would even flirt with the idea.

Chapter 3

Joel's mind was cluttered as he flew through the DMI lobby, past the guards and a few well-wishers. Normally, he would have taken time to acknowledge the guards and the other employees sending greetings his way. Today was different. When Madeline called, his anticipation had nearly overflowed. He got on the elevator and couldn't wait for it to reach the sixth-floor. Executive row had been his home as CEO for over three years. He craved being in the midst of intense decision making and power. The corporate allure was like an addiction that had him groveling to the single individual who'd worked tirelessly to make his childhood and much of his adulthood miserable. Madeline had pulled every trick over the years to knock him down. She'd succeeded and failed in equal proportion, but today none of that mattered. He was praying for a fresh start, a chance to redeem himself for the mistakes he'd made at the company. Madeline was his saving grace. He'd soon see just how much grace she was willing to extend to her husband's other son. `

"She's expecting me. Can I go in?" he asked Madeline's administrative assistant, whose desk was situated off the main aisle.

"Let me check," she told him and dialed Madeline's office.

Joel's enthusiasm was slightly diminished by having to wait for someone's approval to move freely within the company that he had run not too long ago. He set his pride aside and focused on staying positive. He silently meditated and prayed for God's favor.

A few seconds later the assistant waved him on. "You can go in. She's waiting for you."

Joel reached the doorway and paused. He was either crossing into a den of despair or a galaxy of good news. It was too hard to read Madeline's countenance for an immediate answer. He'd have to put on his armor and go behind enemy lines to find out his fate at DMI. Joel took one step, followed by another, until he was standing at arm's length from her desk.

She stared at him, causing Joel to become uncomfortable. "Well, don't just stand there. Have a seat," she offered.

Joel accepted the offer, still not getting a hint of Madeline's mood. Snapping at him was commonplace. So he didn't attach any significance to her small barks. "What's going on? Why did you want to meet with me?"

She took her reading glasses off and set them on the desk without shifting her gaze from him. He felt increasingly more uneasy.

"Your little visit here last month has been needling me since you left."

Oh, boy, Joel thought. *Here it comes.* How had he let this happen? He knew Madeline better than most did, even better than her daughter. He was smart enough not to get caught in her trap. Yet he'd allowed her to lure him into a false sense of hope, into thinking there was a possibility she'd help him resume leadership at DMI. How could he be so silly? He'd let Madeline have a good laugh, and then he'd slink away from shame.

"You must have been out of your mind to ask if I'd let you back into this company, the one your father and I built, with the expectation that my children would run this place."

Joel wasn't willing to hear any more. He'd heard her soliloquy enough to gag. He was desperate for an executive opportunity, but he had a smidgen of pride, and it prevented him from groveling with regret. Madeline could laugh at someone else's expense. So he stood and prepared to tell her goodbye.

"Where are you going?"

"I'm not going to sit here and be the butt of your joke. I'm sorry I asked for your help. I'm out of here."

"Sit your behind down," she said, raising her voice. "See, that's one of your problems. You make rash decisions without getting the full picture."

Joel didn't sit. There weren't nearly enough hours in the day to list his problems, and he definitely didn't want Madeline crafting the list. They'd be there for several days at least. He was ready to go.

"I said sit down."

Joel acquiesced and reclaimed his seat. He might as well sit and finish the meeting since he was there. Zarah would be okay for another hour or so until he and Madeline finished.

"I gave serious consideration to your request, and believe it or not, I'm willing to back your bid to be reinstated as CEO."

"What?" Joel said, leaping to his feet. "You have to be kidding." He'd asked Madeline for help with very little hope that she'd agree. Joy overtook Joel. Before he could harness his elation, Joel had zipped around the desk and hugged Madeline for the first time in his life.

She pushed away from him. "Stop. Get off me. This is an office."

Joel didn't mind if Madeline resisted. The deed had been done. They'd connected for the first time in his twenty-seven years. "This is amazing. When do I start?"

"Not today. You should know this has to be approved by the board."

"Right. So when is the next board of directors meeting? The sooner I get reinstated, the faster we can get moving toward record sales again. Boy, I can't wait to get started," he said, pacing the office as his excitement percolated. Joel recounted his many mistakes, but each quickly washed away as the air of redemption had him soaring emotionally.

"Whoa. Slow down, roadrunner. We have a ton of work to do in preparation for the board meeting. Have you forgotten about your small reputation issue?"

Joel reclaimed his seat as Madeline began slowly stifling the air beneath his wings of hope. "How can I forget? You won't let me."

Madeline began twiddling a pen on her desk. "Don't get snippety with me. You're the one who caused the mess around here. You made your bed, and then you had to sleep on it." Madeline stopped with the pen and interlocked her fingers with them resting on her lap. "The bottom line is that you have work to do, but I'm willing to help you."

He was ready to bolt, but the idea of having Madeline's support was too compelling and kept Joel glued to the chair. "I'll take it. You know I'm thrilled and equally grateful, but I'm curious too. What made you want to help me?"

Madeline seemed to ponder his question before responding. "It's simple. You're the best person for the job. Don is stepping down soon and I have no desire for the CEO role, so that leaves only one capable Mitchell—you."

"I'm flattered, but what about Tamara? You've made it clear that your children come first at DMI. My mother and I are a distant second."

"You might be a distant second, but your mother is not even in the race when it comes to who will own and lead DMI one day."

Joel could have defended his mother's honor against Madeline, but it would be a waste. Madeline's views about his mother stealing Dave Mitchell wouldn't go away if he stood up to her. Their troubles had started long before he was born, and he was pretty sure they would exist until one or both women were dead. "I'm honored that you're choosing me."

"Well, it's only fair that you know everything. You're not the only candidate," she said, pushing against the desk. "Don is recommending Abigail."

"I thought she was resigning from her executive vice president position here to start her own business," Joel replied.

"She is, if we leave her alone."

"I didn't realize we'd be going up against Abigail."

Joel was torn. He and Abigail had fought on many fronts. They'd worked tirelessly, hand in hand, to take DMI to new financial heights, and they'd accomplished their goal. They'd had a few professional squabbles, but the source of her bitterness toward him was purely personal. She was ready to act on feelings for him that he couldn't reciprocate. Early in their professional partnership, Joel had made it clear to Abigail that God and DMI were the most important entities in his life. Admittedly, God had fallen a few notches back when Joel overdosed on power and notoriety, but his commitment to DMI never faltered. Everything and everybody, especially relationships, came second. Abigail didn't accept rejection well, and his getting married, even if it was for business purposes a few months later, was the shove that sent her over the edge. Joel took no pride in hurting his friend. He wanted to make amends, but Abigail wasn't willing. *Perhaps in time,* he thought.

"If you want the job, you'll have to beat her for it. Can you do that?"

"I do want the job, and yes, I'm willing to run against Abigail and win with your help."

"So be it," Madeline said, then stood and extended her hand for him to shake. As soon as he took her hand, her grip tightened. "You better not stab me in the back," she warned him, with a piercing gaze that would make a lesser person shiver.

"I have no intentions of crossing you, Madeline. That would generate a fight which I'm not planning to take on. Abigail is big enough."

Madeline squeezed his hand tighter and then let it go. "I hope so, because I'm giving you fair warning. If you cross me, Mr. Joel Mitchell, you'll suffer my wrath."

"There's no need to threaten me. I get your message and clearly understand the ramifications. You'll see. I'm totally committed."

"You better be, because DMI is my baby." She came around the desk with her arms crossed. "And you know I don't allow anyone to mess with mine and get away with it. Just ask your mother."

It irked Joel, but he had to let the comment go. There was no way he was going to derail this one-shot deal of teaming up with Madeline. She had plenty of clout on the board of directors. "Let's get started," he said without hesitation.

"I'll have my assistant set up some planning sessions with you."

"Great . . . " he replied.

"By the way, I heard about your wife and baby. How's she doing?"

"Pretty good, considering she almost had a miscarriage. Thanks for asking."

"Do you think home life will become a distraction for you after the baby is born?"

"Absolutely not," he firmly stated, enunciating each syllable. Joel headed for the door. "I'll see you soon." Before crossing the threshold, he turned to her and said, "Thank you, and I sincerely mean it. You've single-handedly changed my life."

"Backing you is either the smartest or the dumbest thing I've ever done. Which it is remains to be seen."

"Wait and see for yourself," he stated and walked out.

Chapter 4

Don could have grown weary from fretting over yet another battle over DMI. He had wondered about his father's decision to marry Sherry after Madeline divorced him. If Dave Mitchell had known the family would be fighting long after his death, would he have remarried, anyway? Would the birth of his youngest son, Joel, have outweighed the sting of family discord in his father's eyes? With his father gone for over three years now, no one would know. So Don wouldn't bother second-guessing his father any longer. He had a task to accomplish.

He glided his finger across the nameplate that had been placed outside the office situated several doors from his—ABIGAIL GERARD − EXECUTIVE VICE PRESIDENT. He rapped on the door to get her attention.

"Come in," she said.

"Do you have a few free minutes?" he asked as he entered her office cautiously.

"Sure. What's a few minutes going to hurt? I'll be here late, anyway, working on the quarterly management reports."

Don remained standing as he didn't want to be there long. "That's what I like about you - dedication to the end."

She grunted. "You know I'm always going to do my job, even if it's not always appreciated."

Noting her inflection and her tone, Don took a seat. His appeal might take a tad bit longer than he'd expected if Abigail was already unreceptive two minutes into the conversation.

"See, that's where you're wrong. Not only are you appreciated here, but I want to recommend you for the CEO position."

"Yeah, right! Did every Mitchell in Detroit fall off a cliff? That's about the only way I'd get a shot at CEO."

"Funny. And no, we haven't fallen off a cliff. We're all alive and breathing."

Abigail's head tilted to the side as her body seemed to tense. "So what's this business about CEO?"

"I already told you I'm stepping down," Don stated.

"No, you told me you were thinking about making a change. That's not the same as stepping down. Where are you going?"

"I'm going to work hard at getting you to accept this offer." Don clutched the arm of his chair, desperate to avoid answering her question truthfully. This conversation had the makings of a slippery slope, and Don didn't want to end up at the bottom of it. Their professional relationship was solid but their personal history wasn't as stable. Don was desperate not to let a private failure between them derail this once-in-a-lifetime opportunity for Abigail. He wanted to leave the company in her capable hands. She'd earned the promotion. So he had to think quickly and steer the conversation away from her probing and back to an area he could address without repercussions.

"Seriously? You're not going to answer me? Where are you going, or do I even need to ask?" she said, opening the top drawer of her desk then slamming it shut.

Abigail let her gaze roam around her desk, much to Don's relief. Having her stare at him was too awkward. He didn't want to offend her and would continue dodging the questions and direct eye contact.

"You're going to South Africa, right?"

Don reluctantly nodded in affirmation.

"I figured as much," she said, opening the top drawer of her desk again and extracting a small tube of lotion. She poured some into her palm and briskly rubbed her hands together. "Finally going after that woman, huh?"

"Naledi."

"What?" she snapped.

"Her name is Naledi."

"She's finally hooked you and now you're running across the world to be with her."

Don couldn't figure out why Abigail wouldn't let this go? Didn't she know he was trying to protect her feelings? It was almost like she wanted the pain. Regardless, demoralizing someone wasn't his way. There had been plenty of that to go around at DMI, but he wasn't going to indulge her craving for heartache.

"Can't we talk about this great opportunity that I've laid before you?" he asked, resting his elbows on his thighs. "You deserve my role, and it's about time you finally got your just due."

She didn't respond. Instead, she closed her eyes and pinched her lips.

He didn't break the silence. Don would let her digest the magnitude of what he was asking. Her drive was bound to kick into high gear and overshadow her unrest.

"Are you really going to marry this woman, someone that you barely know?" she finally asked.

"Wait a minute. Why are we talking about marriage?"

"Because not very many men pick up and move across the world, unless it's for a career or a serious relationship. Since you already have a career here, it must be for her."

"If you say so." Don figured it was easier to agree and move on than to get caught in Abigail's clutches.

"Are you in love with her?" Abigail rested her elbow on the desk and pressed her forehead into her palm. "What is it about you Mitchell brothers? Neither of you can find a wife in Detroit. You both had to go to the other side of the world to find a woman." She peered at the desk.

Don's strategy hadn't changed. He aimed to keep quiet as much as possible until Abigail got through whatever she was experiencing. Maybe some of her emotions were wrapped in guilt. He wasn't trying to blame her, but she'd contributed sufficiently to the situation. When he'd been in love with her, she'd chosen Joel. Don had been crushed, but he hadn't blamed her. He'd taken full responsibility for not sharing his true feelings for her when it could have made a difference. By the time he conveyed his feelings, her heart had already settled on his younger brother. Don sighed, letting the past rest.

"Abigail, you need to let it go. You're a beautiful, intelligent, and fun person. Some man is going to be blessed having you for a wife."

"Why can't that man be you?"

Don chuckled. "I don't deserve you," he said, continuing to chuckle. "You deserve a better man than I am." Abigail's blank stare abruptly halted Don's chuckles. "I have to run. Can you give my request serious consideration, please?" Don asked. He lowered his forehead to his fingertips, which were pressed together, as if he were doing a Japanese greeting. "You're the best candidate, and I'd feel a lot better about DMI and my family's legacy if you were in the corner office," Don added as he headed to the door. Just as Don was about to escape for a breath of fresh air, Abigail's words snared him.

"So you're going to give me your job and Naledi your heart. Which is the better deal?" she asked.

Don left the office certain no answer would satisfy Abigail Gerard except a marriage proposal of her own. He was no more certain of her interest in the CEO position than he had been upon entering her office. He schlepped to his office. Nothing came easy at DMI, nothing.

Chapter 5

Tamara had spent the last twenty minutes of her visit with Zarah consumed with wonder. Why was Joel at DMI with Madeline? She knew they were both set on nabbing DMI's West Coast division. Maybe they were scheming to beat her. Nah, Madeline and Joel working together under any condition was a ludicrous idea. There had to be another reason they were meeting, and she would find out.

Within thirty minutes of her cab arriving to pick her up from Zarah's, Tamara was hustling into the DMI office building. Madeline's office door was closed, so Tamara headed for Don's office and found his door partially open. She heard him on the phone.

"Do you want me to let him know you're here?" his assistant asked.

Tamara waved her off and decided to wait quietly nearby until her brother was off the phone. He was bound to have some answers regarding Joel.

"You know, I left your office without you giving me an answer," she overheard him say on the phone.

It felt slightly awkward to stand outside Don's office, but her anxiety wouldn't allow her to leave. She kept watch over Madeline's office door too, avoiding eye contact with Don's assistant, who periodically gave her a hard stare. Her mother's door remained shut.

"Maybe? Is that the best you can give me?" he asked. "Well, at least it's not a flat-out no. Guess I'll take it. We'll talk later," he said and seemed to end the call.

It was none too soon. Don's assistant was about to burn a hole through Tamara. She went into her brother's office without being announced.

"Hey, sis. What brings you here in the middle of the day?"

"Can't I visit my brother without a reason?"

"Not generally," he said, scratching his chin.

"Actually, I'm here to see Mother."

"Oh, man. About what?"

"Zarah told me Joel is meeting with her, and I want to know why. They better not try to steal the West Coast division from me, because I'm ready to fight for it."

"That's not why they're meeting."

"Really? So why are they meeting?"

Don was normally very responsive, but all he could muster was a weird look for a moment. "We need to talk," he said finally.

She tensed. "About what?"

He stood and walked toward her. Let's go to Mother's office. We need to speak with you together."

Tamara followed behind, a flood of possibilities racing through her mind, none of which were positive. Just as they reached the desk of Madeline's assistant, Joel slithered from Madeline's office, sending a chill down Tamara's spine. Her defenses jumped into high gear.

Joel and Don exchanged greetings. Tamara ignored Joel as they brushed against each other.

Niceties weren't in Tamara's stratosphere today. She was strictly about business and delved right in without as much as a hello or a "How do you do?" upon entering Madeline's office. "What was Joel doing here?"

"Have a seat," Madeline offered, closing her portfolio and setting her pen to the side as she sat at her desk.

Don sat.

"I don't want to take a seat," Tamara said with her voice rising. She'd been around these people long enough to smell foul play. The stench was palpable. "I want to know what Joel was doing here. Are you trying to gang up against me?"

"Please take a seat," Madeline said again.

"Answer me," Tamara demanded.

"Calm down, Tamara. Don't get worked up," Don said.

Tamara wasn't going to shut up until they started telling the truth. She wasn't going to be suckered into believing a lame lie, either. She was ready for them.

"Tamara, you need to sit down and lower your voice," Madeline told her. "I'm still the mother. Don't push me," she said, letting her gaze roll all over Tamara. "If you'd act with some sense, we could tell you about the changes going on here. Don is stepping down, and we're appointing a new CEO in his place."

"Please tell me it's not Joel," Tamara said.

"If it's left up to me, yes, Joel will be the CEO," Madeline said.

Tamara shook her head. "You can't be serious."

"Not only am I serious, we're preparing to make a recommendation to the board this month."

"You don't agree with her, right?" Tamara asked Don.

"No," Don replied.

"Thank goodness," Tamara sighed.

"I'm recommending Abigail instead."

"What?" Tamara shouted. The room was twirling faster and faster, and she nearly stumbled. She had to take a seat. "How can the two of you skip over me and offer the CEO position to Joel and Abigail? How can you do this to me?" Tamara alternated between sitting and standing and fidgeted when she was seated. "I'm entitled to a shot at the top spot. Not Abigail, an outsider, and definitely not Joel, the very person who drove this company into the ground. What a joke the two of you are. I should have known not to trust you. Mother, you were so keen on getting me to move back to Detroit and join the family at DMI. For what, so you could stab me in the back?"

"Watch your mouth," Madeline said. "Young lady, have you forgotten? Most of the time you don't want anything to do with DMI. One day you're in. The next day you're out. I practically begged you to take on a serious role from the moment we knew you were coming back to Detroit, and you turned me down cold. The best we could talk you into was taking the junior marketing position. It was never my plan to put you in such a junior role. That was your choice, young lady. So, I'm sorry if you feel slighted, but tough. We can't run a company based on your whims. Grow up. This isn't a day care center where we jump every time you cry foul. You had a chance."

"No, Mother. I was never offered the CEO role."

"Do you really think you're qualified to be CEO?" Don asked.

"Maybe not, but I should have been asked."

"I don't think so, young lady. This is a business, not your testing ground," Madeline said.

"Like I said, I should have known not to put my guard down with you. I was raped once under your care. Now I feel violated again," Tamara told Madeline.

"Tamara, that's enough," Don said.

"No, let her talk. Get it all out, Tamara, because this is the last time I'm going to let you guilt me into feeling sorry for you. I know Andre violated you, and I can't take it back. None of us can. I wish I could, but I can't!" Madeline shouted and smacked the table with the palm of her hand. "Do you think I'm proud that my daughter was raped by my son? Do you think I'm happy that my son killed his brother to avenge his sister's rape and then committed suicide? I lost three children that day includ-ing you. As far as I'm concerned, all of us were raped too."

"No, you weren't," Tamara fired back, too angry to give way to tears.

"Yes, we were. Our family lost its innocence along with you. Sure we had problems before then, but the Mitchell family changed that day, forever. You are my daughter." Madeline rose from her seat and approached Tamara, but then she stopped when her daughter retreated. "My heart breaks for your pain, but the pity stops here. I'm not the perfect parent, by no means. But you know what? I did the best I could with what I had. Now that I know better, I can do better, but you're not going to keep me in the pit with you. No more, baby girl. It's over. Now you can choose to get on board, make a full commitment to DMI, and work together with us as a family, or you can walk away. Either way, I'll love you to the grave, but I'm not going to let you push me there any sooner than I'm intended to go. You understand?"

Tamara wanted to hoof off, defeated. But her need to claim retribution for all she'd suffered as a member of the family held her hostage. "You're no different than Dad. You're doing the exact same thing he did."

"And what is that, Ms. Tamara?" Madeline asked in a tone that came across as sarcastic.

"He chose Joel to run DMI over Don. Now you're choosing Joel over me. What's the difference?"

Tamara's comment cut Madeline like a sharp knife. Her eyes began blinking rapidly. She felt warm. She stared into space, wanting to find the right words. The longer Madeline stared, the less she had to say. She never wanted her children to feel secondary to anyone, but putting Tamara in a role she wasn't equipped to handle was a recipe for failure. To do so would be to replicate Dave's ill-advised appointment of Joel when he was barely twenty-three and too immature and inexperienced to run DMI. Madeline wouldn't repeat the same mistake.

She had to make her daughter understand; otherwise their relationship might be forever rendered unrepairable. Before she could articulate her rationale, Tamara stormed from the office in complete silence.

"That didn't go too well," Don said.

"But it's what we should expect when dealing with Tamara," Madeline said, aggrieved.

Chapter 6

Joel had emerged from Madeline's office, riding a wave of excitement and confidence. He couldn't remember the last occasion when he'd received news this good. Joel continued walking and wearing a grin, this time speaking to the few people he passed on executive row. *Might as well get comfortable,* he thought, because this would soon be his domain again. Nothing would give him more joy. He was close, thank God.

Joel was about to exit the floor but then stopped. He hadn't seen his old friend since his last rare visit to the office. On that occasion Abigail had told him she was resigning from DMI to open her own firm. He'd asked to join her, but she had flat out declined his offer. Thankfully, his circumstances were changing. Back then he was desperate to find a business venture. Now his hopelessness had been converted into sheer adrenaline. He was fired up and found it difficult to contain his exuberance.

Joel casually walked into Abigail's office without fanfare or an announcement, like he'd done thousands of times, but she wasn't there. He stepped back into the hallway and approached the administrative desk. "Where is Ms. Gerard?"

"She's in the break room," the assistant told him.

He tapped the desktop and thanked her, then sought out Abigail near the front of executive row. He found her in the break room, which was off to the right of the elevators. "There you are," he said. She was leaning on a counter near the hot beverages and sipping from a mug. "You're tough to find these days."

"Maybe you shouldn't be looking," she responded.

"Now, now, Ms. Gerard, let's play nice." Joel reached around her to grab a mug and pour some decaf coffee. His hand brushed against Abigail's arm, causing her to move away from the counter.

"What brings you here?" she asked, leaning against the wall about ten feet away from him.

"To see you." Joel closed the gap between them and leaned on the same wall.

Her eyebrows rose as she took another sip. "I'm amazed you have time to worry about me. Last time I saw you, there was a lot going on with you and your pregnant wife."

Joel nodded several times and gulped the coffee in his mug.

Abigail continued. "You were getting divorced and moving to Chicago or something like that."

"Yeah, something like that." He didn't elaborate. Keeping the conversation light was best.

"I see; typical Joel sharing the bare minimum." She eased away from the wall and went over to one of the tables but remained standing.

"What do you want me to say?" he asked, grinning.

"Are you still married?"

"Let's just say that I'm not divorced."

"I see."

Joel sensed a change in her voice. It was subtle, but having a conversation about relationships with Abigail was like lighting a match near a powder keg. An explosion was inevitable. He quickly sought to diffuse the situation to avert disaster. "I don't mean to aggravate you."

"Aggravate me? Please. I'd have to care for this to matter. Fortunately for me, I stopped caring when you eloped and brought a wife back from India to Detroit."

"I admit that wasn't handled well. I learned my lesson."

"Oh, really?" She traced the rim of her mug repeatedly with the tip of her finger without looking at Joel.

"I know that's hard for you to believe, but it's true," he told her.

"Right."

"Really, I'm working on things, including the marriage."

"Interesting. Last time you just dropped into my office," she said as her head bobbed slightly from side to side, "you had major concerns about your faith not jiving with your wife's. Wasn't she worshipping some kind of energy source or something like that?"

"There's more to her religion than that. You make it sound crazy."

"Hmm. Sounds like you've converted to her religion."

Joel appeared increasingly agitated as his neck stiffened. "Nobody said anything about converting. I'm just telling you that there's more to her religion than what you're describing."

She didn't have the details of Zarah's religion right, but it was obvious to her that Joel couldn't explain his wife's faith any better. Abigail could tell he was mad by the scowl plastered across his face. She swirled the contents of her mug and stared at him. "I remember a few months ago you made it seem like Zarah's religion had become a deal breaker. I guess you've worked out your problems and now you're living happily ever after."

"No, I haven't worked them out, and I don't know that I can. God will have to help me resolve that piece of the marriage."

"Maybe you shouldn't have gotten married in the first place."

"Too late for that. We're having a baby, and I won't abandon my child regardless of what anyone thinks."

"Does that mean you're staying married for the baby?"

"I didn't say that," Joel replied with a noticeable edge. "What I said was that I'm not abandoning my child." he added as each word resonated.

"Good for you," she said in a snide tone. Abigail didn't care if Joel was irritated. Maybe he deserved some of what he'd dealt to her over the past three years. She wasn't going to gloat, but she wasn't feeling sorry for him, either.

"Enough about me," he said. "Are you still resigning and venturing out on your own?"

"Maybe, maybe not. Don has asked me to consider the CEO role," she said, sipping from the mug.

"And Madeline has asked me to do the same."

"Madeline! You're lying," she stated and then coughed to clear her throat after getting choked up.

"I kid you not. Can you believe it - Me and Madeline?"

"No, I didn't think that would ever happen." Abigail wasn't thrilled. "This is silly; the two of us fighting for the same job." She hadn't yet responded to Don's request. With Joel's news, her interest in the position had diminished dramatically.

"It's fine with me. If I have to compete with anyone, I'm glad it's with you. You know I respect what you bring to this company," Joel said.

Abigail was disgusted as she listened to his ramblings. Had he forgotten just how little she'd been valued during his reign? She let him talk.

"You've paid your dues, and you're more than qualified to run DMI," Joel told her.

"If you feel that strongly about me, why don't you back out of the race and let me have the job?" she asked.

Joel chuckled. "Now, you know I can't do that."

Of course not, she thought. He was a Mitchell. They never backed down, not even when they should.

Joel strolled closer to her and extended his hand. "I wish you the best, and I can guarantee you this will be a fair fight."

"Humph. Speak for yourself. You can't make any promises about Madeline."

"Good point," Joel said, shaking his index finger at her. Without warning, he kissed Abigail on the cheek. "Everything will be okay. Regardless of what happens with the race, you're guaranteed a job here, and that is a promise." He said goodbye and left.

Abigail took a seat. She thought about the kiss, the CEO role, and Joel's newfound persona. She struggled to retain her composure, but the pressure she felt was pricking at her. She'd worked hard to escape the Mitchell family's clutch, and she was so close to exiting the company. But now she felt Don's corporate pull and Joel's allure. She shook her head. Abigail hadn't dealt with such a barrage of mixed emotions in a while, and she was better off.

The more she considered battling for the role of CEO, the less feasible it became. She wanted no part of starting a fresh war in the Mitchell family. She'd already experienced too many family battles over DMI. However, the CEO position was her dream job, and she would have leapt at the role a year ago. But so much had happened privately and professionally since then. The notion of going up against Joel and Madeline was daunting. They didn't fight fair, and she was too tired to go against two Mitchells, and possibly three, if Tamara got involved. That was suicidal. She wasn't convinced that fighting for the CEO post was the right move. Don would have to do much more persuading. Actually, he might need God to come down from heaven and give her a pep talk.

Chapter 7

Tamara was livid. She stormed out of Madeline's office. She couldn't wait to get out of there and away from these people. Just as her independence was about to be realized, she ran into Joel at the elevators. He greeted Tamara, but she didn't reciprocate. Her disdain for him escalated as she let her gaze slice him up and down. She had a few options: take the stairs and avoid him or take the elevator and ignore him. They both stepped onto the empty elevator when the doors opened. As soon as the doors closed, Tamara's previous options were cast aside as she ignited a verbal firestorm.

"Mother told me about this little arrangement you have with her. You know, I have obviously underestimated just how devious you are." Joel continued staring at the elevator doors as Tamara came close to his right ear. "You are really good if you managed to trick my mother into supporting you." She got closer to him, practically breathing in his ear. "I have to give it to you. I'm impressed, but remember that two can play this game. You have someone holding the cards at your house too, and it's not you."

Joel whipped around, and Tamara was forced to take a few steps back. "You don't want to go there." The elevator stopped on the second floor. Once the doors opened, Joel frantically pushed the CLOSE button. "Can you please catch the next elevator?" he told the person who was waiting to get on. "We're in a meeting," he said as the doors closed.

Tamara went further and pushed the big red STOP button. The elevator alarm buzzed, but it wasn't going to deter the meeting in progress. There was too much at stake for Tamara: her independence and, most importantly, the satisfaction of knowing she'd beaten Joel at his own game, even when he had Madeline's help. He wasn't going to win, because she wasn't prepared to lose.

Joel took a step toward Tamara, but she didn't budge. He had crossed into her personal space. That didn't bother her. She had faced plenty of giants in her life. Joel wasn't the first and wouldn't be the last. She dug in her heels and braced for whatever he might dish out.

"Like I said, you don't want to bring my wife and baby into this." He repeatedly tapped the palm of his open hand against his chest. "You can come at me as much as you want. Bring it on, but back off of my wife, and I mean it," he said with a piercing stare.

"Your wife! *Please.* As if you treat her like a wife. We know she doesn't mean anything to you."

"You don't know what you're talking about," he told her as his voice rose.

"What I do know is that DMI is my legacy. My parents are the founders of this company. This belongs to Don and to me."

The alarm continued buzzing as a voice came over the speaker box. "This is security. Is there an emergency in the elevator?"

"No. We're fine," Tamara shouted.

"Okay. We'll have you out in a minute."

"No hurry," Joel added. Then he returned his attention to Tamara. "I guess you've forgotten that Dave is my father too."

"So that gives you access through one parent. Don and I have two parents in this discussion. News flash, two is bigger than one," she snarled while twisting her index finger in the air. "There you have it. I win. Take your inheritance and move along." She pointed her finger toward the door. "Leave the company to us, the rightful heirs, because you're not running this place without a fight. And I'm willing to do whatever it takes to get you out of here."

"What does that mean?"

"It means exactly what it sounds like."

"You heard what I said. My wife and child are off-limits."

"Nothing and no one is off-limits. My married father wasn't off-limits to your mother. Apparently, it's okay when boundaries are erased if we want something badly enough. Just ask your mom. So, Zarah is fair game, mister," Tamara said.

"Don't make a mistake and cross a line, because I won't treat you like family."

The elevator began moving. Joel turned from Tamara and faced the doors. She moved up so they were side by side.

"Family?" she grunted "If you're that concerned about Zarah and the baby, why don't you remove your name from the list of candidates?" She waited for an answer from Joel but didn't get one. "Why don't you run back to your girlfriend in Chicago? That's what you do best."

The elevator finally made it to the ground floor, and both of them exited. The security guard was standing there, ready to assist, but Joel and Tamara shooed him away. The two parted bitterly in the lobby.

Joel had left the building, but his presence was very much with Tamara. She rehashed in her mind each word they'd spoken in the elevator. She was shattered. One part of her wanted to support Zarah as a true friend and avoid adding stress to her pregnancy. Another part of Tamara wanted to shove the agenda down the family's throat and force them to take her seriously. They owed her. The loyalty in her heart was in conflict with her wounds. Honestly, Tamara wasn't sure how far she'd go to stake a claim on her share of DMI, but the disrespect heaped on by her family might have pushed her pretty far this go-round. If she could move Joel out of the way, Abigail would be simple. She picked up her step. There was work to be done, and she had to get to it.

Chapter 8

Rejection, confusion, and anger swelled in Tamara. She drifted from DMI to what had become her favorite coffee shop in downtown Detroit. A table in the rear corner was as close to a refuge as she was going to get without a plane ticket. Several of the waiters greeted her. After meeting with three Mitchells in one day, she needed something stronger than tea.

"I'll take a latte with a double shot of espresso," she told the waitress who took her order. It was her version of getting wasted, since she hadn't acquired a taste for alcohol. Hopefully, the caffeine jolt would be enough to drown out her gloom.

"You'll want to keep these coming," Tamara said when the waitress set a large mug on the table in front of her.

"Tough day, huh?"

"You have no idea," Tamara replied and didn't hesitate to take a gulp of her mind regulator.

"Let me know when you're ready for round two," the waitress said.

Tamara nodded. Soon she was alone in the corner, and her thoughts refused to be contained. Joel's, Don's, and Madeline's words were like bullets soaring at her from a firing squad. They were relentless, and there was nowhere for her to hide. They were ganging up on her, and she wanted to scream, but her pride was too much of a warrior to allow her to lie down and quit. The Mitchells owed her for twenty years of misery, and she would get restitution, but today was a reminder that her journey wasn't going to be smooth. Being outnumbered meant Tamara had to find a way to fight smarter, not tougher.

She mulled over the latte longer than expected, but no solutions popped up.

The waitress approached her table. "Can I freshen up your cup?"

"Uh, not right now," Tamara responded. The espresso wasn't doing the trick. In fairness, not much was going to give her the wisdom needed to bring down a bunch of self-righteous opponents. She picked up her phone, began dialing, and abruptly stopped.

She pondered her circumstances and fidgeted for over an hour. Finally, she rubbed the palm of her hand across her forehead and her eyelids in frustration. She'd avoided the obvious, but there weren't any other options. Zarah was her best gamble when it came to obtaining something meaningful that could be used as a bargaining chip. Tamara didn't rush to make the call. She simply sat at the table, with her forehead resting against her thumb and fingertips, and stared at her phone.

The waitress appeared again. "Can I get you a fresh latte?"

Tamara didn't bother to look up. "No, I'm good," she said, and the waitress walked away. She wasn't really good, but it was easier for Tamara to send the waitress on her way than risk having to explain her dire situation to a stranger who couldn't help. She wouldn't take the chance. Shutting people out was her specialty, and she did it flawlessly.

Minutes clicked by, and her decisiveness faded. Tamara's overwhelming desire to call her only friend won out. Not only was Zarah her confidante, but she was also Tamara's ticket back to independence. She dialed the number slowly, concerned that Joel had gotten home by now. She'd already had one heated argument with him, and she wasn't looking for two in one day. She'd have to tread lightly. Although Tamara didn't care two hoots about Joel, she didn't want to cause her friend any harm. More importantly, she couldn't alienate Zarah, not now, when there was so much on the line. Pleading her case would be a delicate endeavor, and she wasn't quite sure how to proceed.

Zarah answered after several rings. "Tamara, I am pleased you've called."

"Is Joel with you?"

"No. He's not returned."

Tamara rubbed her hand up and down the mug. "We need to talk."

"Would you like to come back for another visit today?"

"Oh no," Tamara blurted. "I mean, I would like to come for another visit, but not today. I'm a little tired."

"I understand."

"But I would like to come over soon," Tamara responded.

Zarah's Indian accent didn't cover up the disappointment in her tone. It was just as much of a disappointment for Tamara. She could definitely have used some face-to-face encouragement from someone who cared. Zarah was the only one who took her seriously and saw Tamara as a bona fide businesswoman capable of handling a company. Others in the family treated Tamara as a victim or a helpless youth. She couldn't stand either label and would prove her worth by assuming power and running the company better than anyone ever had, including her mother, father, and brothers.

"Let's plan to get together real soon, kind of like a ladies' day out," Tamara suggested.

"But I can't go far from the house. The doctor has me on bed rest for the baby."

"That's right. I didn't forget. I meant that we could spend the afternoon together. I could bring some Indian food, and we can sit around and chat."

"Yes, that would be very nice."

"Then it's a date. Call me when Joel is going to be out for a few hours."

"Joel won't bother us."

"I'm sure he won't, but it will be better if we let him go on his way."

Tamara's plan wouldn't work if Joel was around. He had to be out of the house in order for Tamara to explain candidly to Zarah how important the West Coast division was. Tamara's future depended on Zarah's willingness to sell the division. If Joel got wind of her request, he'd shut the visit down before they had a chance to exchange hellos. He couldn't know. For the same reason, Zarah would have to keep quiet about all of it.

"He'll want you to stay very still, and I understand why," Tamara explained. "But we always have a good time together. We can cheer each other up."

"Yes, that will be good."

"So, we better not mention this to him. Otherwise, he might want you to avoid too much excitement."

"Yes, this will be our secret."

Tamara breathed a sigh of relief. Those were just the words she wanted to hear. They ended the call, and Tamara beckoned the waitress.

"Please bring me a fresh cup with lots of cream and only one shot of espresso."

"No double shot this round?"

"Nope. Don't need it," she said, sliding the old mug toward the edge of the table. "I'm doing much better, much, much better."

Her mission to dethrone Joel was under way, and Tamara couldn't be more pleased.

Chapter 9

Nearly a week flew by, and Madeline was eager to get her candidate confirmed and the selection business over and done. The emotional component of this process was already wearing on her.

Joel appeared in her doorway, having been summoned by Madeline earlier that morning.

"Come in," she shouted as Joel stood at the threshold. "We have a lot of work to do if we're going to nab this job for you."

"I'm ready," he responded and grinned.

Madeline seemed suddenly guarded. "Well, you better be, because I'm putting my name out there on your behalf. You better not fall short."

"I'm all in, and I won't disappoint you."

Madeline motioned for him to meet her at the conference table, which was situated off to the side in her office. "You better not." She halted in mid-step and hurled a stare at him that caused him to pause. "As the saying goes, don't take my kindness for weakness. You know I'm not the one to mess with, Mr. Joel Mitchell."

Joel sensed that Madeline was serious, and he wasn't going to get their partnership off to a shaky start. He would continue tiptoeing around her as his pride sat still. Pretty much whatever Madeline wanted, he was prepared and eager to deliver.

Joel remained silent, and the tension seemed to dissipate. Both of them grabbed a seat at the table.

"We have a week or two to lay out our strategy and get before the board," Madeline told him as she put on her reading glasses and placed the notepad she'd been carrying on the table.

Joel was perplexed. He had expected that they would meet with the board in four weeks or so. But then, of course, Madeline had a way of shaking people up and getting them to move much quicker than they'd planned. For many years, Joel was on the losing end of her influence. In those days he viewed her actions as manipulation. Sitting within arm's reach of his champion, he decided that the term was less fitting.

"You think we'll be ready so quickly?" This meeting was huge for Joel. He couldn't squander it by rushing in unprepared. "I was hoping for a few more weeks to prepare."

"What are you worried about? I'm the one who has to be ready. You just have to show up and keep your mouth shut when someone asks you a silly question. We can't get caught up in deflecting questions about your wayward past. Heaven knows there's plenty to talk about."

Joel didn't find Madeline's comments complimentary, but there was sufficient truth behind her words to keep him humbled. He let her continue.

"You'll have to work on getting very good at changing the subject. When the board raises questions about your tarnished character, we'll aggressively steer them back to your successes. That's where we want to direct their attention."

"Harmonious Energy is bound to be on the agenda," Joel said, remembering how the deal had transpired with Musar Bengali, Zarah's father.

Musar had wanted a prominent husband for his only child, and Joel had wanted to take DMI international. Initially, it felt like Joel had gotten everything he wanted out of the deal. In fact, he had gotten too much. He hadn't wanted to get married then, but Musar wouldn't hear of selling off half his company and putting Joel in charge of day-to-day operations without including his daughter's hand in marriage, especially since Musar was terminally ill. Given the benefits Joel saw in merging DMI and Harmonious Energy, getting married had seemed like a manageable sacrifice.

Although there had been issues, Joel didn't regret his decision to go after Harmonious Energy. He'd done it for the right reasons. His father had longed to expand the company and take it beyond the United States, but he hadn't been able to make it happen. Joel did. The new company could have been a major force abroad. Unfortunately, he'd underestimated how offended the existing customer base would be by DMI partnering with a company that was founded on conflicting beliefs.

"In hindsight, the merger idea was noble. Whether you believe it or not, I did it for a good reason," Joel said letting his gaze plummet. "But in truth, my plan in executing the merger was flawed."

Madeline nodded in affirmation. "And we have to address it before we get to the meeting. We know the company doesn't align with our values and thus it has to go. We know I'm not a holy-roller churchgoer, but that doesn't mean I'm okay with worshipping every religion you drag through this place. Your dad believed in one God. I guess I do too. That means there's no room in here for Zarah's whole bag of gods. That's why Harmonious Energy has to go."

"I agree, but it's Zarah's company. Lately, she's been fixated on running Harmonious Energy in honor of her father. It might not be as easy to wrestle the company from her as we'd like it to be."

Madeline snatched off her glasses and shook them at Joel. "Well, you'd better find a way if you want to be CEO, because there's no way I can convince the board to reappoint you if they're going to get more of the same from you. Look, we have a tough enough job as it is to sell them on the notion that you've changed."

"I *have* changed."

Madeline's eyes widened as her gaze shifted away from Joel. "Humph. It's hard for me to believe. So, I can imagine others will have a difficult time believing this overnight miracle."

"Apparently, you and the board members aren't the only ones who doubt my sincerity."

"Who else?"

"Tamara," he said, grabbing Madeline's attention as she looked up from writing on her notepad. "I ran into her last week, and she let me have it."

"Really—"

"She was angry at me and Abigail for stealing the CEO role from her."

"I see," Madeline said.

Joel couldn't tell if Madeline was shocked or not. Either way, that was her daughter. He wasn't going to express his opinion about Tamara's state of mind. Joel was concerned that Madeline might pull out if Tamara showed too much resistance to the idea of making him CEO. He was wading in deep waters, and his anxiety rose. "Does her reaction change the plan?"

"Not mine. I can't speak for you, but we're proceeding as planned."

"You sure, because I've been honest with you."

"Joel, I told you that I'm going to back your candidacy. Unlike you, I have consistently kept my word." He didn't bother waging a defense. "People might not like what I have to say, but they will agree that I do what I say. You can take my word to the bank," she said. "Hear me good. If Don's out of the picture, then you're the next best candidate for this job, period, end of discussion."

Joel kept his doubts concealed. He was forced to trust Madeline. She was the last person on earth Joel wanted to trust, which was precisely why he'd have to rely heavily on prayer and God's intervention. He wasn't on solid ground spiritually, but Joel was making an effort to reconnect with God for guidance.

"Okay," he said in total submission to her plan. "What's next?"

"Go home and convince that lovely wife of yours to sell her family's business. Then expect to meet with me again in a few days."

"I'll see what I can do."

"You're going to have to do better than that. I suggest you work that Mitchell charm and get her to hand over the keys. I've seen how she looks at you. This shouldn't be too difficult. Woo her, and she'll step to your beat, just like the trail of other women you've encountered."

"Come on, Madeline."

"Oh, don't get defensive now. Besides, this is a time when your womanizing skills will be an asset. So, go and work them," she said, waving her hand in the air. Madeline got up from the table and went to her desk. "Make it happen, Joel. I'm still the founder of this company, and my clout will go a long ways with winning over the board, but you have to help me out here. Consider cleaning up the balance sheet as your first CEO project. If you take care of this problem, you're as good as in."

"I'll call you in a few days and give you an update on my progress," he said.

"Nah, don't call me. I'll call you. Just be ready when I call," she said and picked up the phone.

Joel rightfully took that as a sign to leave and exited her office quietly. Once he was gone, Madeline set the phone down. There wasn't anyone she planned to call, but there was someone she wanted to talk to. Tamara's comments replayed in her head. How could she choose Sherry's child over her own? Madeline was certain Joel was the best fit for CEO of DMI. As much as her heart wanted to promote Tamara, rational reasoning wouldn't dare let her make such a costly mistake. Her daughter needed years of mentoring, training, and experience to come close to being a viable candidate. Abigail would definitely have a better chance at succeeding in that role than Tamara, and Sherry probably would too. Love and wisdom continued dueling within her as Madeline anguished over the situation. She was weakening when it came to Tamara, but she would be sure not to give Joel any indication of that in the next few days.

Madeline was tired of fretting. She picked up the phone to call her assistant. Agonizing for another couple of weeks was unacceptable. "Can you come in here? I need you to set up a few calls for me right away." The quicker their mess was over, the better.

Chapter 10

Several days later the smaller conference room on the executive floor was filled with three of the six board members who weren't members of the Mitchell family. Madeline had managed to coerce them into showing up early in the morning by telling them that she would be presenting plans for a major structural change. In actuality, there was some truth to her appeal. The one detail she'd neglected to share about the meeting was the name Joel Mitchell. It was reason she hadn't called for a full board meeting. Joel was a "structural change" which was bound to stimulate controversy that Madeline wasn't prepared to handle. She'd opted to deal with a sample-size reaction to her proposal to determine just how steep a hill they'd have to climb before Joel's behind could jump into the CEO seat again.

"Can you please tell Don to meet me in the small conference room?" Madeline told her assistant as she walked into the hallway. Then she sashayed serenely into the conference room despite the fact that this group was a pack of wolves eager to pounce on the weak. She ought to know as Madeline was the ringleader in the boardroom on most occasions.

"I'm glad the three of you could join us on such short notice," she said, leaving the seat at the head of the table open for Don and walking to the other end of the room before sitting.

"What's this meeting about, Madeline?" one board member asked.

"Yes, we're quite curious to know why you have called us here," another member added.

"I thought you wanted to speak with me directly," the third board member said. "I didn't realize you were calling a full board meeting."

"Oh, no," Madeline said quickly. "This isn't a full meeting. Excluding Don and me, all seven members would have to be duly notified, and we didn't have time to do that."

She wouldn't dare call a full meeting when there was so much uncertainty. There was another reason Madeline had handpicked a smaller group for her unorthodox meeting. Tamara had been given the empty seat on the board when Joel stepped down earlier in the year. At the time it made perfect sense but not now. Calling a full session of the board would require that Tamara be notified, and there was no way the meeting would have a positive outcome for Madeline, Joel, or Don if that happened. Madeline had always wanted her children to have a voice at the head table. In theory, it was a noble goal. In practice, it had Madeline stressed, and she didn't like the feeling.

"Let's get moving. I have another meeting in an hour," the second board member stated.

Normally, Madeline would rip into anyone who was keen on rushing her meeting, but she would soon be beholden to this group. Soft words and a good attitude were her recipe for success.

"We'll get started shortly. Just waiting on Don," she said. As soon as she made that statement, he arrived. "Perfect timing, son. I saved the seat for you down at that end." She noticed the scowl on his face and sensed his confusion. She knew the source. Madeline hadn't bothered to mention the meeting to Don until the very last minute. He was coming in cold like others in the room.

The greetings between Don and the board members were rapid and curt.

"Mother, I have clients coming in this afternoon. What's the purpose of this?" he said, remaining standing.

Madeline motioned for him to take a seat. "All right, everyone. I understand that you have other obligations. So we'll get right to the heart of this meeting and keep it short."

Bewilderment was evident in each stare hurled her way.

"There is a structural change on the horizon for DMI, and it will require the board's approval," Madeline announced.

Don took a seat.

"What's the nature of this change?" board member number three asked.

"Our beloved Don is stepping down," Madeline revealed. Amid the chatter that broke out, she added, "That means we have to find a new CEO."

"I'm sure we can get the appropriate search firm to provide a shortlist of distinguished candidates for the post," board member number one said.

Madeline shook her head. "No need. We have a candidate."

"We have *two* candidates," Don added.

"Yes, we have two candidates," Madeline said, looking at Don and then quickly shifting her gaze back to the group. "One is more experienced than the other and has a proven track record of success."

Don groaned. "Mother, don't you think that's a bit of an exaggeration?"

"Absolutely not, my candidate has proven that he can deliver unprecedented sales figures."

The sidebar conversations intensified.

"We need a strong successor," one board member commented.

"Agreed. We've suffered a tumultuous year, and we have to regain a solid footing in the marketplace," another board member added.

"If there's a candidate who can step in, once Don leaves and keep us in the winner's circle, you'll have my vote," board member number one commented.

"Mine too," another board member added.

"Who is this fascinating candidate? Do we know this person?" one of the board members asked.

Madeline avoided all eye contact and remained silent.

Don jumped in. "Oh, you know him," he said, snickering.

The board members waited in anticipation for Madeline to reveal the candidate's identity, but she couldn't utter his name. It was too dicey. It was equivalent to pedaling a bike into oncoming traffic. The outcome wasn't likely to be positive. Yet this was the predicament she found herself in. She was about to shout out the name, but Don beat her to it.

"It's Joel," he announced.

"Joel Mitchell?" one of the board members asked.

"One and the same," Don said. "Abigail Gerard is the other candidate."

His smirk irritated Madeline, but what could she do? The room had grown silent, but now chatter erupted once again. Madeline didn't jump in immediately to squelch the uproar. She'd give them a minute to digest the announcement, and then she'd proceed with clearer vision once the electrifying shock wore off.

"It is an outrage that the two of you would bring us here to announce Joel's candidacy," board member number two remarked.

"Wait a minute," Don said. "I didn't call this meeting, and I'm definitely not recommending Joel as a candidate. I'm one hundred percent behind Abigail. She's served DMI in stellar fashion as our executive vice president. She's earned her stripes, and I believe she'd serve DMI well at the helm."

"Listen, once you set aside your personal feelings about Joel and get to the core of what we should be seeking in a candidate, this becomes a no-brainer. He has the experience, the leadership, and the track record that we need." Madeline was firm in her delivery. He also had the Mitchell name, which gave him an extra vote as far as she was concerned. If he were one of her children, his name alone would add four silent votes, which was equivalent to an automatic win. "I respect Abigail as a great second in command, but she's not the right CEO for DMI, at least not now."

Several eyebrows arched around the table, coupled with nods of agreement.

Madeline went on. "We know he had some problems before stepping down last year. That's heavily documented. However, let's be fair. He more than doubled the size of the company in a year. He has what it takes. With the right structure, he could do well for us."

"I'm not sure we should take a chance on Joel Mitchell. He made several compromising decisions," a board member stated. "He merged a company founded on Christian values with one built on conflicting principles."

"We're still trying to unload our stake in Harmonious Energy and remain solvent," added another board member.

More nods and chatter followed.

"Not to mention the excessive debt he took on, which sent the balance sheet toppling. It's good that DMI is privately held, otherwise it would have gone belly up on the stock market," said another board member.

Madeline let them go on and on. The board member was right. DMI was privately held, and she had a major portion of the ownership shares. Madeline was tired of this charade. She wanted to tell them that the decision had been made, and they were going with Joel, because the founder said so. She could only dream that it was that straightforward, as she knew there was more work to be done before they got to the rightful conclusion.

"Reinstating Joel would put the company back at risk, and no one can support him as a sound candidate, especially with Harmonious Energy being on the books," a board member stated.

Madeline wasn't discouraged. She had expected such a reaction. Joel's fall from grace was recent, and the stench of failure still lingered. She'd wanted a sample-size reaction before calling for the live vote. That way they would know where to concentrate their efforts. "Clearly, we'll have to come back to you with a full presentation on both candidates in a week or two."

"Please include the entire board next time," one board member said.

"Of course," Madeline stated.

She had a tough sale ahead. She was encouraged, because it appeared that Abigail wasn't a slam dunk, either. An equal shot at the CEO position was the best she could hope for at this early stage in the process. She'd count this test as a success. Both candidates had strengths and weaknesses, and these would have to be addressed. She wasn't delusional. There was a great deal of work to be accomplished in a short time, but failure wasn't an option.

Despite how much he'd changed, she couldn't muster the resolve to do this solely for Joel. Actually, it wasn't for him at all. This was about her legacy. Madeline wouldn't be able to retire unless a person whom she'd handpicked was running the company. She was confident that Joel would win. How could he not with her in his corner?

Chapter 11

Wednesday morning began the same as the rest. By mid-morning Joel emerged from the guest room that was situated down the hall and around the corner from the master bedroom. His job was to check on Zarah while she was under the doctor's care. After they'd nearly lost the baby last month, he wasn't going to take any chances.

He entered the room and saw that she was tucked under the bedcover, not yet awake. He tiptoed to one of the chairs located across the room and sat down, careful not to make too much noise and disturb her. This had become a familiar scene. Many nights he'd sat in one of those chairs until Zarah fell asleep. Last week he'd considered sleeping on the floor near her bed, but she had refused to let him be inconvenienced on her behalf. He could have opted to sleep on the bed next to her, but it didn't feel right to jump into bed and pretend that they were in a traditional marriage. His lack of affection for her was real, and it wouldn't change overnight.

He believed there was hope for them, but agreeing to stand by her for the sake of their child wasn't the same as eagerly jumping into a satisfying and romantic relationship. True feelings weren't a water faucet to be turned on and off at will. The honeymoon phase wasn't over; it had never existed. If she hadn't become pregnant, he would have already divorced her. Each day they were together was a huge step for him, but there were still significant issues to be worked out between them. He was determined to move slowly and let any budding affection for his wife develop naturally. Until the baby was born and he had a better grasp on the marriage, staying in the guest room was wise. As a backup, Joel also planned to keep his suite at the Westin downtown, the one he had reserved when they separated several months ago.

Zarah stirred slightly and then gave a few moans. He sat on the edge of his seat to determine if this meant she was waking up or experiencing pain. She rolled over but didn't awaken. Joel didn't relax and probably wouldn't until their healthy baby was born in five months. He clasped his hands together and let his chin rest against his fingertips. He gazed at Zarah. He'd seen her many times, but looking at her as the morning light danced around, he saw that she was peaceful, radiant, and delicate. Most importantly, she was a human being with feelings and desires. If only her beauty was enough to move the meter of affection more in her direction, beyond the role of hanging around purely out of obligation. Joel continued to gaze at her. How could he have been so callous as to marry a woman without loving her? How could he have discounted her worth and allowed himself to see her only as a tool required to expand his company?

He closed his eyes and let his head drop, his forehead now resting against his fingertips. Thinking about how he'd been willing to go that far, Joel grew furious with himself. As a result, here they were. He was nursing a pregnant wife whose family and way of life resided more than seven thousand miles away. The weight of their situation could easily overwhelm him, but Joel resisted the notion. Yes, he was in a tight spot, but God was able to deliver him from all unrighteousness. He yearned for stability, for a time when the consequences of his mistakes were far in the distance. He had to believe there was hope. Otherwise, how could he stomach the notion of using someone purely for personal gain? Zarah didn't deserve such treatment. No one did.

She began stirring again, which drew Joel's attention back to the present. He could tell she was disoriented and rushed to her side.

"Good morning, sleepyhead."

She moaned an indecipherable greeting, which was odd. Her accent was slight, and most of the time he understood every word Zarah spoke. He was pleased that language wasn't a barrier between them. At least there was something they didn't have to reconcile. As a matter of fact, it was as if her English had been perfected in preparation for living in the United States, which he found appealing.

"Are you in any pain?"

"No, no pain," she said, directing her attention to Joel.

"Good. That's what I want to hear." She sat up, and he quickly fluffed several pillows and placed the stack behind her back. He gently touched her shoulders as she sank into the pillows. "Let me get your breakfast."

"No, please. I'm not much for eating right now."

"But you have to eat something light. Remember, the baby needs you to be healthy." He placed his hand on her lower abdomen. "I need you to be healthy."

She placed her hand on his. "Then I will have a bit of food."

Joel didn't have to speculate about how she was feeling. The glow on her face spoke volumes. She loved their unborn child, and he knew Zarah loved him too. He slid his hand from underneath hers. *Love* was a complex term. He loved his mother and father. There was a list of people he cared for, like Abigail, Don, and Zarah. Joel wasn't sure what he felt for the baby, besides a sense of obligation and a commitment to be a father. He figured that the right thing to do was to remain married and be there for his child, or was it? If the decision was as simple as staying married to his pregnant wife, he figured there was enough good will and Christ-like compassion in him to stay put. But their dilemma was much more complicated. When his mind was in the right place, he served the God of Abraham, Isaac, and Jacob. Zarah served a different god, an entire set of gods. Therein resided the problem. His Christianity and her Eastern religion weren't dwelling in the same hemisphere without conflict, let alone under the same roof.

Joel didn't fully understand the details of her religion, but he knew it had to do with energy sources connecting with the body, the soul, and the universe. Admittedly, it was too intricate for him to grasp, or maybe he simply lacked any desire to try and understand. Whatever the reason for his reluctance to embrace her faith, the fact remained that it didn't jive with his. He was forced to wonder how they could raise a child together when they did not have the same core philosophies and guiding principles. Staying together seemed impossible, but he wasn't ready to give up. He needed more time to figure out the relationship and his long-term desire. In the meantime, they had to resolve a huge religious issue if they were going to have a legitimate chance at staying together after the baby was born.

Joel wasn't going to compromise on the subject. "What do you think about the baby being baptized in my faith?" he asked.

Zarah fidgeted and let her gaze sink. He already had her answer. "I don't know much about this business of Christianity. I know my language, my culture, my faith. I want our baby to have the blessings of my gods," she said, speaking rapidly.

Joel sensed she was getting worked up. He'd table the discussion until a more opportune time. He recognized there might never be a better time and resigned himself to the notion that only God could give him the answer he sought for such a convoluted predicament.

"Let me go downstairs and get the cook to make you a light breakfast of toast, fresh juice, and . . . I don't know . . . maybe a hard-boiled egg?"

"No fuss, please. I am better with a small bowl of rice and juice."

"If you say so," Joel said.

Zarah grabbed his hand. "I'm very happy that you're here with me. We are a family, and that is most important to me."

"Don't you worry. I promise that you won't have to go through this pregnancy alone."

On the way to the kitchen, Joel pondered heavily. Many couples had survived without mutual love, and his parents were a great example. There was no doubt his mother worshipped his father, but if Joel had to guess, her love hadn't been reciprocated to the same degree by his father. Dave Mitchell had seemed to care deeply for Joel's mother, but his unwillingness to severe ties with Madeline was an indication that his love had been split between two women.

It wasn't an ideal scenario in which to raise a family, but he wasn't seeking perfection. He merely wanted a path forward. Joel yearned for a way to reconcile this mess that he and Zarah's father had created. Musar Bengali had handed his only child to Joel with every stipulation well defined on the business end of their deal, but love had never been a topic of discussion, let alone a requirement. Regardless, there was no one else alive to blame. Her father had passed, and what happened going forward was up to Joel and Zarah.

He returned with her breakfast on a tray and a single rose lying along an edge. Joel didn't want to pick up the conversation where they had left off, and possibly

stress out Zarah. He decided to retreat to his room and
get dressed. That would give her a chance to settle down
completely. He'd barely stepped into his room when his
cell phone buzzed on the nightstand next to the bed. He
rushed to grab it and heard Madeline's voice.

"Get over here to the office. We have to talk," she
demanded.

"What's up?"

"I don't want to talk about it over the phone. How soon
can you get here?"

"I'll be there within the hour."

"Don't keep me waiting. Hurry up," she said and
disconnected the call.

Joel's anxiety level rose. He had no idea what was
going on, but it didn't sound good. He dashed into the
bathroom to get dressed in a hurry. Twenty minutes later
he tore from the bedroom and hustled to Zarah's side. He
found her sitting up in bed, reading a book.

"I have to run out for a few hours, but the cook is
downstairs if you need anything."

"Where are you going?"

"I have to see Madeline." He wasn't surprised at her
puzzled look. "I haven't had a chance to tell you this, but
she wants me to take over as CEO when Don moves to
South Africa."

"I am most surprised that she would ask you."

"Me too, but she did." Joel eased onto the side of the
bed, next to Zarah. He couldn't stay long, but taking a few
minutes to lessen her concern was doable.

"Did you say yes?"

"You better believe I did," he said, unable to contain his
enthusiasm.

"Then you must go to her. Go," she said, gently shoving
him.

"You sure you'll be all right while I'm gone?"

"I will be fine."

Joel darted to the door and shook his cell phone. "Call me if you need anything."

She nodded.

"Anything—"

"Go."

Joel left, and Zarah found herself alone, but she didn't feel lonely. Actually, she was relieved to have him gone for a short period. She reached over and grabbed the house phone and rapidly dialed Tamara's phone number. They'd spoken so often that she'd memorized the number. Hopefully, her friend could come by for a short visit. Zarah was pleased at the possibility.

Chapter 12

Joel rushed to Madeline's office. He didn't try to figure out what she wanted. There were too many possibilities and most of them were negative. With each step he rattled off a quick prayer asking God for favor. It was his single best advantage. Having Madeline on his side was a miracle. Having God on his side was unbeatable. He'd work hard to keep both.

"Is she in?" Joel asked the assistant outside Madeline's office.

"She's in the small conference room, waiting for you."

Joel thanked her for the information and hurried along. He was intent on getting in and out as swiftly as possible. Just as the assistant had said, Joel found Madeline in the conference room.

"I got here as quickly as I could. What's up?"

"Have a seat," she told him, and he obliged. "We have a problem," she said, spinning her Montblanc pen on the table.

Joel braced for the worst, but he wasn't worried yet and didn't shudder. He'd have to deal with whatever was headed his way, but he was sure that God, and Madeline, would help.

"I met with three of the board members today," she said.

Joel sat tall in his seat. This was big. They hadn't prepared properly for such a meeting. And how could she meet with members of the board without him? He was eager to get the results of that meeting, although Madeline's disposition made it clear what had transpired.

"I didn't realize you were calling a board meeting so fast." He had plenty of questions but not much gumption to ask them. Letting someone take the lead on critical decisions that affected him wasn't familiar territory for him. He was tempted to reprimand Madeline for excluding him from an important meeting and crucial decisions, but Joel held back. He'd let Madeline continue and see where she was headed. "Didn't you need me there with you?"

"Technically, it wasn't a formal meeting. We'd have to give proper notification and that whole business. And, no, we definitely didn't need you at that meeting," she said grimacing.

Joel felt a tinge of awkwardness but didn't panic.

"Let's just say the meeting didn't go as well as I would have liked," she added.

"Okay . . ." Joel became irritated. Normally, he couldn't get Madeline to shut up. At a time when he needed her to speak, she wasn't forthcoming. However, he was fully aware of his situation. So Joel continued to exercise patience, perhaps the most he ever had. "What didn't go well?"

"Overcoming your long list of flaws is going to be tough."

"And we expected that going in." Joel intentionally spoke reverently so as not to upset Madeline.

"True, and I'm confident we can sway the board with your past achievements." Her compliment settled Joel's nerves. "There's no question about your poor decisions regarding DMI, but no one can challenge your successes here, either." Madeline began twirling her pen again. "You more than doubled the company's revenue during your first year as CEO."

Joel nodded. "And I increased our exposure in the marketplace."

Madeline grunted. "I wouldn't be too cavalier about that footnote, since it has become our single largest problem."

"How so?" he asked.

"You were bent on dragging this company onto the international scene at any cost."

"I did what my father couldn't do, and that was to expand our territory."

"What you did was expose us in the marketplace." Her tone was stern, causing Joel to wince. "You put us in a compromising position by purchasing Harmonious Energy, and it's not easily reconciled."

Joel groaned. He'd hoped they could get through this meeting without having that conversation. He knew they had to deal with that company, but not in every meeting. "I'll figure something out," he said, wishing to divert them from the path they were headed. "What other concerns came up at your meeting with the board members?"

"Don't you get what I'm saying? There were plenty of questions about you, and they mostly focused on the fact that the members don't trust you. They're not sure if you've changed or if this is merely a smoke screen so that you can regain control of DMI and shove it totally off the cliff this go-round."

Joel didn't readily respond. It was pointless to try to defend himself against others' perceptions and fears. His words were meaningless when held up against his past. His best defense was to show them how he'd changed.

Madeline flailed her hands in the air. "I can convince the board to get past your failures. I can do that, but Harmonious Energy is our main problem. Forget about the board. I can't convince two rookies to support you as long as that company is on our books. We have to get rid of it and show them you're willing to clean up your mess. We have to get rid of Harmonious Energy, and it's too difficult to find a buyer who wants only DMI's half of the company. We have to sell the entire company as a whole entity. You know this," Madeline told him. "Talk your wife into selling her half. If you can get a signed letter stating her intent to sell, that should be sufficient to sway the board in our direction. I'll handle the rest."

Joel didn't know where Zarah's mind was regarding Harmonious Energy. Perhaps this was the ideal time to approach her about it. With the baby being a priority, the company might not be appealing to her. He'd have to see.

"I'll talk with Zarah and see what she wants to do."

"I don't hear the urgency in your voice." Madeline scooted closer to the table. "Joel, we're in a battle, and a heated one, I might add. Remember, Don and Abigail are waiting in the wings. This is going to be tougher than we anticipated. The board is fixated on your involvement with Harmonious Energy. We have to erase your connection to that company," she said, emphasizing each word.

"Won't be easy."

"Well, it's this simple, Joel. Get rid of Harmonious Energy or kiss the CEO title at DMI goodbye. I'm confident that we can finagle a win, but you can't tie my hands by keeping Harmonious Energy in the picture. I'd have to call in too many favors, and even then I'm sure it wouldn't be enough to push us over the finish line." Madeline patted him on the shoulder. "You have your work cut out for you, baby boy. Go home, take care of this, and call me tomorrow with good news."

Joel had heard Madeline's appeal loud and clear. He had to convince Zarah to sacrifice her family business in order for him to have a chance at redemption in his. Feared ignited within him, and Joel wondered if he'd have to sink deeper into the marriage in exchange for her agreement to sell her half of Harmonious Energy. The thought was crushing, and he fought hard to remain optimistic. He rushed home to get the ball rolling immediately with Zarah. He only hoped that God would help him.

Chapter 13

A Pulitzer Prize couldn't have brought Tamara any greater satisfaction than she felt upon receiving Zarah's call. Little brother Joel was out of the house, and she'd take full advantage of her visit with Zarah. The clock was ticking, with Abigail and Joel both plotting to steal her job. Madeline and Don might be planning to go before the board to push their agenda any day now. She was motivated to action.

Her limousine pulled onto Joel's property. For other trips, she'd wait close to an hour for a cab, enjoy the leisurely thirty-minute ride to Zarah's, and have the cabdriver let her off at the end of the winding driveway. Admittedly, perks came in handy under dire circumstances. Her private driver zipped up the driveway and barreled to the front door. They came to a stop, and the driver hopped out to open her door. Tamara didn't have the patience to wait for meaningless gestures. "Wait for me, please," she hollered and jumped out before the driver reached her door.

"Yes, ma'am. I'll pull over to the garage and wait for you there."

"No. Wait right here." She needed the getaway car close. Joel was gone, but he could come home at any minute, and her escape route had to be set.

Tamara trotted to the front door and rang the buzzer. The housekeeper answered.

"Please come in, Ms. Mitchell. Mrs. Zarah is expecting you."

"Is she upstairs?"

"Yes," the housekeeper responded.

Tamara didn't wait for an escort. Climbing the stairs, Tamara had to contain her rising anxiety. Her heart was pounding, and her pulse racing. Sneaking into the house without Joel's knowledge felt like espionage. It brewed an equal blend of intrigue and fear of getting caught.

Tamara called out when she reached Zarah's bedroom. Without attempting to get up, Zarah told her to come in. When Tamara entered the bedroom, she was startled as her friend looked so worn out.

"I'm so glad you called," Tamara said. "How are you feeling?"

Zarah mumbled something.

"What did you say?"

"I'm good," Zarah responded, her words barely audible.

"You don't sound good. What's wrong?"

Zarah was quiet for a while, and then tears formed in her eyes.

"What's going on?" Tamara didn't want to believe the obvious. The prodigal husband had been home for maybe a month. There was no way he could have screwed up already, but then again, they were talking about Joel Mitchell. "What did he do this time?" she demanded.

Zarah wouldn't answer.

Tamara sat on the bed, close to Zarah. "Go ahead. I'm sure this is about Joel, isn't it?" she said.

Finally, Zarah wiped away a few tears and spoke. "It is my marriage."

Tamara knew it. She was getting mad. Why did he always have to suck all the attention from the room? Joel wasn't even in the house, yet he was the main topic of discussion. Tamara became angrier as she thought about how entitled her so-called brother was. He dictated his wife's emotions as if Zarah were a puppet. DMI was Tamara's birthright, but Joel seemed determined to have that too. Her anger was close to boiling over, but she had to maintain control if she was to have any type of meaningful discussion with Zarah about the business.

"I thought the two of you were perfectly happy with the baby coming."

Zarah rubbed her abdomen. "We are, I believe."

"Then what is it?" Tamara had to keep from shouting. She wanted Zarah to get over whatever marital hiccups were going on with Joel and move on. Expending compassion was pointless. This wasn't the only hurt Zarah would experience with Joel. There would be plenty more to come if she stayed in their ridiculous sham of a marriage. If only Tamara could get Zarah to see it the same way.

"Joel is worried about our faiths not matching. He wants our baby to be baptized in the Christian church, and I must have my baby blessed in my faith."

Oh, my goodness, Tamara thought. Didn't they realize they had religious differences before getting married?

"You can always get divorced and make your own decisions about your baby," Tamara said, mostly joking. However, Joel and Zarah splitting up wouldn't be the worst event in her world.

"There can be no divorce," Zarah said with such fervor that Tamara shrank back. "I cannot bring such shame to my family."

Being a friend to Zarah was getting tougher. Tamara had no patience for Joel's shenanigans, but Zarah was annoying her too, with her constant dependence on Joel's validation.

"Why not do both? Why not baptize the baby and have him or her blessed too?"

"We could not do that. No, there must be one faith for the gods to look after my baby."

"I'm sure you'll figure it out." Tamara was done with the matter. They'd burned up twenty minutes already, and Joel could return at any time. She had to commandeer the conversation and address the business at hand. "Have you given any consideration to my bid for the West Coast division?"

"I have not." Zarah, who had been sitting up in bed, laid down. "I'm not keeping well. Maybe I should rest."

Tamara was conflicted. She didn't want to jeopardize Zarah's already difficult pregnancy, but at the same time, with her own survival at stake, she wanted to put their friendship aside and negotiate hard for a business deal. Zarah didn't appear to be in immediate danger. Tamara would continue pressing.

"What about running Harmonious Energy? Are you still planning to buy the other half and run it?" Together they'd worked hard to get Zarah established. Tamara couldn't let her business plans slip away because Joel suddenly had a conscience.

"I'm not sure. I must rest, and we can discuss this later."

Tamara became increasingly agitated. She didn't want to push Zarah too far, but with the couple considering a full reconciliation, her ability to influence Zarah was going to be limited. She had to capitalize on this visit.

"Are you planning to travel soon?" Zarah asked.

"No, I'm not." Tamara was miffed by Zarah's strange question but didn't ask for an explanation. Time was too short. She had to stay on topic. "So what do you think about selling me the division?"

"I look forward to our outings again. We had such fun on our trips downtown."

"Yeah, right. What about the division?"

"You must come to India with me on our next holiday."

Zarah continued trying to change the subject, and Tamara tried unremittingly to steer the conversation back to the business. They went back and forth for fifteen minutes or so, until Tamara finally gave up.

"Zarah, I'm afraid for you. You're changing," Tamara said, speaking as a confidante instead of the desperate Mitchell outcast who was bent on undercutting the rest of the family any way she could.

Zarah had a mystified look.

"Be careful. I know Joel claims that he's changed. Maybe he has." Tamara highly doubted that he had, but she wouldn't convey that to Zarah. "You've done a great job in the past couple of months at becoming your own woman. Remember that Joel didn't show any interest in you until you took charge of your life and got involved in the business. I was the one who helped you do that."

Zarah sat up again. "And I am grateful to you."

"Don't get me wrong. I was glad to help you. But you can't throw away the progress you made . . . that we made. Don't let him control you again."

Zarah nodded.

Tamara took her hand. "My friend, you're in charge, not him. Don't forget that, or he might take advantage of your kindness."

Zarah didn't expect Tamara to understand why her commitment to Joel was unbreakable. She wasn't in denial about his challenges with the marriage. Instead, Zarah believed that if she was willing to wait for however long it took, her relationship with Joel would turn out well. She clung to that hope deep in her soul, because anything less would be too unbearable to imagine.

Chapter 14

Joel was glad to get home. Madeline had him fervently thinking about how to approach Zarah. Should he ask her directly to sell the company, or was it better to utilize the "best for the baby" angle? Both were extreme moves and required a level of boldness that he could have mustered six months ago without blinking. He was working to become a changed man, one who considered the impact his decisions had on others. So it wouldn't be as easy to manipulate Zarah without feeling guilty and awkward.

As the minutes passed, Joel grew tired of playing out a host of scenarios in his mind and practicing speeches. He'd go to his wife, explain their opportunity, and appeal to her for help. Direct and honest was best. He climbed the stairs two at a time. Joel entered the master bedroom and found Tamara sitting on the side of the bed next to Zarah.

"When did you get here?" he asked.

"I'll see you later," Tamara told Zarah abruptly.

"Don't have to leave on my account," Joel said.

"Actually, I am."

"You must stay and have a nice lunch with us," Zarah said.

"Maybe another time," Tamara told her, peering at Joel. Then she dashed from the room.

Joel was relieved. There were serious matters that had to be discussed, and Tamara's presence was a nuisance. He was glad to see her go.

"Why does she always come over when I'm gone?"

He figured his wife had been alerting Tamara whenever he left the house. How else could she be at the house when Joel came home but never pop up while he was there to answer the door? He considered the possibility of Tamara getting too close to his wife. But at least Tamara's agenda was clear. She hadn't concealed her desire to purchase the West Coast division, run off to Southern California, and start a life far removed from the rest of DMI and the Mitchell family in Detroit.

Still, Tamara was dangerous. She was a direct threat to Joel. His fear simmered. Her plan had to be foiled in order for his to succeed. And he reserved the right to impose his will, if necessary. He was too close to realizing his dream of returning to a place of prominence on the corporate scene. No way was Tamara going to derail him. He was annoyed, but he didn't plan on voicing his discontent prematurely.

"I don't want Tamara sneaking around here when I'm gone. It makes me uncomfortable," he told Zarah.

"She's a good friend to me. I am pleased with her visits."

He wouldn't make any further demands. There would be another chance to deal with Tamara. Harmonious Energy had to take precedence now.

Joel sat on one of the chairs in the bedroom. He grasped for words. "You know I met with Madeline at the office."

"Yes. Please tell me about your meeting."

Gladly, Joel thought. "She is determined to have me return to DMI, and I'm very excited to have her support."

"Most surprising—"

Joel moaned. "There's only one problem," he said, interlocking his fingers. He tried spilling it out, but he was too afraid of Zarah's reaction. He moaned and groaned briefly before saying, "The board won't vote me in unless we can get rid of Harmonious Energy."

Zarah covered her mouth but didn't respond. Joel wanted her to say something, anything, to rescue him from his awkwardness. She didn't oblige.

Joel went to the bedside to get closer to her and, hopefully, convey his sense of urgency. "Selling the company shouldn't be a problem since you'll want to stay home with the baby anyway."

"We've already spoken of this, and I've not decided," she said.

He took her hand. "What is there to decide? Don't you want this marriage to work?"

"Yes, of course."

"Then we have to address the religious issues between our companies first and then deal with our marriage." He was keen to pursue whichever angle gave him an edge in the conversation without going too far.

Zarah drew her hand away. "We've also spoken of this." She tried to get up from the bed, but Joel gave her a light tug on the arm. "Remember, you have to rest."

"How can I rest with so much talk of business?"

She sounded frazzled, but Zarah was stronger than he'd initially believed. He'd seen her show a lot of gumption in recent months. He chose to continue this conversation, confident that she and the baby weren't in danger. Besides, if he stopped every time she seemed uncomfortable, most likely they wouldn't get the religion or Harmonious Energy issues resolved until their child was in junior high school.

"Zarah, we have to sell Harmonious Energy."

"I'm not ready to sell my father's company."

"What choice do you have?" Joel pressed his fingertips against his temples. He wanted to scream. Didn't she hear him? Neither their marriage nor their future had a legitimate shot unless she made the sale. "When you were in the hospital, I got a call from India. They wanted me to oversee Harmonious Energy while you were ill, but I refused."

"That was not their right."

Joel didn't care if they were right or wrong. He was pleased with his personal growth. The old Joel would have assumed the leadership role of Harmonious Energy and sold the company before Zarah was released from the hospital. If Joel had taken the covert route, he could have avoided his fruitless appeal. He wasn't letting up. He had to get his point across.

"Unless you're able to go into the office tomorrow, the team in India has to appoint someone else to oversee their stake in Harmonious Energy. We both know you're not able to handle this." Zarah slumped in the bed. Joel knew this was a strain for her, but that came with playing on the big corporate stage. He slumped down in the bed next to her and intentionally spoke in a lower tone. "Let me help you. Let me help us."

She wrestled the covers over her head. He kept talking. "DMI is ready to sell their half of Harmonious Energy, but no serious prospect will want a fraction of the company. They'll want all of it. So I just need you to give me permission, and we'll get Harmonious Energy sold for a huge profit."

"I don't care about the money," she muttered. "I have plenty."

"Then maybe there is something that you do care about—me, our family, and our marriage." He hadn't wanted to play his trump card, but Zarah had forced him into a corner. Madeline's mandate repeatedly played in his head. When Joel thought Zarah was softening, he said, "Let me call India and get a deal going. We can have a letter of intent by Friday and have this behind us. You'll feel much better when this is over. I promise you."

Joel waited for her answer. She said nothing, and he took her silence as an endorsement. "I'll make the call," he told her and headed toward the door, feeling relieved.

Zarah let Joel walk out of the room without bothering to stop him. Her thoughts were swirling, and the confusion was overwhelming. She didn't want to sell the company, but Zarah wasn't sure about keeping it, either. She wanted to help her husband, but she also wanted to keep her corporate fire burning. She pulled the covers tighter over her head. Her anxiety increased. She'd rest for now. Come tomorrow, she'd figure out how to save both her marriage and Harmonious Energy. Maybe Tamara had some ideas. She'd wait until Joel left the house tomorrow to find out.

Chapter 15

Zarah peered at the alarm clock, which brightly displayed the time. One thirty. She flipped over, yearning for a good night's sleep, desperate to clear her mind of unpleasant thoughts. She drifted off, then woke up again and rolled over to see the clock. Two fifteen. She sighed, sat up, and turned on the light situated next to her bed. The talks with Joel and Tamara remained on her mind regardless of what she did. Peace was not to be hers this night. Maybe she'd go downstairs for a cup of tea.

She maneuvered to the edge of her bed and put both feet on the floor. She sat there, leaning against the pillows. Downstairs was too far. Maybe she'd read a book to block out her worries. She glanced at the books on her nightstand but didn't find one that interested her. Zarah moaned and leaned back on the bed again in total frustration as she succumbed to her worries.

Time crawled by. Around 4:00 a.m. Joel peeked in. "How long have you been awake?" he asked, sailing into the room.

"For a bit."

"Are you all right?" he asked, rushing to her side. "Any problem?"

Yes, there are plenty, she thought, but her husband didn't understand her troubles. She had no energy to explain her desires again. "Maybe I should go to the hospital."

"Why?" he asked.

"It is peaceful there, and I can rest."

"You can rest here," he told her.

Usually she was happy to have him nearby. Tonight his presence didn't bring her much joy.

"There is more time for troubles than for rest here."

"You shouldn't be worried about anything. I'm handling everything for you. All you have to do is relax and deliver a healthy baby."

She shook her head frantically. "I feel ill."

"Then I will definitely take you to see a doctor."

"The doctor can't help me with my troubles."

Joel appeared confused.

Her pain came from constantly being pulled between her husband and his sister. "So much talk about business with you and Tamara has been unsettling."

"Tamara? Is she still bugging you about the West Coast division?" Joel didn't wait for her to answer. "She never stops," he said, rubbing his head. "When will she let the division go and move on?"

Zarah knew he wasn't expecting a reply, so she remained silent.

He went on. "I tried being nice to her for your sake, but I'm going to let her know that you can't handle this pressure. This stops in the morning."

"No, you mustn't speak harshly to her. She's been my only friend."

Joel stared into her eyes. "Well, if she's not the problem, who or what is? Is it me?"

Zarah grew emotional and couldn't bring herself to tell the truth.

"Am I the one making you sick?" he questioned.

"I don't want anyone making my decisions for me. No more. I want to make decisions for myself and my father's company."

"So you feel like I'm pressuring you?" Joel asked, spreading his palm across his chest. "I thought you wanted to let go of the business."

"I didn't say that. I'm not sure, but if I do, it must be my decision."

"So what are you saying? You want to keep Harmonious Energy?"

"Maybe."

"Even if it goes against my beliefs and those of DMI?" He wanted to shout out of frustration, but he resisted the urge.

"*I* must make the decision, no one else."

"Okay," Joel replied. He was caught off guard by Zarah's response, but he was not surprised with Tamara filling her head. "I understand, and I definitely don't want to upset you, but please tell me you aren't still considering letting Tamara have the West Coast division."

Zarah didn't answer right away, which made Joel tenser. He couldn't sit idly by and let her drag them down that road.

"Come on, Zarah. Please tell me you're not." The tension in the room was thick. "No, don't bother. I already know the answer." He stormed out.

Joel was steaming and had to relieve the pressure before he burst. Why couldn't Zarah understand how important the role of CEO of DMI was to him, to them? She was going to benefit as much as he was. He was making sacrifices to keep the marriage going. It had to be a two-way deal if they were going to raise their child together. What didn't she understand? By selling her company, they would be one step closer to bridging the religious chasm between them that prevented him from loving her completely. Several months ago she would have listened and they'd already be drawing up sales papers by now, but thanks to Tamara's poisonous influence, his wife had changed. Admittedly, he had been drawn to Zarah's strength a month and a half ago, upon returning from Chicago, and had found himself attracted to the woman she had become. But now he struggled with that part of her, as it was preventing him from going back to Madeline with a signed declaration of intent to sell.

Joel lamented over not being able to close the deal with Madeline. It was brutal to watch his second chance—or was it his third or fourth chance?—slip from his clutches when his hopes had been soaring so high. He had to wonder if this was a test from God before his breakthrough came or if it was one of the consequences resulting from marrying outside his faith purely for professional gain. He didn't know and didn't feel much like praying. He preferred to wait awhile before approaching God, afraid of what he might hear. Joel schlepped toward his home office, not quite sure where to go. He yearned for support.

There were two people on earth who could give him the encouragement he sought, and they were his mother and Sheba in Chicago. Sheba had been his faithful confidante for nearly three years. Her faith in him had been unwavering. Because of their closeness, some might erroneously label her a girlfriend. He preferred not to give their relationship a label. Sheba was simply a safe haven, warmth in the cold, and a cool breeze on a hot day. She had been a constant for him. What he valued most was her ability to be present without judging, confining, or smothering him. Through his ups and downs she had stood by him without judgment or expectations. Being with her allowed him to exist freely, and he craved those visits.

He reached the library and kept walking toward his office. If history was a road map, this was the moment when he packed an overnight bag, grabbed his keys, and put the Lamborghini on the highway, seemingly headed in no particular direction. However, most often his road to nowhere ended at Sheba's penthouse in downtown Chicago, his place of refuge when the challenges in Detroit were too much. Sheba was the boost he needed at this moment. He picked up the phone, dialed most of her numbers, and then froze. He desperately wanted to push the last few buttons, but his fingers were stuck. They wouldn't move in the direction of Sheba. Her comfort called to him, but Zarah's pregnancy and his newfound commitment to do right by his child screamed louder. He put the phone down.

Joel was reminded of the pledge he'd made to himself as he stood outside Zarah's hospital room last month. Maybe it had been out of emotion, but the fact was that he'd committed to giving the marriage a chance to get better for the sake of his unborn child. Regardless of his reasons for taking her as a wife, or how he'd gone about it, she didn't deserve to be left on her own to carry his child. He had turned away from God for several years and had made many misguided decisions. Yet he was wise enough to know that things had to change if he wanted stability. He had to try something different. Sheba couldn't be his safe haven anymore, not if he was serious about moving forward and trusting God.

His soul was rattled, and his spirit could have brought him calm, but Joel still wasn't ready to pray specifically about the religious issue. He already knew that God didn't want him fraternizing with other gods or energy sources. But he didn't know what God wanted him to do about Zarah's religious differences, and Joel was afraid to ask. What if the marriage was unfixable? Would he be reduced to a weekend dad who had to fly to India on occasion to see his child for a few days? As bad as becoming an absentee father seemed, honestly, Joel could survive without living under the same roof as his kid. Madeline's kids had lived without their father when they were growing up.

Being an absentee parent was manageable, but if Zarah left the marriage without selling Harmonious Energy, his career aspirations were dead. There were as many reasons for him to leave the marriage as there for them to stay together. Frankly, Joel was confused and unsure which way to go. As long as he was ignorant of God's direction for him, he could make mistakes without feeling any guilt. Once he had knowledge of God's plan for him, then he was accountable for his actions. In his confused state, it was hard for him to tell which was better: following God's lead down a difficult path or taking the easier route by forging ahead on his own, unprotected by God. His torment increased in proportion to his confusion. He had to get some air.

Joel darted upstairs and quickly changed into a pair of jeans and a loose-fitting shirt. He ran back to his office, snatched the keys that were sitting on his desk, and hurried to the garage. He climbed in his Lamborghini, opened the garage door with the control, pressed the button to start the car, and jetted from the garage down the long driveway. He hit the road at full speed. Thankfully, it was early, and few cars were on the road in his exclusive neighborhood.

Running away from his problems afforded him instant relief. But four blocks later his torment caught up with him and hopped into the passenger seat. Joel didn't bother trying to kick out his companion. Positive thinking and hope weren't sufficient to free him. His reality was paralyzing. He had to do more to free his mind from the barrage of dueling emotions.

He maneuvered his car to the shoulder of the road, then leaned on the steering wheel and shut his eyes. He realized that running away wasn't going to fix his problems.

Regardless of how many miles he drove, his problems with Zarah and Harmonious Energy would be waiting for him when he got back home. Exhausted, bordering on desperation, and certain that he had come to the end of his rope, Joel was left with no choice but to return to his source of strength, something that had worked flawlessly for him in the past.

"Lord, I need you. I don't know how to piece my life together. I want to fix things," he said, gripping the steering wheel so tightly that the bones of his knuckles practically protruded. He harbored worry and anxiety deep inside him, and they felt like liquid careening through his veins. "I want to make things right, but I'm struggling. Nothing is going my way." His marriage was set up to fail. Zarah believed one thing, and he another. It was an impossible scenario.

"You know I can't change Zarah, and she can't change me. I don't know what to do about the marriage or about DMI. I don't even know if there is a way to fix this, but you're God." He shook his fists in the air. "I want to be back in your grace." Joel was naked spiritually, with no tricks, pride, or ego pushing to the forefront. Humbled, he was willing to trust God, even if it meant severing a marriage that compromised his faith. God didn't like divorce, but Joel was sure He didn't want His children living under the same roof as other gods, either. Joel's head hurt as he thought about the mess he'd created. "Please, Lord, help me. Help me and Zarah figure this out, if there is a way out."

Joel didn't know how long he'd sat in that spot along the roadside before he pulled away. He couldn't say that peace consumed him once he finished his prayer, but there wasn't any additional feeling of unrest, either. He took that as a win and drove down the hill to the local coffee shop. He wasn't hungry or thirsty, but there weren't many places open at 6:00 a.m. He crept into the parking lot, and a lady pulled in next to him a second later. She and Joel got out of their cars simultaneously, and their gazes met.

"Nice car," the woman said, shooting him a wink.

Joel acknowledged the compliment with a nod. Several months ago he would have turned on his charm and engaged his admirer in a heavy round of flirtatious bantering. The chase had always given him a rush of excitement; it was almost like a drug. The more Joel had, the more he craved.

"You're up and about quite early," she said.

Joel couldn't muster the energy to engage in a conversation. The woman's tall stature was captivating, and she had quite a few curves thrown in to make her stand out in a crowd. He noticed how softly her hair fell along her face, and silently acknowledged her beauty. He chuckled. She had no idea how effortlessly he could snag her in his web.

"Cat got your tongue?" she asked.

He flashed his grin, the one that usually made women gravitate toward him. "Something like that." Joel let the woman enter the shop and then turned around to leave.

"Aren't you coming in?"

"No. I have somewhere to be."

"Too bad," she said, giving him another wink.

Joel didn't reciprocate the flirting. Women were great—always had been to him and always would be. But he had to keep his mind uncluttered with frivolous notions. Zarah and DMI were plenty to handle. There wasn't room for anyone or anything else.

Chapter 16

Zarah grew weary of her confinement, and Joel's departure made it worse. She was determined to keep the marriage afloat, but there were instances when the effort was daunting. The walls were closing in, and what should have been her baby's safe haven had become a prison. She couldn't breathe freely in her bedroom. She had to get out of there. Zarah grabbed her robe and flung it over her shoulders as she maneuvered to the doorway and into the hallway. She hadn't gone far, but Zarah was pleased with her initial steps toward freedom. She decided to go downstairs and fix a pot of tea. One gingerly step at a time was the plan.

Eventually, she reached the main floor and found herself winded. Her instinct was to panic, especially since there wasn't anyone in the house to help. It was just her and the baby. Although Zarah was physically drained from walking down the stairs, she gathered her strength and held on to the banister. She was prepared to stand there for as long as necessary to ensure her baby's safety. It was her job and no one else's.

She peered around the foyer and soaked in the truth. Her future was no longer going to be left to others to decide. She had once worried about having to return home to India a divorced woman. The shame associated with such a failure had caused her to spiral into a deep depression right before she became pregnant. But now she was motivated and felt eager to make decisions.

There was a fire burning inside her, and it caused her to release the banister and stride down the hallway, toward Joel's office.

Tamara urging her to take control came to her remembrance. Support from her sister-in-law served as a welcomed blanket. She strode into Joel's office and sat in the chair behind the desk. With little concern about the late hour in southern India, Zarah placed a call to Kumar. He had been the family's attorney for many years, and he alone handled their business matters. She trusted him.

She rushed right into the discussion as soon as he got on the line. "We must talk about plans for Harmonious Energy," she said.

"I asked Joel to run the company while you were in the hospital."

"Why did you ask him without asking me? I am still the major shareholder, and I must be consulted about such decisions," she firmly stated.

"Indeed, but—"

"But I am half owner," she interrupted. "I am my father's sole heir. You mustn't discount my voice."

She knew Kumar was probably confused about her reaction. Usually, she went along with his direction and avoided conflict. But now she wrestled with so many individuals. Between Joel, Kumar, and Tamara, she was being pulled in many directions, and sometimes she felt like she was being ripped apart. She yearned to find her own voice, the one her baby could follow. She hadn't been keen on taking charge of her business affairs until Tamara pointed out how important it was for the Bengali legacy. And she was especially motivated by the fact that Joel had found her more attractive a month and a half ago, when she began doing interviews and showing an interest in the business. She hadn't experienced such attention from him previously.

"I'm sorry, Zarah. I didn't want to cause you to worry when you were in the hospital. Your husband was the right choice."

Wasn't Kumar getting her message? His lack of faith in her wasn't hurtful, just irritating. He could join the list of people who didn't think she was strong enough to handle a job and a baby at the same time. "Before my baby problems, you were helping me learn the details of Harmonious Energy. Let's continue with the training. There is no time to lose."

"I don't believe this is wise. We must let you rest, and the board will appoint a temporary leader, since Joel declined the offer."

"Did he tell you why?" she asked.

"Yes, because he wanted to give his full attention to you."

"That is quite nice," she said. Zarah was pleased to hear that Joel was concerned about her. Her tone softened, but her earnestness didn't wane.

"He also doesn't believe that DMI's board will retain their half of the ownership of Harmonious Energy. So we must appoint leadership until a decision to buy or sell is made directly."

"I have not changed my decision. I will have the lead position and will work with DMI until we figure this business out."

"Zarah, in good faith and out of a commitment to your father, I can't advise you to proceed in this way."

"You don't have a choice."

"As the executor of your father's estate, I could legally have the company remain in my control."

"But you won't."

"Why not, if it's in the best interest of the company?"

"Because you would not dishonor my father by challenging his pregnant daughter for control. I am not concerned about your threat, Kumar. I'm sure you will help me stand for my father's legacy, or else you will be cursed. The gods will not bless you for your act of selfishness."

After an elongated pause, Kumar answered. "Please, take several days to rest. We can continue the knowledge transfer next week. It will be my pleasure to honor your father."

Zarah thanked him and disconnected the call. She sat behind Joel's desk, in no hurry to do anything. She was steadfast in not wanting Kumar and Joel to join together and sell the company without counting her vote. She was not going to be discounted any longer. Harmonious Energy belonged to Musar Bengali, her father. As his only child and his only living heir, she had all the rights and would use them fully. They'd see. She was inspired, and she contemplated the next steps. Since her sister-in-law had many good ideas, she'd give her a call and get some more advice.

Chapter 17

It was pointless for Joel to drop by his hotel suite at the Westin. There wasn't anyone there to console him. Instead he'd wandered around for about an hour after leaving the coffee shop in search of meaningful dialogue. After praying for peace and guidance, he didn't want to go home and get drawn into another disagreement with Zarah over her father's company.

Around nine o'clock that morning he walked into the Mitchell estate, the place his mother had claimed as her home after Madeline divorced his father and moved out. Since his childhood, not much had changed in the massive house situated on Mayweather Lane. The familiarity of the place was comforting, and Joel felt it might provide the solace he sought. Sherry didn't understand him as well as Sheba, but his mother was a strong second option when it came to support.

"Mom, where are you?" he called out. Joel weaved through the dining room and ended up in the kitchen. "Mom," he called out again.

"Why are you yelling for me this early on a Thursday morning, mister?" Sherry said, entering the kitchen in her casual wear.

Joel embraced his mother and held her longer than usual.

"Okay, what's going on?" she asked.

He finally released her. "Why do you ask that? Can't I stop by to see my mother and give her a hug?"

Sherry snickered. "You can, but most of the time it means there's something serious going on." A worried look appeared on her face. "Is it the baby?"

"No," he quickly responded.

"Oh, good," she said, and then the worried look reappeared. "Is it Zarah? Is she back in the hospital?"

"No, Mom, nothing like that. Zarah and the baby are okay." Joel sat on one of the tall stools surrounding the ten-foot-long marble-covered island. He'd solved countless problems at that counter over the years. He was hoping for the same today. He tapped his foot on the stool next to him. Sherry sat down.

"So tell me, what's going on?"

"I'm hungry. Do you have any breakfast cooked?"

"Uh, no," she said and giggled.

"Where's the cook?"

"At home, I guess," Sherry responded. "Last year I stopped her from coming in daily."

"Last year? Why? Aren't you lonely being here by yourself every day?"

Sherry touched his hand and gave him a light smile. "I'm not lonely, if that's all you're concerned about. Don't worry about me. I'm fine. Now, tell me what's going on with you, and don't say, 'Nothing,' when I can see that something is clearly bothering you."

Joel's gaze dropped. "It's DMI and Madeline."

Sherry drew her hand back. "Oh, boy. What's she done now?"

"Actually, you'd be surprised."

"I doubt it. I've known Madeline since she hired me as Dave's assistant at DMI over thirty years ago. I know her well, and I wouldn't put anything past her."

"Except asking me to return as CEO."

"What?" Sherry asked.

"You heard me right. She wants me in the CEO role. Can you believe it?"

"No, I can't, and you shouldn't, either." Sherry stood and walked across the room and leaned against the wall. "You can't trust her. It has to be a trap."

Joel watched as his mother's pleasant mood evaporated. Seeing her standing there reminded him of the woman who, years ago, had cringed at the mere mention of Madeline's name. He remembered how upset his mother would get every time his father let Madeline have her way on issues pertaining to their children. Sherry had worked hard to gain her independence. Joel was thrilled to see her thriving after his father's death. She didn't crumble, as most thought she would. To see her shudder in fear now about what Madeline might do was disheartening.

Joel went to his mother's side. "Mom, you don't have to worry. I truly think Madeline is sincere about this."

"How can you say that after everything she's done to us, to me, to your father, and to you?"

"What choice do I have but to go along and see how this plays out?" He wasn't 100 percent sure that Madeline's offer was legit, but his gut said she could be trusted on this one. Hopefully, his desperation wasn't clouding his vision and blindly drawing him like a fawn into the lion's den.

"No, this doesn't sound right." Sherry folded her arms tightly, and Joel could tell distress had a grip on her. "What's she going to do? Kick Don out?"

"No, he's moving to South Africa and stepping down."

"Okay. What about Tamara? Madeline would never choose my child over hers to run DMI, never in a million years."

"I thought the same thing."

"So what are you thinking, then? Madeline's not going to choose you over Tamara."

"She already has."

Sherry buried her fingers in her hair. "No way."

"I'm sure Tamara was her first choice, but Madeline admitted that her daughter doesn't have the experience to run DMI. I agree, but I wasn't about to tell Madeline that. I'm just glad she recognized Tamara's shortcomings and didn't try to force her into the role, anyway."

"Clearly, she's convinced you, but not so fast for me. I have good reason not to trust Madeline. She hates me, and that will never change." Sherry shut her eyes tightly and interlocked her fingers. "I used to be bothered by how she treated me. When Dave was alive, I had to put up with her. I've tolerated her constant antics against you. She was incorrigible when your dad appointed you CEO. I sat quietly and let her torment you, but those days are over. You, Zarah, and the baby are my only family. I won't let her harm you again, not without a serious fight."

Joel grabbed Sherry's shoulders. "Don't worry about Madeline. I can take care of myself." He hugged her. "Besides, she's not the one giving me problems."

"What do you mean?"

"Tamara is the one I have to watch. Influencing Zarah has become her life's mission," he said and chuckled. "Thanks to Tamara, my wife doesn't want to listen to reason. It wasn't too long ago when her primary goal was to be a supportive housewife."

"Well," Sherry said, shrugging her shoulders, "most women don't take on the traditional role anymore. Most of them are educated and want to work."

"You stayed at home, and I guess it was okay for you."

Sherry moaned. "Maybe, maybe not. You might not know this, but I'd worked for several years before meeting your dad. I didn't make a great deal of money as a secretary back then, but I was very proud of my job and budding career."

"How did you end up as a housewife?"

Sherry fidgeted. "That was my choice. It's a long story, but the short version is that Madeline fired me after the affair with your dad. After we got married, your father wouldn't dare rehire me. Madeline wouldn't hear of it, and he didn't want to upset her. So, I decided to stay at home for a while. It wasn't long afterward that you arrived. I wasn't about to go to work and leave you with a nanny or a stranger. No way," she said, squeezing his forearm.

"See? That's what I'd like Zarah to do, put the baby first. She needs to step away from the corporate scene for the sake of the pregnancy, but Tamara is filling her head with other ideas."

"Joel, I don't think you have to be concerned about Zarah. She loves you. She'll come around."

"I'm not so sure."

"I am. I know her type. That was me when I met Dave Mitchell. I was so naive and so captivated by your father that I willingly surrendered my identity. If you care about her, be patient and give Zarah the space she needs to grow into the marriage."

He leaned against the wall next to Sherry. "Space is exactly what I'm afraid of. If I step back, Tamara is going to pounce on Zarah." There was no telling how far Tamara would go in manipulating his wife. Since Harmonious Energy was a key component of his CEO bid, he wasn't willing to be hands off with Tamara hovering like a buzzard.

"Joel, you're playing a dangerous game. Zarah is fragile. You need to tread lightly. Too much pressure and a miscarriage is a real possibility. I know that's not what you want."

"Of course not."

"Then you have to be patient, like I said. I've had a miscarriage, and I don't wish that on anyone. Thank goodness I was able to get pregnant right afterward with you, but it doesn't dissolve the pain I suffered in losing my first child." Joel watched her get teary eyed.

"Enough about me. Let's talk about you," he said.

"What about me?"

"I don't want you to be alone. Dad is gone, and you deserve some happiness. Why don't you start dating?"

"Whoa! Dating isn't for me. I was married to your father for twenty-five years. That's enough for me."

"Mom, come on. I didn't say, 'Get married.' We're only talking about dating."

She shook her head and giggled.

"Well, I'm going to create a profile online for you," Joel told her.

"A profile? What is that?"

Joel laughed. "I'll post your photo and tell a little bit about you. The online system will identify men whose profile matches yours. It's simple."

"Sounds crazy to me. If I do begin dating, we'll stick with the old-fashioned method of meeting someone at the library or through a friend. I'm not open to meeting a stranger online. No thank you," she told Joel.

"We'll just have to see," he said.

"I guess we will."

They laughed simultaneously. Briefly Joel felt better, but nothing was settled, and he knew it.

Chapter 18

Madeline parked her convertible Bentley in DMI's executive row, in the spot labeled MRS. MITCHELL. It was the same spot she'd had since the inception of DMI. She recalled the time, fresh after her divorce from Dave, when Sherry parked in the spot. Before lunch that day Madeline had threatened to have Sherry's car towed, but Dave intervened, rescuing his woman's car. On that day it was established that Madeline's role at DMI would never be comprised, regardless of what bimbo Dave married. There was only one legitimate Mrs. Mitchell, and she parked up front. The others could crawl several rows back and settle for an obscure spot near the rear of the lot.

Madeline cackled at the thought and peeked at herself in the rearview mirror. There wasn't a strand of hair out of place. If only the rest of her life was in the same shape. She sat in the car, dreading another run-in with her daughter, but it was bound to happen. She knew that Tamara's fury was smoldering. Madeline wasn't happy about excluding Tamara from the CEO candidate list, but she wasn't going to change her mind. Yet there had to be another way she could get Tamara involved in the company. Madeline sighed in defeat. She opened the car door and delicately set her four-inch stiletto heels on the ground.

It was after 9:00 a.m., and everyone in the office was in rapid motion. Madeline made her way to Don's office.

"Are you just getting in?" Don asked his mother.

She set her bag on a chair and gripped the back. "I got a late start this morning."

"I guess so, because you're here no later than seven every day."

"Well, let's just say I have a lot on my mind."

"Like what? Or do I already know?"

"You know it's Tamara. I'm failing her, but what else can we do?"

Don shrugged his shoulders. "I feel badly too, but we both know she can't run this company. Appointing her CEO would be worse than Dad appointing Joel."

The words seared her heart and went on to burn her soul. "Tamara said exactly the opposite." The correlation was piercing for Madeline.

"But at least Joel had worked at DMI for several years while Dad was alive. Tamara is totally green. Before coming home, she was an artist who drew pictures, for goodness' sake."

"I'm aware of all that," Madeline said. "But it doesn't change the fact that I feel badly about shoving her out. She was gone too long . . . fifteen years out there on her own, bouncing from country to country like a vagabond."

"At least she's home now."

"For how long?" Madeline said, taking a seat and crossing her legs. "I'm terrified that Tamara's going to run away again if we don't give her what she wants." Madeline winced. "I can't bear to lose her. Anything might happen to her out there without our protection. I haven't forgotten that nutcase Remo, who had the unmitigated gall to show up in Detroit and stalk my daughter." Madeline popped up from her seat and paced the room. "He better be glad I let your uncle Frank handle the situation, because I would surely have ended up in jail if I'd gotten my hands on him."

She stopped pacing and pointed her index finger at Don from across the room. "I'm not going to let anyone hurt you or Tamara, nobody. I'll fight God for my children." Madeline meant every word she said, which was why she ached from the knowledge that the choice she had made caused Tamara to be unhappy. Madeline had to think harder. She was determined to appoint Joel the CEO of DMI, while also finding a way to appease Tamara. She didn't have any ideas at the moment, but Madeline was determined to come up with something.

"Sounds like you're changing your mind about Joel over Tamara."

"I'm not, but this is complicated." Madeline was proceeding with Joel, but not with as much fervor as she had a few days ago.

"Good. I hate to toss fuel on the fire, but we can't drag out the selection process. I'm resigning soon, and we need to have my replacement set."

Madeline was saddened by Don's imminent departure. Both of her children were fleeing Detroit. There would be little motivation for her to stay behind. That was a new challenge, one she hadn't anticipated. But she'd deal with the next chapter of her life after the immediate crisis was resolved.

"Then I guess we better get moving," Madeline told him. She picked up her bag and left his office.

His mother was gone, but thoughts of the conflict with Tamara didn't leave Don. His family was like a teeter-totter, constantly up and down, although it seemed like they experienced the downside with greater frequency. He wondered if his family would realize long-term peace or if the Mitchells were doomed to a life filled with hatred and an unwillingness to forgive. He would have contemplated this dilemma longer if Joel hadn't popped up.

"Can I come in?"

"Sure," Don answered, beckoning Joel. "Have a seat."

Joel flopped into a chair. "I came by to see Madeline, and I figured we could chat a few minutes too."

"Why? What's up? How are Zarah and the pregnancy?"

"Both are good so long as she stays on bed rest for the next five months."

"Oh, boy. That's a long time to be in bed. Can she get up at all?"

"She can, but the less the better."

"I hope everything works out."

"Me too," Joel responded. "We'll have to see what happens with the baby and the marriage."

"I thought you decided to stay with Zarah?"

"In theory that's true, and I honestly want to give the marriage a legitimate shot. But honestly, I have to work on rebuilding my own faith. I can't do that if Zarah is chasing her gods in the house and I'm seeking mine. It won't work, and that's my major concern." Joel rested his elbow on his upper thigh. "The spiritual vibe is so off in my house that I find it hard to pray without sensing heaviness around me."

"That's not good," Don replied.

"You're telling me. How do I honor God's desire for us to stay married when Zarah and I live in two extremely different spiritual worlds? I'm seriously beginning to wonder if staying in this marriage is the wrong thing to do if I want to get my life right with God." He pressed his index finger against his lips as though he was contemplating what to say next. "This is so jacked up. I'm a jerk if I leave my wife and child, but I'm a heathen if I share God's space in my house with other gods. I can't figure this out. Honestly, what should I do?"

"I don't know what to tell you. That's a tough one. The best I can do for you is pray."

"I appreciate that, big brother. Actually, prayers are what I need and tons of them. I've been reminded of that quite a bit lately."

Don smirked. "God sure has a way of getting our attention. He starts with a whisper, followed by a shout, and only God knows what comes after that. Personally, I don't want to find out."

"I hear you. I'm glad I stopped in. I better get to Madeline's office," Joel said rising from the chair. "You know she doesn't like to be kept waiting."

Before Joel could duck out, Don said, "Have you considered pulling out of the CEO race since you have so much going on at home? Mother would understand if you have more pressing obligations at home. It would be a win-win. DMI would get Abigail in our hour of need, and Zarah would get a dedicated husband when she needs him the most. What do you think?" Don wasn't expecting a favorable response, but he had to ask.

"There's no doubt that Abigail has been valuable to DMI. I have an enormous amount of love and respect for her, but she's not the best candidate for the job. I am."

"Which remains to be seen?"

"Brother, this is life and death for me. Resuming the role head of DMI will allow me the opportunity to restore the Mitchell name and erase the stain I placed on this company. This round I'm committed to letting God lead me, instead of my personal desires."

"Easier said than done," Don observed. "But if you're sincere, your actions will prove it," he added, leaving Joel with something to ponder.

Chapter 19

Joel refused to feed into Don's negativity. He wasn't delusional. There were obstacles to overcome in his bid for the CEO post, including proving to Don, Madeline, and the board of directors that he was trustworthy. The uphill battle for redemption wasn't going to be easy, but so long as God gave him a chance, the decision makers at DMI had to as well. His confidence perked up when he shook off Don's comments and boldly headed to Madeline's office. He wanted to pick up the pace and get over the selection process.

He burst into Madeline's office after getting clearance from her assistant. She heard him enter the room, but she didn't give Joel her full attention. Last week he would have waited for her to conclude whatever she was handling and shift her focus to him. Today he wasn't waiting. This was his day. Opportunity was banging on the door, and he was answering it.

"Do you have a few minutes? We need to talk," he announced.

"Give me about ten minutes, and I can carve out a small window for you," she said without making eye contact.

Joel approached her desk and leaned on it. Madeline shot him a glance filled with irritation. Joel wasn't swayed. He gripped the desk tightly.

"I only need a few minutes. I'd prefer to meet right away and get this over."

Madeline set her fancy pen down, closed her laptop, and slid her pad of paper to the side. Joel's anxiety stirred when he realized he'd poked a sleeping bear. Fight or flight might be his most critical decision at this juncture, because Madeline was too calm. He had to worry.

"Let me tell you this one time and one time only," she said barely above a whisper.

Joel's heart raced. He couldn't afford to alienate his quasi-ally. Joel wished he could rewind the tape and enter the office with a more subdued disposition, but he knew too well that the past wasn't erasable. It might be forgivable, bearable, and recoverable, but it was not erasable. Madeline was already wound up and was blowing out steam. He gripped the desk even tighter, until his fingertips tingled, and decided to let Hurricane Madeline blow over.

"Don't you ever come in here, making demands. I'm calling the shots here, little boy." There was a time when Joel would have fought back, but wisdom and necessity told him to shut up. Humbly, he listened to Madeline, like a young schoolboy being corrected by a teacher. "Don't mess around and have me kick your behind out of here and let Abigail have the CEO position."

Joel stepped away from the desk. "Madeline, you're absolutely right." Joel pressed the palms of his hands together and touched his fingertips to his chin in a gesture of humility. "It was disrespectful and foolish of me to approach you with so much bravado. Please accept my apology."

Without saying a word, Madeline picked up her pen and twirled it on the desktop for a bit. The silence was sobering for Joel, yet he had to wait for her forgiveness.

"Fine, I accept your apology. Just don't approach me like that again."

"Believe me, I won't." Thank goodness the storm had passed and he was still standing, with no significant damage. His relief was consuming.

"Pipe down and be patient. Did you forget the opposition we got in our unofficial board meeting? You have to let me do this my way. I can get you confirmed, but it has to be on my terms."

Joel listened intently, although it was difficult to acquiesce and be patient. Didn't she realize that he had one shot at securing a better future and that waiting around wasn't a good idea, especially with Tamara on the prowl? Despite his fears, he knew Madeline was his best strategy. He'd have to trust her, which was a seemingly impossible feat several months ago and a taste of bad medicine even now.

Chapter 20

Tamara stepped frantically up to Zarah's front door. She'd been hoping for a chance to speak with Zarah alone to work out a deal. Watching her future become more elusive with each passing day wasn't fun. She couldn't stand playing the waiting game any longer. If it was only a matter of compelling Zarah to meet her demands, Tamara had no reservations. As much as she'd probably hate the process, their friendship would have to take a backseat to her obtaining a piece of DMI. But she wasn't heartless. Tamara had fretted all week about how to take her next step. She'd been ecstatic when she got the call from her sister-in-law a half hour ago.

She assumed Joel was not at home, but she wasn't absolutely sure. When the front door opened, Tamara was stunned to find Zarah standing there. "What are you doing out of bed?" she asked. "The housekeeper or cook should be answering the door, not you." Tamara strolled inside.

"Don't worry about me. I feel very strong today. It is a good day."

Tamara stayed near the door until she determined that Joel was gone and it was safe to stay. She couldn't quite figure out what was going on with her friend. "I'm glad to see you're feeling better. Where's Joel?"

"He's meeting with Madeline at DMI."

"Whew!" Tamara cried. "Thank goodness I don't have to deal with him today."

She followed Zarah to the library. Tamara was miffed about Madeline and Joel conspiring to nab the CEO post for Joel. She resented them both immensely, but she'd get her chance to get even. She'd show them, especially that conniving brat of a man.

"No offense, but Joel irks me every time I see him," Tamara confessed. A smidgen of her soul wanted to accept him out of respect for her friendship with his wife. The problem was the rest of her wouldn't dare allow it.

"Yes, I am very well aware."

Tamara waited for Zarah to say, "But I would like for you to get along," which was her typical response. Fortunately, she didn't utter those words. Instead, her friend was poised and seemingly not bothered. Tamara wondered from where Zarah's spark of energy had come.

"What's going on with you?" Tamara asked.

"I feel well; better than I have in several weeks."

This made Tamara anxious. Perhaps Zarah wasn't so fragile, after all. With her newfound energy, her friend looked good. Thoughts trotted around Tamara's mind. Was this the moment to make her move?

"Can I get you a cup of tea?" Zarah asked.

"No thanks." Tamara became increasingly antsy. There weren't going to be too many more opportunities to meet with Zarah before Madeline and Don called the board meeting. She wrestled with her thoughts. Finally, she succumbed to her own pressure and blurted out, "Zarah, please sell me the West Coast division. I desperately need your help. It's my best shot at keeping a portion of my father's company. I'm sure you can relate to that."

Zarah took a seat and remained silent.

Tamara wasn't close to giving up. She had much more pleading to do. "You're my closest friend, and I really need your help."

"Joel has asked that I not sell the division."

Joel, Joel, Joel, Tamara thought. He didn't deserve to have everything. "Zarah, please don't let him tell you what to do. Remember how far you've come. He likes when you're making decisions, embracing the media, and throwing yourself into your father's business. When Joel saw how independent you were becoming, remember how fast he ran to you. Don't change now. Let him keep running after the woman who clearly has her own mind and uses it."

Zarah's head rocked subtly from side to side. "I'm not certain the sale is best."

"Zarah, I have to get out of town, but I can't go without the division."

"You mustn't go. Stay and we can figure this business out."

"I have to go. Otherwise, I'll surely go crazy."

Zarah's head was still rocking, and this was beginning to annoy Tamara. Everything was beginning to annoy her.

"I would be unhappy if you left. I will find a way for you to stay in Detroit with me."

"I love you," Tamara cried. "I helped you when no one else would. Now I need your help. I need this division, please. And don't worry about the money. I can cash in the inheritance my father left me. I can write a check," she said, fumbling in her purse. "I have about twenty million."

"No," Zarah said, raising her hand.

"If you want more, I can get more." She didn't know from where, but she was sure there were ways.

Like a lightning bolt, Joel burst into the library. He didn't break his stride until Tamara was within his reach. "How dare you come to my house and pressure my pregnant wife about a business deal!" Joel rubbed his entire head vigorously over and over with one hand, while the other was latched to his side. He kept walking in a circle, ranting on and on. He didn't let Tamara sneak a word in.

"I thought we could trust you to do the right thing and just be a friend to Zarah. I should have known better," he shouted, getting in Tamara's face again.

"Joel, no. Please don't. I called Tamara and asked her to come for a visit," Zarah said, reaching for his arm.

Joel gave an eerie laugh, which sent a chill through Tamara. There wasn't anything that funny. She figured he'd gone bonkers, and was hoping he would pipe down.

"You really don't care about anybody," he snarled.

"Look who's talking," Tamara muttered in return and stepped closer to him. "Don't come in here playing the devoted daddy and the loving husband, because the three of us know it's not true. You're bound to leave any minute, if and when a better offer comes along."

"You don't know anything about me," he responded.

"Please, let's sit and talk," Zarah pleaded. Neither Tamara nor Joel listened. The fire of discord between them was burning way out of control. Zarah reached for Joel's arm, and he flung her hand away.

"Don't toss her aside like that!" Tamara screamed. "I won't let you treat her badly in my presence, buster. You better get it in your head. I'm not afraid of you, and Zarah isn't, either."

"I'm sorry. I didn't mean to hit your hand. I'm really sorry," he told Zarah. Then he immediately returned to the argument in progress with Tamara. "Don't try to turn this into an issue. I have not laid a hand on Zarah and never will. You know it, and I know it."

"Who knows what you're capable of doing?"

"I'm capable of throwing you out of my house, and that's exactly what I'm going to do. Get out," he demanded, pointing toward the hallway. "You're not welcome here."

"Joel, please! She's my friend. I don't want her to go."

"Zarah, I can't let her get you stressed out again. You should be resting right now, and I wouldn't be much of a husband if I didn't take care of you. She has to go."

"Yes, but let's talk first," Zarah urged.

"There's nothing to talk about. Tamara has to go. Either she goes or I go," he told Zarah.

Despair laced Zarah's countenance, and it touched Tamara deeply.

"No problem, Mr. Big, Bad Joel Mitchell. I'm leaving for now, but you know this isn't over by a long shot. Tamara snarled before storming out of the house.

Chapter 21

Madeline yearned for stability in her family. She felt drained from constantly clawing to maintain what was rightfully hers. Rest was calling out to her with a resounding shout. Don was stepping away from DMI. Maybe it was time for her to do the same. As soon as Joel took office, she might take a long cruise along the French Riviera, or maybe she'd catch a plane to the South Pacific and island hop after making a brief stop in Hawaii. She had been to her vacation home only once since Dave died, and she was overdue for a stretch of pure relaxation. The notion of bouncing from one beachfront to the next was alluring. She'd have to give it serious consideration.

She slowed down to make the turn from Grand Boulevard onto Jefferson. It was the long route, but Madeline wanted some extra minutes to collect herself. A few extra turns enabled her to prepare for the rush of emotions that came with each visit to Dave's gravesite. She crept along the main road and finally reached the cemetery's entrance. The large sign read HISTORIC ELMWOOD CEMETERY & FOUNDATION, WHERE DETROIT'S HISTORY ENDURES. She stopped to read the sign again. The word *history* sparked a rush of memories. She held back her tears. For the past couple of years, she'd visited the cemetery on their anniversary in September. She'd decided to go on his birthday this year. Her tears pushed forward, and Madeline pushed back, determined not to let her emotions takeover.

Madeline slid her foot off the brake and pressed the gas pedal lightly. She inched into the parking lot and drew in a deep breath. She parked the car, then peeked at herself in the vanity mirror and patted down her hair. Of course, Dave wouldn't object to a hair out of place, but she did.

Tired of sitting in the car, she got out and sauntered along the babbling brook that led to the mausoleum. The tranquil rhythm of the flowing waters calmed her as she entered the complex. She walked directly to Dave's crypt without assistance with directions. Madeline delicately kissed her fingertips and then pressed her hand against Dave's crypt. She longed to have peace in her family. Being close to the man who had once held her heart and had fueled her ambition made her feel better, even if only for an hour. With the mess going on with Tamara, she'd gladly claim an hour of solitude. *Thank goodness for the mausoleum,* she thought. Madeline was finally in a place where she could think. She grabbed a seat near Dave's crypt and relaxed.

Out of nowhere, Madeline heard heels clicking against the floor. She looked up and was rendered speechless.

"What are *you* doing here?" Sherry asked.

"I guess the same as you," Madeline responded. Was there anywhere she could go to avoid running into a Mitchell? She was instantly agitated. This was supposed to be her moment with Dave to reflect and gain insight. Sharing Dave with Sherry in this private moment was out of the question. Madeline got up to leave.

"Where are you going?" Sherry asked.

"I have work to do. He's all yours," Madeline said.

"Can you believe he's really gone?" Sherry responded, as if she hadn't heard Madeline.

"Not really. Seems like yesterday when he was getting on my nerves and being Dave."

Sherry smirked. "Twenty-five years of marriage."

"Fourteen for us," Madeline said, which didn't count the years Sherry had robbed from them. But who was counting? Madeline wanted to be cavalier in her retorts, but her deep-seated grief didn't let her. At that moment memories of her deceased sons, Andre and Sam, crushed her soul like waves against a shoreline, rapid and uncontainable. She plucked a tissue from her purse and dabbed the corners of her eyes.

"Are you crying?" Sherry asked.

"I'm just feeling sorry for myself. The dreams Dave and I had for our children have failed. Nothing turned out the way I'd planned," Madeline said, dabbing the corners of her eyes again as she sat in her original spot. She didn't want to tackle talking when she was in such a vulnerable state. Madeline hated letting any signs of weakness show for fear of vultures circling.

Sherry sat next to her. "Madeline, I want to apologize for getting involved with Dave while you were still married."

Madeline wasn't prepared for a heavy conversation that wasn't likely to generate a winner. Besides, she was running out of tissues. "That was many years ago. I'm done with that business," she told Sherry.

"Maybe, but please let me apologize. I've never told you how sorry I am. I was young then and had no idea what I was doing or the pain I was causing. I won't apologize for loving him. That I won't do, but how it happened wasn't right. I deeply regret getting in the middle of a marriage."

"Well, I've blamed you for a long time, but the truth is that Dave and I had problems before you came into the picture. I'm not endorsing what you did, but Dave and I also played our parts in ruining our marriage." She cleared her throat and searched for a dry spot on her tissue. "Dave wanted to work out our problems, but I asked for a divorce and refused to budge. He pleaded with me to drop the divorce, and I said no."

"I never knew that," Sherry said as her voice dipped.

Madeline contemplated what would have happened if she'd stayed with Dave after the affair. There would be no Joel; perhaps Tamara wouldn't have been raped by Andre; and surely Sam wouldn't have killed his brother before committing suicide. She had no way of knowing and didn't feel right in blaming Sherry for all the tragic events in their past. "Now here we are, two losers lamenting our failures at the foot of a man we both loved and despised."

"I did love him, but I lived in humiliation, knowing that he was always going to be your husband. You were the person he discussed business with every day. He valued your opinion, and I know he loved you more than he did me." Sherry pulled out a tissue too.

"Huh, you weren't the only one dealing with humiliation. I was mortified when he left us to be with you during your first pregnancy. I was devastated, embarrassed, and flat-out angry. If I could have plucked Dave's eyeballs out with my fingers, he would have been walking around blind."

"I hadn't thought about your breakup like that before," Sherry stated. "I guess being married to Dave was a happy and sad time for me."

"Who are you telling?" Madeline said, sniffling. "I spent plenty of happy and sad years with him too."

"You're right. I'm sorry. I didn't mean it the way it sounded."

Madeline waved her tissue, as if to say she wasn't offended. "Everyone has paid the price for our choices," she said, pointing back and forth between herself, Sherry, and Dave's crypt. "Especially our children. All of us have suffered rejection in this family. We crushed our children's dreams before they got started."

"Even though our dreams for them haven't come true, they can still find happiness. Dave is gone. Our children are adults. Maybe it's time to step away from our children and focus on our happiness," Sherry said.

"I agree." Madeline coughed to clear her throat. "I think we've suffered enough losses to last a lifetime."

"You're right."

"It's time to turn the page, as they say."

Sherry stared at Madeline, making her uneasy. "That's why I have to thank you for helping my son."

"Sure. Although I don't like some of his past mistakes, he's best suited for the job."

"Thank you."

"But he better not cross me. I'm keeping a tight rein on baby Mitchell this time."

"I'm certain that he'll do fine."

"Actually, I think so too." Madeline glanced at her watch. "It's getting late."

"I won't keep you." Sherry rose. "I've enjoyed talking with you. When I think about it, we haven't interacted on a personal level since you hired me at DMI when I was in my twenties. We should do this again."

Madeline stood too. "Let's not get ahead of ourselves. Remember that you slept with my husband and had a baby, two babies. Let's face it. We're not going to be best friends. I can't trust you, but it doesn't mean I have to hate you." Madeline flung her purse over her shoulder and quickly patted her hair. "I see no reason why we can't be civil for the sake of our children."

"That's a start. The way I see it, there's a new generation of Mitchells in our future, and they shouldn't have to shoulder our problems."

Sherry threw a kiss at Dave's crypt. Madeline did too.

"Guess what my son is forcing me to do?" Sherry said.

"I have no idea when it comes to Joel," Madeline replied.

"He's setting me up with online dating."

Madeline roared, "Good luck with that."

"Think you'll date or get married again?" Sherry asked.

"No. Through it all Dave was the man for me. Then again, who knows? Stranger things have happened, especially in this family. Who would have expected me to recommend Joel over my own child for the CEO position? So, apparently anything is possible. But I'll wait for you to try out the online dating and let me know what you think. Perhaps I'll give it a shot."

Together they walked out of the mausoleum and went to their cars. Madeline felt invigorated, and honestly, she had to thank Sherry, a person whom she had once considered a bitter pill but who now seemed much more tolerable.

Chapter 22

Don's cry for freedom had begun as a faint rumbling and had rapidly transformed into deafening thunder. He wasn't confused about his purpose for being in Detroit. When Abigail and his mother had begged him to return from South Africa last year to help rescue DMI from Joel's clutches, he'd been reluctant to forfeit his newfound happiness and contentment. He'd been doing well before he got the SOS signal from Detroit. The initial anger he'd felt toward God and his father for appointing Joel as CEO of DMI had subsided. During his hiatus in South Africa over three years ago, he had embraced Nelson Mandela's teachings on forgiveness and had restored his relationship with God. Dave Mitchell died before Don got a chance to reconcile with him. Maybe that was why Don had fought so hard to promote unity in his family. He wanted the Mitchells to realize that they didn't have forever to work out their differences. Tomorrow wasn't promised.

As he sat behind the desk in his office, mulling over his past, Don began to focus on his blessings. Despite what he'd endured, God had been good to him. His company in South Africa, LTI, was growing at an incredible rate. He'd even found love in a radiant employee, whose support had been a lifeline during his initial estrangement from the Mitchell family and DMI.

Don shut his eyes and reared back in his chair, with his fingers locked. The sweet sound of Naledi's African and Indian accent, splashed with a dash of French, spoke to his soul from across the Atlantic Ocean with such undeniable passion that he couldn't concentrate on work. They hadn't spoken in close to a week, which was much too long. He needed to hear her voice constantly, and the only way to make it happen was to get on a plane headed for Cape Town soon, not next quarter or next year. He had to go within a few months. He sincerely believed that the next leg in his destiny was with Naledi.

He hadn't gotten full confirmation of this from God, but there was a peace in his spirit when he thought about her and their future together. His yearning overtook Don. Disregarding their different time zones, in an instant he was dialing a string of numbers, eager to reach his confidante. Other than God's, no voice was more desired or appreciated than that of Naledi. The phone rang several times, and he anxiously waited for her to answer. Don was about to give up when he heard a greeting that stirred his affection.

"Naledi, I'm glad to reach you."

"Me as well. It's been a very long while since we've spoken."

"I have to apologize for not checking in more frequently."

Don was grateful to have such a competent executive running LTI in his absence. He didn't like it, but the truth was that DMI had always monopolized his time, leaving only a tiny amount for LTI and his personal desires. Without Naledi, he wouldn't be able to run two companies successfully on different continents. Relying heavily on her made him feel guilty. He had her full support, and she deserved his.

"I have to talk with you about something very important," he told her and then paused. There was a host of words swirling in his mind. His affection for her nearly took control of him, but this wasn't the way he wanted to convey his plans for a future with her. They had to meet in person. "I'll be in Cape Town very soon."

"That is excellent news. We will be most pleased to have you here. *I* will be pleased," she told him.

Don's heart warmed.

"On what date will you be traveling?"

"As soon as matters are wrapped up here with DMI," he replied.

Don desperately wanted out. He found it disheartening that he was not able to commit to an exact date with Naledi, but he promised himself that he would solidify his travel plans shortly and get out of town. He just needed to get Abigail confirmed. However, his confidence wasn't soaring as high as it had been several weeks ago. Madeline was difficult to beat when her mind was set. She was a pit bull, but Tamara seemed worse. At least his mother could be won over with a rational argument. Tamara operated purely on impulse, hurt, and revenge. He suddenly felt very discouraged as he thought about the state of his family. He was at a loss about what to do and had to pray for guidance.

It was good for DMI that Don wasn't impulsive, or he would be on a plane tomorrow. That thought was fleeting. He understood that it was unwise to move too quickly and topple the building blocks God had used him to erect in the Mitchell family. No matter how honorable or intense his personal desires were, he couldn't override God's purpose and timing for his life, not even when the Mitchell clan seemed demented and their differences irreconcilable. His faith said that as long as they were alive, there was hope. He enveloped that notion in the bosom of his spirit and held on. He couldn't see it, but positive change was coming to his family.

Chapter 23

Time was running out. There wasn't much more Tamara could do to convince Zarah. She'd presented her best proposal, hoping that the priceless value of their friendship would sufficiently make up for her modest financial offer. She was hopeful but not confident. Nobody was off-limits when it came to finding a strong ally. Tamara believed a weak opponent worked just as well. She slithered past the security desk in DMI's lobby before reaching the stairs. Six flights wasn't a deterrent. She'd get to Abigail in whatever way was required.

Tamara was slightly winded after climbing the stairs. She avoided contact with as many people as she could, hoping especially to avoid Don and Madeline. Tamara wasn't sure how she'd react to seeing them in person on such a desperate occasion. If it hadn't been for the two of them betraying her, she'd already be sitting in the big CEO seat. *That's okay,* she thought. *They will be dealt with in due time.* Tamara approached Abigail's office and discovered that the door was shut. The assistant who sat near Abigail's office wasn't at her desk. Tamara waited five minutes. Growing impatient, she approached another assistant nearby.

"Do you know if Abigail's assistant is coming back?"

"I think so, because she didn't ask me to cover for her. She probably went to the ladies' room."

Tamara waited a few more minutes, to no avail, before knocking on Abigail's closed door. She heard a faint "Come in," and entered Abigail's office.

"I wasn't expecting to see you," Abigail said. "What brings you by?"

"To talk about the CEO position," Tamara responded, shutting the door. She wanted to glide in and out of the building without being noticed by anyone else.

Abigail's smile melted, and a serious look took its place. "What about it?"

"I can't seriously believe you're trying to become the CEO of DMI."

"I don't know why it seems strange to you. I've been with the company for eight years. Your father hired me as an intern before I finished business school and mentored me personally. I know this business better than most," she said. "I'm a solid candidate."

"Really? You think so?"

"Most definitely," Abigail said with a tone of indignation.

Tamara wasn't bothered. "But you don't possess the most critical attribute," she stated as her confidence oozed.

"And what would that be, Tamara?"

"You're not a Mitchell, plain and simple."

Abigail flicked her wrist, discounting Tamara's comment. But denial didn't change the truth.

Tamara hoped to intimidate Abigail to the point where she caved and withdrew from the race. "Deep down you know the name matters. The Mitchell name carries clout in this place."

"Integrity, loyalty, and experience do too," Abigail retorted.

"Fine. Believe whatever you'd like, but I can guarantee your feelings will get hurt before this is over, because my mother will not turn her back on me. Don won't, either. I can tell you that with one hundred percent confidence. The name matters. You're a fool if you think it doesn't."

Abigail reached for the calculator situated near the edge of her desk and began pecking at a few keys. Tamara wasn't to be ignored. Victory was too close. She could smell it in the air. Abigail was weakening. Tamara would go in for the kill.

"Don't take my word for it. Look at the history of DMI. How many non-Mitchell family members have served in the top position?"

Abigail kept pecking at the calculator and jotting numbers on what appeared to be a report.

"None." Tamara allowed this realization to marinate. "Only three Mitchell men have held the position, not a woman and definitely not anyone from outside the family."

Abigail gave Tamara a fiery look.

Tamara's intent wasn't to be cruel to Abigail. It was to help her face reality and move on. "Look, I understand why you want the job. That's easy. Who wouldn't want it? But this job and this place isn't for you," Tamara said, spreading her arms in grand fashion. "If I were you, I'd walk away from DMI with some dignity. There's no wisdom in fighting for a job you'll never have." She hoped Abigail was caving. To make sure, Tamara would give an extra nudge. She stepped closer to Abigail. "And if by some twisted fate you were appointed CEO, I would never accept you in that position and would fight you to the end."

"Can you please leave my office?" Abigail demanded.

"Gladly, and I really hope you hear what I'm saying. Save yourself the aggravation. Drop out of the race and let a Mitchell have the job, since one of us is going to get it, anyway."

"Get out!" Abigail yelled.

"All right. I'm going."

Tamara couldn't draw any conclusions from Abigail's last reaction, but the likelihood of Abigail bailing was high. The seeds of her inadequacy and impending rejection had been planted. Tamara crept off the executive floor and scurried from the building, undetected and satisfied. Step one, Abigail, was complete. Step two, Joel, was next.

Chapter 24

Tamara wasn't the most diplomatic person Abigail had ever met. Yet her perspective bore a healthy element of truth. Unless her last name was Mitchell, Abigail didn't believe she had a substantial shot at the CEO post. Don was a worthy opponent against anyone except his mother. It was a fact that Madeline got what she wanted at DMI 99 percent of the time. Abigail searched her soul to figure out how much she truly wanted the gig and to what extent she was willing to go. She pondered this until she finally felt drained. This job wasn't for her. It would require too much fighting, and Abigail wilted at the mere hint of a battle.

Without any hesitation she soared into Don's office. She had to share her decision before she had a chance to mull it over and perhaps change her mind.

"What can I do for you?" he asked.

"I'm withdrawing my name from the CEO candidacy."

"What?" Don bellowed before collapsing into his seat. "Please tell me you're kidding."

"I'm sorry, but I'm serious. I can't go any further with this." Abigail felt awful. Don's cheek and chin were cradled in the palm of his hand. She couldn't take the disappointment on his face. He deserved better from her, but she wasn't able to honor his request. "You know I'm grateful for the offer, but there's too much opposition for me to be comfortable proceeding."

"What happened between yesterday and today? Huh? Tell me. Did Joel get to you? He did, didn't he?"

Abigail discounted his assumption frantically.

"It had to be him," Don insisted. "What did he promise you?"

"It wasn't Joel."

"Then who?" Don yelled.

She was about to tell him about the eye-opening conversation she had had with his sister, but she stopped herself. Tamara wasn't her sole motivation for withdrawing. She might have stirred the pot. However, competing against Madeline and Joel already had her doubting the decision to go forward. Alone they were treacherous when it came to business dealing. Together she couldn't imagine how far they'd go to win.

Don came around the desk and approached Abigail. He gently placed his hands on her shoulders. "Please don't do this to me. I have your back on this. You don't have to worry. We're going to win this. There's no one more qualified."

"Except Joel."

"Joel has baggage and a reputation to overcome. Trust me; it's nearly an impossible feat to win over our conservative board of directors with such baggage. He made fools out of them before. They aren't eager to get pounced on twice. He's out, which means the door is open for you. You'll be a dream confirmation."

"What about Tamara?"

"What about her?" he asked, removing his hands from her shoulders.

Abigail wasn't going to reveal details of Tamara's recent rant, yet she wanted Don to be aware of what they were up against. "Tamara is very upset, and I personally wonder if you can withstand her determination to claim the role as head of DMI." Abigail questioned whether

Don was unaware of his sister's fervent opposition or was simply in denial about it. Neither scenario gave her the confidence required to fight the DMI battle. "It's clear that Tamara feels entitled to the position and is willing to trample anyone in her way," Abigail stated.

Don rested his hands on her shoulders again. "Abigail, I'm begging you not to back out. This is personal. If we can't get you appointed, we'll need to conduct a full candidate search."

She tried shifting her glance away from him, but Don's gaze followed hers. She couldn't wiggle free. He had a tight grip on her due to their friendship and the dormant affection they had for one another which resided deep within.

"A full search could take months, even years," Don told her. He let her shoulders go and moved away, scratching the back of his neck. "I can't wait months or years. I have to get you confirmed now so that I can get out of here, knowing DMI is in good hands."

She could tell he had more to say and therefore chose not to interrupt.

"It has to be you in charge, someone I trust. I can't afford to run back if something falls apart at DMI again. With Joel, that's a strong possibility. I came back once because God led me here. Don't think I'm coming back after my mission in Detroit comes to an end. That's why I prefer to have you as CEO. I like the odds of you being successful better than the ones for Joel. If you have a heart for DMI and share my father's vision, you need to take this job."

Abigail graciously waited for Don to finish before she spoke up. "Again, I'm sorry this isn't going to work out as you'd like. However, for the sake of my sanity, I have to keep my resignation intact."

"That's too bad," Don told her, allowing his disappointment to be seen and processed. There wasn't much he could do in the way of convincing her to see his perspective. "Close my door on your way out, and please tell my assistant to hold all calls."

His gaze was tranquil, much to Abigail's bafflement. "Are you going to be okay?" she asked.

"I will be soon, once my plane lands in South Africa in a few weeks."

Abigail wasn't quite sure how he planned to transition out of his position at DMI without a confirmed replacement, but she wasn't about to inquire. Don definitely didn't appear to be in the mood for conversation. She quietly retreated into the hallway and left him to ponder his family's complicated lives. She walked away, relieved. Abigail hated disappointing Don, but it was either him or her. Four years ago she would have acquiesced. Thanks to Tamara, saying no felt better.

Chapter 25

Don watched helplessly as his replacement slipped from his grasp. He sat down and moped. His family was twisted, and he didn't know how to fix them. He let his mind settle down by concentrating on the South African air blowing across the Atlantic Ocean, carrying the allure of his future. The tug was strong, and it was getting stronger with each breath. Usually, this was the point when Don had to set his desires aside and put the family first. He'd sacrificed countless times before, believing with each episode in his family's drama that this would be the last time he'd be required to rescue a brood bent on dwelling in turmoil. He reflected on so many different events over the years. After a while, he was overwhelmed. It was too much, and he knew it.

Don got up and went to see Madeline. He found his mother in her office, where she was meeting with a client. Not wanting to interrupt, he stopped in the doorway, intending to leave, but she beckoned for him to come in. He entered as she continued the conversation.

"Don, you remember Mr. Mullins from Faith Keepers International?"

"Of course." Don shook the client's hand. "It's good to see you."

The greetings concluded, and Don took a seat at the conference table across from Mr. Mullins. Madeline approached the table and then stood there with her arms folded. Her reading glasses rested on the bridge of her nose.

"How many times do you think we're going to give you the new client discount?" she asked.

Mr. Mullins replied, "Please don't misunderstand. I'm not asking for a special discount."

Madeline pressed her tightly closed fists against the table. "Then what are you asking for, because that's what it sounds like to me?"

Don squirmed. He'd seen his mother in action on numerous occasions when she felt a client was trying to take advantage of DMI's generosity. Mr. Mullins didn't have a chance. DMI was her baby, and she protected the company's integrity and reputation as only a lioness could. Don was silent, realizing she didn't need or want his help. She could handle this lone chief financial officer from Faith Keepers on her own. Don relaxed in his chair and watched the fireworks.

Madeline continued lashing out at Mr. Mullins. "What do you think DMI is? A charity—"

"Wait a minute," Mr. Mullins interrupted.

Madeline ignored him and went on. "We provide leadership and financial management training to churches and other religious entities." Madeline's voice was crisp and somewhat controlled, but her words were like darts thrown at a dartboard. "That doesn't mean we're offering handouts."

"Please don't misunderstand," Mr. Mullins said. "I'm asking for a discount in good faith in exchange for a significant chunk of additional work in the neighborhood of three hundred and twenty-five thousand, if we include all our satellite locations. The discount is merely a way for us to share the risk."

"What risk?" Don asked.

Mr. Mullins gulped. "We've been very pleased with DMI's services, but the issue your company has faced over the past twelve months gives you an air of instability."

Madeline scooted close to the table. "Instability . . .? Are you crazy? We have stabilized our operation, and we're moving forward with expansion plans."

Don wasn't aware of any expansion projects, but far be it for him to interrupt. He was trying to loosen the DMI knot around his neck, not tighten it by getting too deeply involved in matters that were already being handled by a top executive. He was perfectly fine with being quiet and letting Madeline handle the mess. He was tired.

"Perhaps I misunderstood the financial reports we received on DMI," Mr. Mullins said.

"There is no misunderstanding," Madeline replied. "We went through a structural change in our senior management last year. As you know, that's when Don was appointed CEO."

The client nodded in affirmation.

Madeline pushed slightly away from the table. "Leading up to that change, we are all well aware of the problems DMI encountered. That's the truth." She threw her hands up. "I'm not sugarcoating our temporary corporate set-back. Not only do we teach full transparency, but it is also a presiding core principle here at DMI that we actually put into practice."

Don knew she was referring to Joel's stint as CEO and his botches. Hearing the client express concern about this made Don wonder how Madeline could possibly support Joel in his CEO run. He had too much baggage, and customers had too little forgiveness which was a recipe for Joel's failure.

Madeline continued. "We're on track now and in the service of helping troubled groups with their financial challenges. If you want our help, we would love to work with you. If not, I challenge you to find a better service provider. Either way, what we're not going to do is let you strong-arm us into a one-sided deal because you think we're desperate. You can kindly walk out of here if that's your strategy."

Mr. Mullins seemed to dwell on Madeline's statement before responding. "Thank you for the honesty. I believe we can work with you."

"Wise decision, because if you chose otherwise, it would have been your loss." Madeline slid a pen and a contract to Mr. Mullins.

Don didn't have to wonder if it was a Montblanc. He knew it was because that was what Madeline preferred. Whatever Madeline preferred, she generally got, which would certainly have been detrimental to Abigail's bid for the CEO post. His anxiety slowly began rising as he contemplated Abigail's withdrawal from the shortlist of CEO candidates. Don wasn't thrilled that he had to tell his mother about Abigail's decision. He cringed as he anticipated Madeline's reaction. She'd gladly accept an uncontested confirmation for Joel. Don's heart sank, until he realized it was better not to care about DMI once he got on a plane heading out of Detroit. That day was coming sooner than anyone at DMI dared to believe.

Mr. Mullins interrupted Don's musing. "Don, Faith Keepers International and I look forward to doing business with you."

"Likewise. I'm sure you'll continue to be pleased with our services."

Don shook the client's hand again, and then Madeline escorted Mr. Mullins from her office to the assistant's desk. She closed the door upon reentering her office.

"What a jackass," Madeline said.

"Mother! Why would you say that about a client?"

"Well, he is one." She returned to the conference table. "I don't appreciate clients who think they can take advantage of us because we suffered a few losing quarters. That's it, only a few quarters."

"It's business, Mother. Everyone looks for a deal."

"Humph. It's not becoming for a church leader. He should be straightforward and honorable in his negotiations. I deal with snakes all day, every day. I don't need to face them from the church."

Don considered telling Madeline that not every person working with a church knew the Lord and had committed to living by God's guidelines. He could have shared his insight with her, but he didn't want to get her riled up in a debate over religion. He'd let her think as she wanted. God would correct her if and when He chose. Instead, Don focused on a topic that was much more pressing.

"I had a talk with Abigail about an hour ago." Don paused.

When the silence persisted, Madeline said, "And . . . ?"

"And she wants out of the CEO pool of candidates. I desperately tried to convince her not to pull out, but her mind is set. She's out of here."

"I see. Well, that leaves Joel," Madeline said with a wide grin. "No problem. I can call a board meeting by Friday and have Joel in the office next week."

"Not so fast, Mother," Don said, slowly raising his hand. "Tamara is the reason she's running scared. Apparently, Tamara is so upset about not being considered for the post that she confronted Abigail."

Madeline drew in a deep breath of air and released it very slowly. "I had no idea she was so upset." Madeline fumbled with her pen, letting her gaze remain low. "Actually, I thought she would come around to our way of thinking and would continue in her junior-level marketing position. It's an ideal place for her to learn the business. In the meantime, I would personally mentor her. She's a smart girl. In a few years, I'm sure she'd be ready for a manager's position. That child of mine," Madeline said punctuated with a heavy sigh. "Tamara could make executive vice president in no time if she'd put half as much effort into improving her skills as she puts into scheming about how to climb to the top." Madeline sighed again. "Nothing is easy with my child."

"What do you want to do? Abigail is out. As you saw with Mr. Mullins, clients are still edgy about our credibility and stability. If Joel is reinstated, you might lose customers, or you'll have others, like Mr. Mullins, who'll want a heavy discount in exchange for trusting us to do the right thing. If you ask me, we can't afford to have Joel in charge."

"Then you'll have to stay longer, until I can figure this out with Tamara."

"Oh no," Don said, leaping to his feet. "I'm leaving."

"When?"

"As soon as I get the green light from God, I'm out of here."

Madeline giggled. "What are you waiting on, for Him to come down and discuss your travel plans over dinner?"

"Something like that." Don wanted to make sure he wasn't operating on emotions and fleeing because the Mitchells were draining. He definitely wanted out, but he refused to get ahead of God. Don would wait until his confirmation came in the form of a dream, peace in his spirit, or clarity in his prayers. He was open to however God wanted to reach him. Hopefully, it would be soon.

Madeline's giggle turned into a full bout of laughter.

"Mother, what I said isn't that funny."

"It is for me. I have to laugh to keep from crying."

Don understood. He'd felt that way on many occasions when dealing with his family. He was thrilled that another Mitchell was getting a taste of his plight.

Chapter 26

Tamara was bored with playing a game of cat and mouse with Joel. He'd leave, Zarah would call her, and Tamara would rush over to their house, hoping to complete a deal on the West Coast division before he returned home. She wasn't able to count the number of near misses they'd had.

Fired up, Tamara popped out of the cab at the main entrance to Joel and Zarah's house. This was it. "Can you pull to the end of the driveway and wait for me near the exit please?" The driver appeared reluctant to do so. "I'll pay you the full fare. Just keep the motor running," she said and hurled a wad of crumpled twenty-dollar bills at him.

The driver's face lit up, punctuated with a smirk. "Where did you say you wanted me to wait?"

Tamara repeatedly pointed toward the end of the driveway. "Down there is fine. I should be out in thirty minutes."

"No problem," the driver said, straightening out the money. "Take your time. I'll be right here."

Tamara smirked too as she walked away. This was a reminder that everyone had a price. When it came to Zarah, the incentive to sell might have nothing to do with cash. That was understood, but regardless of race, gender, religious beliefs, or culture, every person valued something. For some, it was money; for others, love. In her worldly travels, Tamara had learned that in some cultures the gift of a goat represented the highest form of appreciation. She knocked on the front door, determined to wrap up this lengthy match play and get on with existing beyond the Mitchells' territory. She giggled. There wasn't a goat in the cab to offer Zarah, but Tamara had something better. She was certain of it.

The housekeeper answered. "Good day, Ms. Mitchell. Mrs. Zarah is expecting you."

Tamara pushed past the housekeeper and hustled across the foyer. "She's upstairs?"

"No, Ms. Mitchell. She's in the library."

Tamara wasn't expecting that answer. Zarah was on strict orders to stay on bed rest until baby Mitchell was born. Tamara went into the library and found her friend sitting there, dressed in a deep royal blue sari trimmed in gold. "My goodness, you're fully clothed. Where are you going?"

"Nowhere."

"Sure looks like you're going somewhere. Aren't you still on bed rest?"

"Yes, my doctor has asked me to stay calm. I have done so, but staying in the bed every day has become more than I can bear."

Tamara understood and gave no admonishment. Besides, she didn't have time to chastise Zarah. Minutes were streaking by. Tamara plopped into a chair and sat on the edge, eager to review the terms of her proposed deal and then duck out. "How long will Joel be gone?"

"Two to three hours."

"Where did he go?"

"I'm not sure. I went for a nap earlier. When I woke, our housekeeper gave me his note."

Tamara couldn't care less about where Joel was and what he might be doing. Unlike Madeline, he hadn't conned her into thinking he'd changed. It was a ridiculous notion given that snakes didn't change. They just shed their skin, giving the illusion of change, which was precisely why Tamara had to act fast. Joel was fooling too many people too quickly. If she didn't act this very moment, it might be too late. Despite her best mentoring efforts, Joel could swoop in, woo his wife, and entice her over to the dark side. That would push Zarah and the West Coast division too far out of Tamara's reach. She couldn't handle the idea of losing a friendship and a piece of the company simultaneously. Tamara's stress was building. She couldn't allow Joel to have this much control over her livelihood. She had to act fast.

"Zarah, I am begging you on our friendship. Please sell me the West Coast division. I have to get out of here. It's my only chance to have a fresh start. If I didn't have to ask, I wouldn't." Tamara had to use every tactic available. She could lie around, feeling poorly later. "But you're the only person on earth who can help me. Please," Tamara said, balling up both fists and tapping her thighs. "I can't rely on anyone else to help me. You're my very best friend, my only friend," she wailed.

Somehow Tamara managed to squeeze out a few tears. It was literally just a few, but she magnified their effect by asking for a tissue. Zarah obliged, and Tamara wiped her eyes for an extended period, although not another drop fell after the first few tears.

"You must not get upset. Please, let me get you a cup of tea. It will help you feel better."

"No thank you. All I need is the West Coast division, and I'll get out of here and let you rest."

"Is the division this important to you?"

"Yes," Tamara bellowed. "I lost fifteen years with my father. When I was moving from place to place, running from my family, I didn't have contact with my dad." She dabbed the area below her eyes with the dry tissue. "He died without seeing me as a successful adult." She dabbed again, as her eye had become slightly sore from continually rubbing. "The division gives me my one chance to honor my father and to make him proud. This is the most important gift anyone can ever give me."

"I'm not sure my husband would agree with selling the division. He was very angry last year, when I considered selling."

"You don't have to worry. Remember that he's changed since last year. He won't mind if you help a friend. He appreciates loyalty. I do too. If you sell me the division, you can believe I'll be indebted to you forever. I'll return your kindness at the very first opportunity. I've told you before. You can count on me to always be here for you." Tamara was exhausted. She'd expended enough emotional energy to win a sports championship. She sat quietly, having told Zarah every possible reason for saying yes. There was nothing left to add. Tamara had done all the convincing that she could. Her future now rested in Zarah's hands.

"You have been a very good friend," Zarah said. "I am in your debt as well. I will sell you the West Coast division."

"Zarah, please help me. I need the division. I have only twenty million, but you can have every penny. Please help me," she pleaded.

"Did you hear me? I said yes. I will sell you the West Coast division."

Tamara couldn't move. Had she heard correctly? "What did you say?"

"The division is yours, my friend."

Tamara slapped her open palms repeatedly against her face. She felt as if Zarah's answer was dangling in midair. Tamara had to snatch the words and hide them in her soul for safekeeping. "Are you serious?"

"Yes, I am most serious."

Tamara wanted to jump for joy, but she couldn't get too excited. They'd gotten close to making a deal about a month ago. Before Zarah could sign the papers, she was admitted to the hospital with symptoms of a miscarriage. Tamara had her doubts but proceeded with as much hope as she could that the deal would actually happen.

"How soon can we get this done? Can we call your attorney now and get the papers going?" Tamara asked.

Zarah glanced at a small clock on the center shelf of one of the built-in bookcases. It was 4:15 p.m.

"It is close to three a.m. in the south of India. I will call my attorney later this evening, when it is morning for him."

"What time?" Tamara asked, sitting on the very edge of her chair. If she scooted forward any farther, she'd fall on the floor.

"Nine thirty. That will be around eight in the morning. He's usually in the office by then."

Tamara wanted to leave nothing to chance. "I can give you a wake-up call."

"That's not necessary. I will be awake."

Tamara reluctantly replied, "Okay, if you say so, but promise to call me after you've spoken to the attorney. I don't care how late. Call me. I won't sleep a wink until you call." Tamara jumped up and squeezed Zarah's hands so tightly, the blood rushed to her fingertips. Both of them smiled.

"I know the division is worth ten times what I can pay," Tamara continued. "But I promise to pay you the rest in a few years. I can also sell my fifteen percent stock ownership in DMI. It's got to be worth a couple hundred million. Don't worry. I can get more money. Really, I can."

"The money is no issue. There are no money problems as we are family." Zarah looked intently at Tamara, as if peering into her soul. "You're both my family and a friend. I will take what you have. It is good."

"Are you sure? We're talking about a lot of money."

"Yes, I'm sure," Zarah affirmed.

Tamara hugged Zarah briefly without thinking. "Thank you. Thank you for everything. I am grateful to you forever."

It was like a dream. Tamara's war was coming to a close, and not a day too soon. She was worn out and felt too depleted to fight Joel this afternoon. She'd better get out of there before he got home.

"I'm leaving now, but you might not want to tell Joel about this until our deal is final."

Zarah grinned and didn't respond, which caused Tamara's zeal to diminish rapidly. Joel was a huge danger. Until the deal was signed, he had the upper hand. And Tamara knew it.

Chapter 27

Madeline leaned against the set of drawers firmly mounted in the center of her closet and took off one shoe at a time. She swayed a bit before regaining her balance. There had to be a few empty slots for shoes among the 150 that had been erected when she had the custom closet designed and installed. She was familiar with every inch of the house. Rochester Hills, an exclusive town situated to the north of Detroit, was supposed to be a safe haven for her children during the years that the family had to be rebuilt. She'd carefully selected the quiet neighborhood lined with trees and the award-winning private schools. She was particularly pleased with the decent amount of distance between their new home and the old one on Mayweather Lane. In a dreamland, she could have imagined a house filled with the laughter of four impressionable children who were showered with love from both their parents. No matter how sweet her dream was in the beginning, it always ended with the screams of Tamara, Andre, and Sam, each of them crying out for help. They needed help that she and Dave weren't able to give.

She unhooked her string of pearls and placed it in the five-foot-high jewelry case, which she'd organized by gem type. Surrounded by plenty, Madeline battled a tremendous lack in her soul. Her heart ached and her head too. Barefoot, she crossed her arms and sat in front of the full-length mirror situated in the corner of her closet.

Fatigue set in. Leaving work early had to become the norm and not the exception. She couldn't get Joel confirmed fast enough. Filing the upcoming vacancy in the CEO assignment flooded her mind like a gigantic tide repeatedly crashing against the shoreline. She couldn't get a moment of peace. Don wanted out. As much as his leaving created a monumental problem for her, she appreciated her son's desire to walk away while he was still on top. Despite the ebbs and flows over the year, Madeline was pleased with the son she'd birthed and raised. Not everything had been damaged in her life, and there was cause to celebrate briefly before the other challenges met her at the doorway.

Wearily, she eventually emerged from the closet into the open space. The large mansion swallowed her up and seemed more like a mausoleum. It was empty and void of liveliness, exactly the opposite of what she desired. Madeline draped her body across the chaise lounge in her bedroom. Maybe after the fate of DMI was secure, she'd consider selling her house. Might as well. Don wasn't coming home. He was moving to the other end of the world. And Tamara hadn't set foot in the house since running away over fifteen years ago.

Madeline picked up a magazine from her reading table and turned the pages. She was too tired to do much and too energized to sleep. She put the magazine back on the reading table and then puttered around, waiting for energy or sleepiness to get the edge and shove her in one direction or the other. Either was fine so long as she wasn't stuck in neutral. She detested being in neutral; nothing was worse than being awake and not enjoying life.

The security panel located near the entrance to her room buzzed. Madeline checked the time on the clock that sat next to the bed. Seven thirty. She wondered who in the world could be dropping by unannounced. She went to the screen situated next to the panel, and saw that there was a cab sitting in front of the ten-foot-high gate leading into her property. Madeline became concerned. She was about to press the emergency button, which would connect her directly to 9-1-1, and get this stranger away from her house when the buzzer rang again. Curiosity got the best of her, and she pressed the SPEAK button.

"Can I help you?" Nobody responded, causing Madeline to become immediately irritated.

"Can you please get away from my gate, or I'm dialing nine-one-one."

"Mother, it's me."

"Tamara!"

"Yes, it's me. Can you please buzz me in?"

Madeline frantically punched in the code on her keypad, and the two sides of the gate parted for Tamara's cab, which coasted up the driveway. Madeline flew downstairs as her thoughts roamed. Before she reached the door, Tamara had rung the bell repeatedly.

"All right, okay. I'm coming," she said, hustling. She snatched the door open. "Are you all right?"

Tamara pushed past Madeline. "I'm fine."

"Excuse me, young lady. You could say hello or something before pushing past me and barging into this house."

"We need to talk," Tamara said in a demanding tone.

Madeline eased the door closed. She didn't appreciate her daughter's tone but wouldn't react, not yet. "Great. Let's sit down and talk."

"No!" Tamara shouted. "We can talk right here."

Madeline didn't pressure Tamara. It was surreal having her daughter back in the house. Whatever she had to talk about had to be monumental. Madeline didn't think her daughter would cross the threshold for anything less significant.

"What is this about? Is Remo bothering you again?"
The terrorizing threats he'd hurled at Tamara during his
last visit to Detroit were fresh in her mind. Madeline had
paid her brother-in-law Frank to take care of Tamara's
stalking ex-boyfriend. She had hoped he'd leave her
daughter alone, but judging by Tamara's demeanor, he
must have returned. What else could have Tamara so
wound up?

"No, it's not Remo. I haven't seen him."

"Good." Madeline was relieved. "Then what is going
on?"

"I came to tell you that I'm leaving town."

"Why?" Madeline asked as Tamara's statement punc-
tured her feelings.

"Zarah is selling me the West Coast division. Once we
close the deal, you won't see me in Detroit or in this house
ever again."

Madeline was crushed. "Tamara, are we so awful that
you can't stand being in the same state with us? Are you
so wounded that you want us to hurt as much as you
obviously do?" Madeline didn't know how to feel. She was
angry, shocked, anxious, and scared at the same time.
She knew that if Tamara left this time, it was for good.
Madeline couldn't let that happen. "What can I do to
change your mind?" she pleaded.

"Nothing. I'm out of here." Tamara turned to leave. "I
stopped by to remind you of the fact that you betrayed
me."

"That's not true," Madeline replied, clinging to any
hope of convincing Tamara to stay.

"You chose Joel over me."

"Tamara, you know that's not what happened." Madeline reached for her daughter. Tamara pulled away.

"It's exactly what happened. Face it, Mother," Tamara
said, spewing her words. "My leaving is on you. This is
your doing. I'm gone."

Tamara turned the doorknob. Madeline intervened and pressed her foot against the front door, preventing it from opening.

"Please move your foot. I want to get out of this hellhole. Move!" Tamara screamed.

Madeline didn't want to let her child walk away under these conditions. Tamara had too much anger to be out in the world alone.

"Move," Tamara ordered again. This time she yanked the door open, knocking Madeline off balance. Tamara darted from the house and hopped in the cab. The cab skidded down the driveway, sliced through the open gate, and bolted into the exterior world.

Madeline stood paralyzed in the doorway for what felt like an eternity. Her baby was gone, and the pain was unbearable. She dropped to her knees, drowning in sorrow. Each breath was laced with a reminder of her mistakes and the family's personal failures. They'd been ravaged by one battle after another, with no respite. Pride kicked in and enabled her to stand, close the door, and swallow the realization that the world as she'd known it twenty minutes ago was no longer. The notion was beyond devastating. She just couldn't let Tamara go without trying to save her. There was only one way to fix the situation. She scurried upstairs to grab her cell phone and quickly retrieved Joel's number to call him.

When he answered, she took the direct route. It would be better for him and for her too. "I'm sorry, but I'll have to rescind my offer to support your candidacy for CEO."

"This is a joke, right?"

Madeline gulped. "I wish it was, but I'm serious."

"Come on, Madeline. Don't do this to me. I need this job."

"I'm sorry." And she was. Joel was the most qualified candidate, but not at the expense of Tamara. As much as Madeline's heart wept for DMI, it was severed by the mere idea of losing her daughter forever. Madeline would let Tamara have the CEO post. So what if she ran DMI into the ground? As long as she stayed in Detroit, Madeline would eagerly make that sacrifice.

"Why are you backing out? You at least owe me an explanation."

"Joel, I really am sorry. Come by the office tomorrow, and I'll personally make sure we find another suitable position for you."

Joel snickered. "Are you kidding me? I'm not looking for a job in the mail room. I can submit an application online myself to do that. You know there's only one job that's right for me at DMI, and it's CEO. You know it, and I know it."

She agreed, but there was little Madeline could do. His appeal was falling on deaf ears. Her greatest allegiance was to Don and Tamara. Others had to squeeze in if and when the opportunity arose. Unfortunately, there was nothing more Madeline could do to appease Joel. She ended the call.

Joel was enraged as he held the phone. Madeline had hung up, but he couldn't put the phone down. He was shattered and didn't know what else to do. He reeled and rocked in his office, hibernating in there for hours. He was completely lost and had to pray for relief from his rage. How cruel to dangle a bone in front of a starving dog and then yank it away just as the smell reached his nostrils. He felt like a fool. Madeline's supposed support had been a lie. His mother had warned him not to trust Madeline's motives. In his desperate need for restoration, Joel had let his guard down and had gotten taken for a ride. He didn't know if he felt more contempt for losing the CEO position again or for letting Madeline con him. Both were devastating losses.

Joel yearned to handle this challenge as he had others. Instinctively, he would usually resort to crafting a shaky deal, attempt to secure questionable and possibly illegal funding from Uncle Frank, or head to Chicago to garner emotional support from Sheba. Not this time. He was willing to stand alone without running. It was unpleasant but necessary. He knew it and acquiesced to the valuable lesson rising out of his disappointment.

Chapter 28

Madeline still hadn't recovered from the windstorm that had sailed in and totally obliterated her dreams. For weeks her rational thinking had successfully kept rash, emotional decision making at bay. The logical reason for selecting Joel over Tamara was unchanged. However, her heartstring for Tamara was pulling rank over her "do the right thing" philosophy. Madeline couldn't let her daughter walk away if there was a way to keep her home. She found a phone and pecked the keys in record speed. She doubted that Tamara would answer her call, but Madeline had to try.

A grand mixture of delight and surprise consumed Madeline when she heard Tamara's voice. "Tamara, are you there? Tamara," she cried. "Please answer me. I know you're there."

"Mother, what do you want? We said everything that had to be said."

That couldn't be farther from the truth. There was much more for Madeline to say. She had heard her daughter's plea and aimed to honor it. She had kicked aside her pride and was willing to apologize, plead, or negotiate. The love she had for her daughter had no limits, and as of this moment, Madeline was open to any tactic or plan to save her relationship with Tamara. "What can I do to keep you here?"

"Nothing. It's too late, Mother."

"It's never too late when there's love involved," Madeline replied.

"We're not going to do this. I'm not going to do this."

"Do what?" Madeline asked.

"Let you try to guilt me into staying. Can't you accept that there's nothing here for me?"

"What do you mean? Don and I are here. We're your family."

"Really? Then why did you choose Joel over me?"

"I didn't choose him. I recruited the best candidate to run our company."

"Fine. Then why are you calling me?" Tamara said with a distinct edge in her voice.

Madeline didn't attack in response. She was completely restrained and terrified that Tamara would drop the call any second. Madeline clung to each word Tamara uttered as if it were a lifeline to her daughter.

"Look, I'm sorry. I made a mistake in choosing Joel, but you have to give me a chance to make this right. Please believe me. If I had any idea that becoming CEO was this important to you, I never would have nominated Joel. Please understand that you come first." Madeline was frustrated, because her love for Tamara was too vast to be summed up in a two-minute phone call. "I want you to know that Joel is no longer a problem. I've withdrawn his name. No decisions will be made without your involvement."

"Thanks, but no thanks. I'm not getting suckered into thinking you're going to make me CEO or make me any other officer at DMI. Nope. I'll take my division and go on about my way," Tamara replied.

Her efforts to change Tamara's mind weren't working. Yet Madeline was built to win battles for which, on the surface, the odds of success seemed low. Giving up on this fight to win back Tamara wasn't even a remote possibility. "I'll talk to Don. Between the two of us, we can provide the mentoring you'll need to assume the CEO position. You can do this."

"Mother, that's our problem. We don't hear one another. As soon as the transaction is finalized for the West Coast division, I'm gone."

Madeline gasped.

Tamara must have heard her, because she responded, "I don't want to hurt you, but I'm not changing my mind. I want to get out of here. I have to. Please let this go. Let me go."

Madeline's soul cried out as her feelings got the best of her. "Don't ask me to give up another child. I've already lost two. I can't bear to lose a third. I can't. Don't ask me, because I can't honor such a request."

"Then you're on your own. Bye."

The line went silent. Madeline was cemented to the moment. She couldn't go forward or backward. Her pulse pounded, and a massive amount of pain left her heart empty. The room was spinning rapidly, in a wild fashion. She struggled to retrieve a memory that could help stabilize her thoughts. Nothing sprang to mind. She dragged herself to the wall and braced herself, searching for an answer. She really didn't know what to do, in spite of being known for her quick wit and creative problem-solving skills. Albeit some of her approaches bordered on being unethical and illegal, Madeline didn't allow obstacles to prevent her from getting the job done. She was aggrieved from bearing the weight of the moment. This was her greatest challenge, and when she needed to devise a creative solution from her brain, there was nothing.

She adjusted the cell phone in her hand amid her tumultuous despair. Her eyes were watery, but she managed to punch out Don's cell phone number on the keypad. When he answered, she broke down emotionally.

Amidst her sobs and incoherent words, she heard him yelling.

"Mother, calm down and tell me what's wrong."

She winced and sighed repeatedly, until she achieved a semblance of control. "It's Tamara," she managed to blurt out.

"What about her? Is she hurt?"

"I'm the one who's hurt!" she told him, attempting to clear her throat.

"Do you need me to call an ambulance?"

"No, my physical body is fine." Madeline wished it was that kind of hurt, the kind that could be erased by taking a pill. She'd prefer to have a leg ripped out of its socket without anesthesia than to deal with heartache. "I'm upset about Tamara. She stopped by here a few minutes ago."

"I thought you left the office early today. Did you go back?"

"No. I'm at home. She came over here."

"Tamara came to the house!"

"Can you believe it? So you know her visit was serious. I honestly think she'd rather die than come to this house again." The mausoleum feeling was creeping in again. The walls were closing in on Madeline. The beauty she'd once seen in the house had been eradicated with each bad memory. "She came to tell me that Zarah is selling her the West Coast division."

"I'm sort of surprised."

"Actually, I don't care about the division. I just don't want to lose Tamara. She plans to settle the deal and leave town, and us, for good this time. So, I told her she could have the CEO position."

"Ah, Mother, you didn't. What about Joel?"

"Based on what you'd told me earlier and how upset Tamara was when she came by, I had to call Joel and rescind my offer of support."

"Oh my goodness Mother, how could you do that? You know Abigail has pulled out of the running. Now, we're forced to find someone on the open market. That could take months, even years to get the right person."

"Look, I wasn't happy about going back on my word, but I didn't have a choice." Sorrow enveloped her. "I'm going to lose her for good, Don." Sobbing ensued. "What else could I do?"

Don gasped. "I don't know . . ."

"Thanks a lot."

"Mother, you didn't let me finish. I was going to say that I don't know what to do except to pray. When we don't know what to do, I turn it over to the Lord."

Madeline thought about his suggestion, assessed it carefully, and tried to figure out her other options. She came up blank. *What the heck,* she thought. She figured that Don's prayer couldn't hurt. Besides, in her state of total desperation, Madeline figured she'd be foolish to turn down any reasonable help. "Yes, I'd like you to say a prayer." Nothing else had worked. Perhaps she'd try something new.

Chapter 29

Joel was reeling. He drove aimlessly through downtown Detroit without a legitimate destination. Time stood still, and all sounds were drowned out. He replayed in his mind Madeline's vicious retraction of her support for his candidacy. Then he remembered his mother's words of wisdom, how she'd told him not to trust Madeline. He was shocked to realize that she was right. Joel drove slowly, his fury rising and mostly directed at himself. How could he have been so gullible? He should have been prepared for Madeline retracting her offer. Yet he hadn't been. She'd completely blindsided him.

He wanted to wipe out this fresh failure as it clawed at him. His foot was itching to press the gas pedal hard against the floorboards and keep it there until he rolled into Chicago. The itching intensified as he fought against it. Joel maneuvered his car onto the shoulder of the road and put the gear in neutral. He had to clear his head in order to function.

An hour later Joel shuffled into the house, too dazed to spend a second in his office attempting to concoct a plan B. Instead, he'd go upstairs and hibernate in the guest room, hoping to block out his circumstances for the evening. He climbed the stairs gingerly. As Joel reached the landing upstairs, he noticed through the partially open door that Zarah's light was on indicating she was probably awake. He was tempted to dart past and avoid seeing her. That was his initial instinct, before concern kicked in and directed Joel into her room. He found his wife reclining on a side chair, reading a book.

"It's good you are home," she said. "I didn't know where you were. You've been gone a long time."

"I'm home now," he said. Joel didn't want to relive the trauma he'd suffered earlier. The wounds he'd suffered were too raw for him to discuss the details glibly, particularly with someone who had no means of helping him fix the setback. "Can I get you anything?" he asked, anxious to get to his room and sulk in private.

"Nothing."

"Call me if you need me."

Joel was leaving the room when Zarah called out, "Wait. I must share a bit of news with you."

He wasn't particularly excited about more news. With the way his day was going, he suspected more bad news was on the way, and braced for the worst. "What is it?"

"I'm selling Tamara the West Coast division."

Joel scratched behind his ear with his index finger. "Excuse me?" He couldn't possibly have heard her correctly.

"I'm selling the West Coast division to Tamara. It is most important to her, and as her friend, I choose to honor her request."

Joel cackled uncontrollably. It was official. This was arguably the worst day of his existence. "How could you betray me too? You know I didn't want Tamara to get her hands on the division. She's spiteful and reckless. How could you?" he asked.

"It is my right to make the decision. It is best to let her move to California and start her business. We have plenty of the company remaining."

"Zarah, don't treat me like a child. You had no right to let Tamara go behind my back. I trusted you." How did they expect him to keep on standing when he got one punch followed by another? If this was God's way of getting Joel's attention, then the mission was successful. "Call her for me please and tell her the deal is off. You've changed your mind."

"But I haven't changed my mind. The division should be hers."

"Don't you hear me? I need you to hang on to the division for us."

It was his only bargaining chip. DMI wanted to restore the division. He wanted the top spot. An equal exchange with the division for the CEO role was his best hope. By handing Tamara the division, Zarah was single-handedly putting a choke hold on his plan B. He didn't have any recourse against Madeline's betrayal. Zarah was different. She was his wife and owed him the courtesy of being more loyal to him than to Tamara.

"Remember that the two of us and our baby are family. We have to stick together. I'm here in this house to support you," he said, pointing at the floor. "If it had been left up to me, I'd have been back in Chicago a month ago. But I'm not there. I'm here with you. You see that I'm committed to you," he added, his volume rising out of frustration. "Why aren't you committed to me?"

Zarah reached for the glass of water sitting on the small table nearby and bobbled the glass a few times before taking a sip. "Please excuse me. I'm not keeping well." She gingerly made her way to the bed and lied down.

Joel wasn't sure if she was being honest. In the past she'd become sick at the most opportune time to avoid conflict. He proceeded with caution. "You want me to call an ambulance?"

"No. Please no fuss. I'd like to lie down."

He remained uncertain about her current health. If he had to guess, he'd say she was fine. However, the threat of a miscarriage was constantly looming. Wisdom told him to err on the side of caution. "If you don't need anything,

I'm going to my room. Call me if anything happens." He took her phone from the table across the room and placed it next to her on the nightstand. The tension mounted as he walked out of the room.

Joel made his way to the guest room and began pacing back and forth. He was outraged and wanted to take action. He couldn't continue arguing with Zarah. The risk to her pregnancy was too great. That left Tamara. He could call her and share his frustration, but it wasn't going to give him the satisfaction he craved. His pacing and fretting got the better of him. He had to get out of that house before the walls caved in on him and crushed the bit of spirit he had left. Without uttering goodbye to Zarah, he left the house, climbed in his car, and sped from the driveway with his tires screeching. He drove down the hill and was grateful to see that the local coffee shop hadn't closed for the evening. He parked his car in the parking lot, went inside, and was shown to a table.

"Can I get a shot of espresso?" he asked the waitress.

"Coming right up."

"Don't tell me this is my lucky day. If it isn't my favorite CEO," Joel heard a voice whisper over his shoulder.

He turned to face the person. "Samantha Tate, what are you doing in my neck of the woods again?"

She tossed a sheepish grin his way. "Maybe I stopped in hoping to run into you."

He grinned as his worries lightened. "Twice in two months. What are the odds?" He recalled running into her, last month, after she'd interviewed Zarah for an article featuring local businesswomen. "Careful or I'll think you're stalking me."

"What if I am?" she said, punctuating her remark with a wink. "Let's grab a table and chat for a while. It will be good to catch up on you and that lovely wife of yours."

It didn't take long for Joel to respond since he wasn't eager to go anywhere else. "Sure, why not.."

Once Samantha had her cup of coffee, they grabbed a table in the back and chatted as the hour ticked by.

"Why haven't I heard from you?" Samantha asked. "And don't say you lost my information, because I gave you my card the last time I ran into you here."

He didn't answer. Joel had thrown the card away as soon as she left the parking lot after their last run-in.

The conversation moved on to other topics. The two talked freely. Their exchange was sprinkled with loads of flirting. The waitress refreshed their beverages several times. Joel was intrigued with Samantha and was more relaxed now than he'd been earlier. He was glad to spend some time with someone who'd been with him during the height of his success. His ego was happy.

"Why don't we grab dinner and maybe a few drinks for old times' sake?" Samantha suggested.

Joel was feeling loose but didn't take the bait. "I can't stay much longer. I have to check on my wife."

"That's right, the lovely Zarah Bengali Mitchell. I was quite fascinated with her during our interview. She's captivating."

"She is all of that," he said, taking a gulp of coffee.

Samantha rubbed her foot against Joel's leg.

"Don't do that," he said.

"That's a first," she told him with a pout.

"Like they say, there's a first for everything."

"You mean to tell me the debonair Joel Mitchell is loyal to his wife?"

He chuckled. "You're the reporter. You tell me."

"Sounds like it."

"I guess pregnancy has that effect on a marriage."

"Pregnancy?"

"Yep, I'm going to be a dad. Can you believe it?"

"No, actually, I can't."

"Me, either, most of the time, but it's true. Zarah is pregnant."

"Wow. What a shock. The most eligible bachelor gets married and has a kid in not much more than a year. You move fast."

"You could say that."

"Congratulations."

"If you say so." His statement hit the airwaves before he had a chance to rephrase it.

"What do you mean by that?" she asked.

"Nothing, actually. I have to get home and check on my wife. It's good seeing you."

"Likewise."

"Who knows? Maybe I'll run into you here again," Joel told her.

"Never know," she said, letting her eyelids flutter which he interpreted as flirtation.

They exchanged goodbyes and departed.

Samantha was off his mind as soon as he drove out of the coffee shop's parking lot. Zarah was monopolizing his thoughts. He wasn't getting everything right as a husband, but Joel was trying. He felt bad about the argument they had had earlier and was eager to get home and reconcile. His car zipped up the hill as fast as the speed limit allowed. Joel wanted to forget about this evening, as if it had never happened. He was still open to building a marriage with Zarah if they could solve their looming issues. There was at least a fifty-fifty chance of them staying together. Zarah might not think those odds were great, but compared to the zero percent chance she had before the pregnancy, Joel saw hope on the horizon.

Chapter 30

Zarah braced against the pain that had erupted in her abdomen. She sucked in deep breaths, determined to alleviate the pain and silence her fears. Instead of relief, each gasp ignited a fresh wave of pain. Zarah screamed as memories of the last miscarriage episode flooded her. She had to protect her baby but didn't know what to do. She frantically patted the sheets underneath her to see if they were wet. There wasn't any blood like there had been the last time, which was a relief. Her heartbeat slowed down. She leaned against the headboard, shut her eyes, and breathed while gently rubbing her belly. Zarah was comforted by thinking about how much the baby meant to the marriage and to their family. Without the baby or Joel, her life was meaningless. As her body calmed, Zarah drifted off to sleep.

When he got back to the house, Joel poked his head in the bedroom to check on her. He saw her sleeping and quietly walked into the room for a closer look, to make sure she was okay. She was resting peacefully, which was refreshing. His day had been disastrous. Ironically, taking care of Zarah afforded him a brief reprieve from his turmoil. Joel kissed her on the forehead and then went to the guest room.

He paced around the room aimlessly and turned on the TV, then muted it. Joel plucked a book from the small built-in shelves in the corner. He paced some more and then grabbed the TV remote and flipped through several

channels. He sat and stood repeatedly. The grip his turmoil had on him was too strong for him to think clearly.
Prayer was calling out to him, but Joel didn't answer.
What more was there to ask? He'd sought forgiveness
several months ago. After countless failed attempts to
rebuild his career, he'd humbled himself and reached out
to God for help. Joel wasn't ignorant. Yet, nothing related
to his marriage or restoration into DMI was working.

He pressed his palms against the dresser and let his
gaze roam across the floor. Doubt was very present. He
expected to suffer the consequences of his arrogance and
poor decisions. But Joel refused to believe that this latest
setback was some kind of punishment from God. Besides,
where would the punishment begin and end? The list of
his mistakes was too long—they ranged from marrying
outside his faith to giving his relationship with God low
priority. It would be impossible for him to recant all his
errors.

Joel was in a bind. He needed to pray but was too
ashamed to ask for more from God. He sat on the bed and
rocked back and forth until it was clear to him that there
was no other path forward. Joel felt like he was going
mad. He became increasingly desperate. Without overthinking, he mumbled a few words to God, completely
surrendering. There wasn't an audible response from God
vibrating throughout the room. There wasn't a whisk of
wind sailing around the room and blowing peace at him.
But Joel did feel a smidgen of change, as if his load had
been lightened a bit. It was unexplainable. He attributed
his rising calm purely to faith. Even if God didn't end up
rescuing Joel from his botched circumstances, he was
absolutely convinced that God was able to do it. He found
solace in his belief.

He rose from the bed and decided that he would check
on Zarah in a few minutes, before turning in for the night.

Suddenly his phone rang. Joel jerked the phone from his pocket and answered it immediately. Maybe it was Madeline calling to reinstate her support for his bid on the CEO role. *God sure works fast*, he thought.

But all he heard on the other end of the line was moaning and groaning. And then a faint "Help . . ."

"Zarah," Joel called out and darted from the room. He sprinted to the master bedroom and found her folded into the fetal position on the bed, holding her phone. "Zarah, is it the baby?"

The excessive sobbing made her incoherent.

"Are you in pain? Are you bleeding?" he asked and felt around the bed. Finding nothing, he sprang into action. "We have to get you to the hospital. I'm calling an ambulance."

She grabbed his collar. "Please don't take me to the hospital. I will be well here. Just stay with me until the pain is gone," she pleaded.

"Don't you worry. I'm not going anywhere. I'm right here," he said, sliding onto the bed and resting her head on his lap. "But we have to go to the hospital. They can take better care of you than I can. We have to go."

Her cries intensified. Joel didn't know if fear or pain was fueling her cries. He had to get help. Joel dialed 9-1-1 without waiting for Zarah's approval.

"We can't lose our baby. This pregnancy is most important to me. Our baby is good, yes?" Zarah said through her pain.

Joel cradled Zarah as critical minutes ticked by. He didn't have an answer for her or possess the ability to heal her physically or emotionally. But he knew someone who could. He placed his hand on top of Zarah's and began praying. He didn't seek her permission, because he realized that she might be offended. He had to use what worked.

Zarah interrupted him as he prayed. "We must pray to the fertility gods and cure the problems we're having with my pregnancy."

Joel had been married to Zarah for eight months. During that span of time he hadn't seen her gods perform any miracles on her behalf. He'd known his God since childhood. Dave Mitchell had made sure that Joel formed a personal relationship with God and learned to rely on the Heavenly Father during good and bad times. Joel had personal knowledge of what God was capable of doing. If the marriage was to work, they'd have to figure out whose faith was going to govern the household. Being pulled in different spiritual directions was a guaranteed recipe for failure, one that he no longer cared to facilitate. Joel had failed enough professionally to curb his desire to repeat the same mistake personally. He was tired of losing. He wanted to taste victory again. Returning to what he knew worked was the idea.

Despite Zarah's protests, Joel continued praying. "Lord, please forgive me for my sins. I ask for your mercy and grace over Zarah and the baby. Please take away—" Joel was interrupted by the doorbell. "Must be the medical team," he told Zarah and removed his hand from hers.

She clawed at him, wanting him to stay by her side, but he pulled away. "Don't leave me," she pleaded.

"I have to open the door, or they'll break it down." She seemed to understand and acquiesced. "I'll be right back."

He dashed from the room, bolted down the stairs, and opened the front door. "Come on in," he told the two emergency medics after giving them his name. "My wife is in the master bedroom, at the top of the stairs," he said, leading the way.

"Is she conscious?" one medic asked.

"Yes, but she's in pain. I hope you can help her."

"We'll do our best," the other medic said as they entered the bedroom.

Zarah hadn't moved from the fetal position. She reached for Joel as soon as he entered the room.

"You're okay. I'm here. They're going to take care of you," Joel told her. He wasn't leaving her. They'd face their fears together by his God's grace.

Chapter 31

The ambulance ride should have taken fifteen minutes, but Joel had demanded that Zarah be taken to Henry Ford Hospital instead of Providence Park Hospital. The request added an extra twenty minutes. Although she'd received decent care at Providence last month, he figured at Ford she would have access to more specialists and technology since it was a much larger hospital.

After calling his mother, Joel waited in the emergency room for his wife to return from having a battery of tests performed. Worrying and praying simultaneously was counterproductive, and he despised being ineffective. He had to choose one or the other—prayer or worry—but not both. After a brief assessment, he opted to pray, as worrying had never produced the kind of results needed to solve any situation.

About twenty minutes later Joel looked up at the doorway and saw Sherry walking in. He stood and welcomed the big hug she gave him.

"I'm glad you called me," she said, still holding on to him. She eventually let go.

There was only one guest seat in the room, not counting the doctor's stool. "Here, Mom. Have a seat," Joel told her, moving out of the way.

"No, you sit. I can stand. I'm too upset to sit. What have the doctors told you so far?"

Joel swiped his hand across his forehead. "They haven't told me anything yet. They took her to have some tests done. We should know something any minute." Worry was clamoring to regain an equal footing with prayer and faith, but Joel wasn't relenting. Prayer was all he had.

Sherry pressed both palms against her face as tears began streaming down her cheeks, and then she burst into soft sobs.

"Mom, please sit down," Joel told her. "Don't worry. Zarah is going to be okay. I don't want you to be this worked up."

"I'm sorry." She followed his suggestion and took the seat as the sobs continued. "This room takes me back twenty-nine years ago, when I was admitted for problems during my pregnancy." Joel didn't know what to say. "I know exactly how Zarah feels." Her sobs were slightly louder.

Joel wanted to comfort his mother, but how could he dissolve a deep-seated sorrow, one that had resided in her heart for three decades?

"I'm praying for both Zarah and the baby," Joel said.

"Your father did the same thing. I remember him going to the chapel and praying for the baby."

"That sounds like my father."

"But what good was it?" she blurted out, with a tinge of what sounded like contempt. "My baby died, anyway. So forgive me if I don't join you in prayer." She patted her eyes with the moist tissue in her hand.

"You don't have to join me, but I have to pray. I don't have another option. God has always answered my prayers when I've asked for the right thing."

Gloom hung over the emergency room. Joel ducked and dodged it. He was inclined to stay positive. At one point he ran to the chapel and was back in the room within ten minutes, eager for an update. He was hoping Zarah would have been back by now.

"Did the doctor come in yet?" he asked Sherry.

"No one has been here."

"I'll be right back. I'm going to find the doctor or Zarah's nurse. Somebody ought to tell us something." Joel dashed into the hallway, looked for someone who could help, and found no one free. He slipped back into the room, deciding to leave worry on the other side of the threshold.

"Did you find anyone?" Sherry asked.

"Everybody was running around with other patients."

A few minutes later Zarah's gurney was wheeled into the small room. She appeared to be asleep.

"How did the tests go?" Joel asked the nurse at Zarah's side.

"The doctor is on her way to see you," the nurse replied. She wouldn't make eye contact with Joel, which made him nervous. Worry hadn't fully entered, but it had one toe in the room. Joel clung to his faith, hoping for a miracle.

"What can you tell me while we're waiting?" he asked.

The nurse hooked the IV bag in place and stuck to her original answer. "The doctor is on her way."

Joel was forced to wait for answers, but he wasn't happy about it. As promised, a petite black woman entered the room shortly after the nurse left.

"I'm Dr. Bernice Green," she said.

"Are Zarah and the baby going to be all right?" Joel asked.

"I'm sorry, but the privacy rules won't allow me to discuss Mrs. Mitchell's condition publicly," Dr. Green replied.

"It's okay to talk in front of my mother," Joel assured her. "Please, tell me what's going on with my wife."

The doctor hesitated and then leaned against the counter. "I don't have good news."

Joel stiffened. Sherry gasped.

"We made every effort to stop your wife's premature labor, but she began bleeding. We couldn't stop the bleeding, and as a result, the pregnancy terminated."

"What are you saying?" Joel asked.

"She lost the baby?" Sherry cried.

"Yes, and I am sorry for your loss, Mr. Mitchell. We gave your wife a light sedative to help her rest."

Joel was too stunned to reply.

"Your wife is young and appears to be in good health. You can try again right away," Dr. Green told him.

Joel thanked the doctor and watched as she left the room. He let his head hang low, like his spirit.

Sherry was balling, Zarah was asleep, and he was lost.

"I told you that praying is foolishness. All it does is get your hopes up and then lets you down," Sherry told him.

Joel wasn't falling into that trap. God was the same when He answered a prayer and when it appeared that He hadn't. *Let His will be done,* Joel thought. He didn't expect his mother to understand and didn't attempt to preach at her in their moment of grief.

"I'll be back," Joel told his mother.

"Where are you going?"

"To get some air. If Zarah wakes before I return, please let her know I stepped out for a few minutes and will be right back."

Sherry nodded.

Joel was crushed. He was suffering more than he had expected he would. This was his baby, true enough, but he couldn't help but to go back to the beginning. Initially, Zarah's revelation about the pregnancy had been a dagger in his independence. Several months ago he would have been thrilled about the baby vanishing and granting him his freedom. The issue about how to reconcile his and Zarah's religious differences would have been instantly solved.

Now that the baby was gone, he had to rethink his decision to stay with Zarah. Was it as simple as saying, "No baby - no marriage"? Perhaps it was. Before Zarah became pregnant, he'd wanted either to fix their marital issues or leave the marriage. But while she was carrying the baby, he didn't see a way forward that entailed leaving his child behind. Now there wasn't a child, and he was free.

Joel hesitated before celebrating. He wasn't getting off that easily. Losing a child was tragic, and he had to swallow the agony of it. His thoughts came in rapid succession as guilt tried latching onto him. Perhaps the pressure Zarah had endured, when he tried pushing her away from Tamara, contributed to the miscarriage. Joel wasn't clear on why the miscarriage happened, and he didn't have a yearning to question God for answers. He'd prayed and asked for His healing touch to cover Zarah and the baby. What more could he have done? If God wasn't going to save the baby, no one on earth could, either. He had to accept God's will.

Joel roamed the hallways until he landed in front of the double doors leading outside. He went out and stood in the open space. Serving God was simple. Accepting His will was hard for Joel, especially when it conflicted with his desires. Joel was aggrieved and longed to speak with someone who could help calm his raging soul. He didn't hesitate to call Don. He needed a family member, a big brother with whom to share his moment of grief. He knew that Don loved the Lord, and despite their challenges, he was certain that his brother would set aside his pride and provide encouragement. It was the only thing Joel wanted at that moment.

Chapter 32

Don had fallen asleep on the couch in his living room, with a pile of DMI documents to his left and a smaller stack of papers related to his company, LTI, to his right. He was sandwiched between the two and couldn't wait for the day when he would be able to focus on one challenge at a time. The ringing phone startled him, and it took Don a few seconds to react and take the call. He wasn't expecting to hear from Joel.

"I'm sorry to call you this late," Joel said.

"What time is it?" Don asked, searching the room for a clock.

"Close to ten o'clock."

It was later than Don thought, but not too late for someone to be calling. "What can I do for you?" he asked, figuring Joel wanted to talk about the CEO post. Don wasn't really up to it. They'd talked plenty over the past few weeks. "I'm a little tired."

"I'm sorry to bother you, but there isn't anyone else I can call. We're at Henry Ford Hospital. Zarah lost the baby."

"Say what?" Don sat up and plopped his feet on the floor, sending folders and papers flying.

"She miscarried."

"Joel, man, I'm sorry. I don't know what to say."

"I just wanted to call someone who would have a kind word for me. Honestly, I don't know what I need."

"I might not know what to say, but I know what to do." Don prayed aloud for Joel and Zarah.

"That's why I called you. You have a way of helping people put situations into perspective."

Don rubbed his head as humility covered him. "I can't take credit."

"Well, I can honestly say that I felt led to call you. This is a bad situation, but I still believe God is with me."

"And He is." There weren't sufficient hours in a day for Don to share the countless times God had created a positive situation out of what had started as a negative one for him. "God doesn't change just because we don't get the outcome we want. You know that God is God regardless, and that means somehow or someway you and Zarah can get past this and come out stronger. Maybe not right away, but definitely in time."

"I hear you, and in my spirit I know you're right. But I feel badly about what's happened. I married Zarah and got her pregnant, knowing we weren't spiritually yoked. She has her gods, and I have my God."

Don acknowledged silently that it wasn't the best scenario for a successful marriage. But pointing out the obvious wasn't useful for Joel, so Don didn't. The least he could do was offer a listening ear to a man who seemed filled with despair.

"When there's a crisis in our home, we pray to different divine powers. What kind of sense does that make?" Joel remarked.

"That's tough," was all Don said.

"I don't know. Maybe it's best that the baby died, instead of coming here with a job to do. No child should be the glue holding his or her parents together. I've been there, and it's no cakewalk."

Don continued to pray silently as Joel spoke and searched for meaningful encouragement. "I have no idea why your baby died, but God is able to comfort Zarah and to strengthen you. That much I do know."

"Yep, your right. I'm just feeling sorry for myself. Seems like when one thing goes well for me, three things fall apart."

"I'm sure that's not quite true."

"Maybe not, but I sure miss the days of living under God's favor and anointing. The world was a different place for me then. I had the confidence to walk on water. I knew God was with me. It gave me tremendous confidence. When people saw me as arrogant, I saw it as being confident in God's ability to let me do what He created me to do. Nothing bothered me." Joel got quiet.

"Are you there?" Don asked.

"Yes, I am," he said sighing. "I really messed up by leaving the Lord, and now I'm paying the price."

"But God doesn't hold mistakes over your head. You know He's a loving God. I don't have to tell you this stuff. Even when we mess up big-time, He is quick to forgive us once we repent."

"I have repented and asked for forgiveness for everything."

"Then trust God to keep His word. He said that He'd never leave you or forsake you. Trust Him now. Remember when Adam sinned in the garden?"

"Of course. They were kicked out of the garden and couldn't fellowship directly with God anymore."

"Okay, but before they were kicked out of the garden, God clothed them. He made sure their needs were met even when they messed up. He is always a Father, always. That's what you have to cling to now."

Joel took a deep breath as the sound resonated on the phone. "See? That's why I called you. I had a feeling you'd get me on the right track. I've never said this, but I'm honored to be your brother. We've never been close, but one day maybe that can change."

"Maybe," Don responded, feeling hopeful and in-trigued.

"I've been gone long enough. Zarah might be awake, and I need to be with her. Please keep us in your prayers."

"Consider it done. Before you go, has Tamara gotten the news? I know she and Zarah are close," Don said.

"I haven't told her. We're not exactly on speaking terms."

When would it end? Don lamented, thinking about his family's inability to cast petty matters to the side and rally together during times of adversity. How long did they think God was going to keep him in Detroit to maintain the peace?

"Joel, take care and call me if you need anything."

"I will, and thanks."

Don meditated and prayed for a solid thirty minutes after hanging up. He wasn't thrilled about calling Tamara. He believed she'd want to know about her friend, but he was concerned that his sister would run to the hospital and have a confrontation with Joel. She tended to operate on passion instead of logic. Nobody needed the drama, especially Zarah. Don contemplated calling Tamara for quite a while. Finally, he dialed the phone. Tamara was an adult, and he aimed to treat her as such.

"Why are you calling me so late? What's going on?" Tamara grumbled.

"I thought you'd want to know that Zarah had a miscar-riage. She lost the baby."

"Oh, no!" she bellowed. "That's awful! Where is she?"

"At Henry Ford, but you might want to consider hold-ing off on a visit. This is a tough time for Joel and Zarah. It might be better for you to stay away for a day or two, until they can deal with this on their terms."

"You don't have to sugarcoat it. Joel and I don't get along, and my being there might be a problem."

"Precisely—"

"I get it," she said. "You're probably right. I'm not happy about it, but I understand."

"Good. I'm sure Zarah will be glad to see you in a few days. She'll need a lot of support."

"You know, she was selling me the West Coast division. A few hours ago there wasn't anything more important to me. Now, it seems lame to base my future on a corporate division when the only friend I have is suffering."

Don was pleased to hear Tamara express concern for someone. She had a ways to go before embracing the Mitchell family, but this was a great sign of her potential.

"This changes everything. Honestly, I don't know what to do or where to go from here. I have to regroup and figure this out," she mused.

"Don't make any hasty decisions."

"I won't," she said.

Tamara ended the call. Her decision to leave might be perceived by Don and Madeline as hasty, but in actuality the matter had been marinating for months. Maybe thoughts of leaving had been in the recesses of her mind since the instant she landed in Detroit. What had she done? Why had she come back? This was her birthplace and the town in which her family lived, but it wasn't home for her any longer. Many of her pleasant childhood memories had been drowned by treacherous ones. There was only one entity nudging her to stay here, and that crippling tie to Zarah had to be severed.

Tamara opened the closet doors in her tiny apartment and pulled out a suitcase. She could perform the packing routine in her sleep, having done it ten to fifteen times in fifteen years. Leaving Detroit wasn't difficult. Saying goodbye to Zarah would be, and she was already experiencing the hurt. Tamara didn't fret. Next time she would be more careful and would keep away from relationships that caused her heartache. From the rape and her brother's betrayal, she'd learned not to let people get too close. Tamara had broken her rule with Zarah and had to be reminded of why she couldn't let it happen again. It hurt too much, and Tamara was intent on not hurting.

Chapter 33

Don called Madeline to share the news about Zarah and the baby. He wasn't sure which was worse: Zarah losing the baby or Madeline losing her daughter. He was grateful that the sadness in the Mitchell family didn't have to be ranked. There were generally too many front-runners to prioritize one over the other.

"Mother, I just got off the phone with Joel."

"I know he's upset about my withdrawing the offer of support, but I didn't have a choice. I couldn't let Tamara run away mad. She wouldn't come back next time. I'm sorry he bugged you with this."

"Actually, he called about Zarah. She lost the baby."

"Oh no. That's awful." Madeline exclaimed. "Poor Joel. I think he's really trying to get back on track. Seems like he can't catch a break, but most of this he brought on himself. All that nonsense about expanding into international territory with no regard for the damage he was doing to DMI and the Mitchell name. His junk might finally be catching up to him. Maybe God is punishing him."

"Whoa. Be careful what you say. We have quite a few problems of our own in progress. God must be punishing us too."

"Wait a minute. I'm not trying to get you worked up, preacher man. I'm just saying Joel hasn't done himself any favors by marrying into a different religion and dragging our company with him. I wanted to help him out, but nobody can save Joel if God is dealing with him."

Compassion kicked in. Don wasn't willing to dissect Joel's woes and sit in a position of judgment. Each family member, including his mother, had committed his or her share of mistakes. Joel wasn't alone. His challenges just happened to be more public.

Madeline went on. "You have to wonder if Sherry's family is cursed. She entered into a taboo relationship with Dave and had a miscarriage with her first child. Didn't Joel's wife go and do the exact same thing? What is going on with this family?"

"We're not jinxed or cursed. We can't blame any external sources for our mess. Joel and Sherry, you and Dad, and Tamara and I each had our hand in driving this family straight off a cliff. We've made choices and decisions that have landed us smack-dab in the middle of chaos. You'd think we'd have learned after you and Dad split."

Don had to contain his admonishment so that he didn't sound too confrontational, but it was difficult. He was fed up with the nonsense. "Instead of accepting reality and finding a way to work with Sherry as our stepmother, we treated her and Joel very badly. And after Sam and Andre died, you'd think we'd have figured out as a family how to come together. But no, that wasn't enough of a lesson. We had to stick to our unforgiving, prideful ways and take our fighting to a grander level after Dad passed. When will it end?"

"I didn't mean to get you so worked up. I agree that we've made some mistakes, but it's easy for you to point fingers. There is no way you could have expected me to embrace my husband's mistress after he left me for her."

Don knew more than his mother realized. Madeline had put Dave out after she became aware of his indiscretion. He'd found out last year that his father didn't want a divorce. Apparently, Dave had begged Madeline for forgiveness and for an opportunity to restore their family. Madeline wouldn't hear of it. Her pride kept his father at a distance. When it was clear that Madeline wanted a divorce and a future without him, Dave Mitchell fostered a serious relationship with Sherry a year or two later. His mother had definitely been wronged with his father's act of adultery, but Madeline had also contributed to the final breakup.

"Nobody is exonerated in this family, including you, Mother. I love you, but you're not an innocent victim in the scenarios that have played out over the years."

"Well, easy for you to say, young man. You've never been married, and you don't have to worry about providing for your children and setting an example for them."

"Maybe not, but we all have to get our priorities right."

"Now, I can agree with you there."

"Then you agree that we have to stop fighting over DMI? It's ripping our family apart."

"It's worth fighting for."

"Not to me. Not any longer. I'm done. If you ask me, maybe we should let DMI go bankrupt."

"You're out of your mind," Madeline replied.

"Seriously, if DMI closes, then there's nothing to fight over."

"Well, I can tell you that won't happen as long as I'm breathing. I've worked too hard to build this company. I'm not going to watch it collapse because you're going through a sentimental patch."

"Fine. It's your company to do what you'd like with, only without me. This is it."

"I get that you're ready to go, and we're working on a replacement," she stated.

"Before, I told you I was leaving, but I never gave you a specific timeframe. I've been going back and forth about when to leave. Now I have a plan. I'm resigning in a few weeks, with or without a CEO replacement."

"Calm down. You're not going to walk out and leave us in the lurch."

"Mother, please take me seriously. I mean it. My last day is coming fast. Mark it on your calendar. I have to get out of here. Unless God comes down from heaven and tells me differently, I will soon be out of here. So do whatever you want to confirm my replacement, but be clear. I'm not going to put my future on hold because you want me to follow your plan regardless of what I want. It won't fly this time."

"I'm sad that you and Tamara can abandon me so easily."

Don wasn't falling for her sad story. Madeline was a survivor. She'd shown resiliency through a multitude of disappointments and adversity. He wasn't worried about her or DMI. His plan was set, and he was unwavering. He felt good now that he had abandoned his perpetual limbo status. Feelings for Naledi poked at his heart as he anticipated their upcoming reunion. Joy draped his soul.

"You're my mother, and I love you whether I'm here or in South Africa."

"Yeah, sure. I see where your heart is, and it sure isn't here with me."

"And that's a good thing, since I'm thirty-five. It's time to cut the umbilical cord and let me get on with my life. As far as DMI goes, you can either back Abigail or assume the CEO position yourself."

Don didn't typically speak so firmly to his mother, but his outlook wasn't the same. He had realized that something had to change if they wanted a different outcome. He was ready to change, and he hoped his mother was too.

Chapter 34

Since she'd gotten the news last night, Tamara had debated back and forth about going to see Zarah. She wanted to pack up and get out of town immediately, but she didn't want to leave while Zarah was in the hospital. She fought against the strong urge to bolt and decided to hang around for a few days.

Tossing caution aside, she headed to the hospital. She was on her way up to the maternity ward when it dawned on Tamara that her friend might have been moved to a different ward. Hopefully, the hospital hadn't left Zarah in the maternity ward, where she would be surrounded by a bunch of giggly mothers cooing over their newborns. The image was uncomfortable even for Tamara. It would have to be unbearable for Zarah. So Tamara went to the nearest courtesy desk to find out where Zarah was.

"Can you please give me the room number for Zarah Mitchell?"

The elderly lady at the courtesy desk typed a few letters on the keyboard and then drew closer to the computer screen. She appeared to be struggling to see clearly.

"She might be in the maternity wing," Tamara added in an effort to push the search along.

"Did you say Martin?" the lady asked.

Tamara frowned. "No. Mitchell," Tamara replied and spelled the name.

She was becoming irritated when the elderly lady said, "Oh, I see it. Zebra Mitchell."

Tamara didn't bother correcting the lady. She got the number and saw that the room was located in a private wing of the hospital. Tamara's legs couldn't get her to the room fast enough. She wanted to see Zarah right away and offer some form of comfort. Suffering in silence after a trauma was quite familiar to Tamara. Being raped and miscarrying a baby weren't the same, but despair looked alike. Tamara understood the shame and darkness Zarah might be experiencing. When she reached the private wing, Tamara rushed to Zarah's room and ran into Joel, who was standing outside the room. She tensed.

"Oh, I didn't know you'd be here," she told him.

"Where else would I be?"

Tamara wasn't up for fighting. Her goal was to see her friend and offer support. "I'm not here to cause trouble."

"Good, because I'm not going to let you," Joel said, staring at her. "Zarah couldn't handle that. Me either."

Tamara remained true to her word by not countering. "How is she doing?"

"As best as can be expected, I guess." He hesitated. "You know she lost the baby?"

"Yes, and I'm sorry."

"Thanks," Joel said in a more cordial than usual tone. "She'll be glad to see you. Just don't bring up business."

"Give me some credit," Tamara replied.

She entered the room quietly. The shades were drawn, and it felt morbid. She began opening the shades, and Zarah blurted out, "No, please, no light."

"Are you sure?"

"Yes, please. No light. I don't want to see the day."

Zarah's grief was thick, and it was almost more than Tamara could handle without slipping into her own despair. She fought against the dark and all it represented, determined to be there for Zarah. It was difficult, and every second was grueling, but she was determined to remain strong. Putting someone else's needs above hers was new, and oddly, it gave her a sense of vitality. She mattered in someone else's life, and it was gratifying. It was rough being in that room, but Tamara felt good. She eased into the darkness and met Zarah in the depths of her despair, feeling connected. Tamara hadn't lost a child, but cruelty had stolen her innocence. She sat next to the bed and held Zarah's hand, knowing how it felt to hurt deeply.

"I lost our baby."

"Shh. We don't have to talk if you don't want to."

Tamara could hear Zarah whimpering, which prompted her own tears to flow too. She wasn't sure if she was crying for Zarah or over her own deep-rooted wounds. Either way, this emotional cleansing was necessary. Tamara had been carrying a heavy load lately and needed to put it down. She quietly laid her head on the edge of Zarah's bed and let their genuine friendship massage her soul. A dab of relief resulted.

Several hours passed before Tamara left. When she did, Zarah was left alone with Joel and her troubled thoughts. Losing the baby was unimaginable, and she was in agony. The threat of her marriage failing was equally as painful. She ached in her heart believing that Joel wasn't going to stay without a baby to bond them together. She had nothing more to offer him. She wanted to cry but refused to fall apart in Joel's presence. She took Tamara's advice from last month to heart: Joel was attracted to a strong, independent woman and not to a weak, crying girl. Her mind wandered until Joel asked her a question.

"Can I get you anything?"

"Yes. Another baby," was what she wanted to tell him. She resisted and instead decided to speak boldly. She shoved her emotions deep inside and said, "We have no baby."

"I know," he immediately answered and stroked her hand.

She withdrew her hand, not wanting to be coddled. She stood on her courage and took control of the conversation. Zarah had to get her concerns out in the open, because she might weaken later. "What will happen with our marriage? I didn't give you a child."

Joel winced. "We don't have to deal with this. You need to rest. It's been a rough day for you."

She wouldn't be discounted. Zarah felt that she deserved an answer and didn't retreat from their awkward discussion. She'd rather get all her unpleasant news in the same day, instead of being bombarded day after day. She swallowed her pride and pressed for answers.

"I want to know if you will stay in the marriage without a baby."

"I told you we don't have to talk about this."

"But we must," she said, raising her voice, causing Joel to sit up in his seat. "I must know if I am to be your wife."

"What's the hurry? Why are you so determined to discuss this right now, when you clearly have not fully recovered from the miscarriage."

"Because it is too much worry for me not to know."

She felt there was no cause for Joel to stay in the marriage. He wasn't happy with her, but given time and a family, Zarah believed Joel would have found contentment. She wrenched her hands and looked away from Joel. Her emotions were kicking and shoving their way to the surface. Loneliness crept in. There were no parents sitting by her side, no siblings, no baby, and no husband. The sheer burden of living alone was crippling. She wanted to die and would have prayed to the gods for a gentle passing, but Zarah didn't want to dishonor her father's name with such a selfish act. She'd hold on a while longer.

Joel patted her hand, and her gaze slowly returned to meet his. "Don't you worry about anything, just rest."

Just then Sherry walked into the room. She had been to the hospital earlier and had gone home for a short period. "I'm back," Sherry said, approaching the bed and Zarah. "How's our patient doing?" she said in such a pleasant voice that Zarah began to relax.

They spoke for a few minutes, and then the room quieted and the shades were drawn. Zarah slipped into a slumber.

"She's finally resting," Sherry whispered to Joel after they moved away from the bed. "That's good. That's what she needs most, rest for her body."

Joel beckoned for his mother to follow him into the hallway, and she did. "What about her feelings for the baby?" he asked.

"That will come later," Sherry said. "Trust me when I tell you that it will take time for her to recover. Really, you never recover, but she can learn to live with it, especially if the two of you work on getting pregnant again right away."

Joel stared at his mother. They hadn't gotten over this child. Who was talking about another one so soon? "I don't think you can replace one baby with another."

"No, you're right. You can't. But her pain can be lessened if she's supported by a husband who loves her and wants to build a family with her."

Joel couldn't tell if his mother was fishing for an answer. If she was, he couldn't give her one. Twenty-four hours ago he had been in line for the CEO position at DMI and had been committed to the loving husband and father role. Things had changed dramatically. He didn't have a job prospect or a child on the way, factors that previously gave him a reason for staying in Detroit and in his awkward marriage. He was gravely disappointed about both unfortunate situations and wondered if this was a sign for him to return to Chicago and start over.

Joel leaned his head back against the wall and bent his leg backward, his foot pressing lightly against the wall. He wrestled with his marital situation. "Can you stay with Zarah? I want to go home and get cleaned up. I've been here all day."

"Of course. Go. I'll be here until you get back."

"I'll take only a few hours." He hoped that was the case. There was no guarantee how long it would take for him to gain peace of mind amid his rapidly fluctuating set of circumstances.

"No rush. Take as long as you need. I'll be here. We'll be fine."

Joel believed that his mother and Zarah would be fine. Would he be fine? That was the question.

Chapter 35

When the sunlight burst into his room, Joel was sprawled out on top of the bedcovers and fully dressed. He woke slowly and got up fifteen minutes later. Unfortunately, a night's rest hadn't brought him any clarity about his marriage. He wanted to erase yesterday and start over, since much of it was a blur. When he'd returned to the hospital last night to relieve his mother, Joel had stayed until Zarah was sound asleep around ten thirty. Afterwards he'd gone straight home and collapsed on the bed. He'd intended on getting to the hospital early this morning but the energy wasn't there.

Joel tried to force himself to stand, without success. He wasn't in the right mindset to sit in that hospital room with Zarah. She was bound to ask questions he couldn't answer. Joel mulled over his predicament and came up with no answers. He sat on the edge of the bed and slumped over. He yearned for some good news and a break.

After several minutes, Joel glanced at his watch and jumped up. He darted into the bathroom and turned on the shower. He had fifty minutes to get dressed and drive to Greater Faith Chapel if he wanted to make the 11:00 a.m. service. Joel hurried, exhibiting more vigor for attending a church service than he could recall having in years. There was something drawing him to Greater Faith. He had prayed but hadn't heard from God. He'd go the extra step and meet the Lord in His house. Confusion was debilitating, and he'd had enough. It was time to get clarity.

Fifteen minutes later Joel was straightening his tie as he fired up his Range Rover. He cruised to church, anxious to receive whatever God had for him. Joel was like a kid waking up to an array of gifts on Christmas morning. He could hardly wait to park and get inside the building. He had serious business to handle, and peace was calling his name. Joel wasn't leaving Greater Faith until he got a breakthrough.

"Good morning," a greeter said as Joel entered the vestibule. Joel had been to the church on several occasions alone, plus a few times with Abigail. Each visit had netted him valuable advice from a very special person. Mother Emma Walker was a tiny woman who packed a wallop in terms of wisdom and encouragement. She often spoke in rhymes. Joel didn't always understand her right away, but when he reflected on her message later, it made sense. Joel wasn't ashamed to admit he was desperate for a word. He lingered in the lobby, secretly hoping she was at church and would run into him.

"Excuse me. Is Mother Walker here yet? I'd like to see her," he asked the greeter.

"You mean Big Mama?"

"Right." Joel remembered the name that most people affectionately called Mother Walker, but he felt awkward addressing her by a nickname when she was so much older.

"She's around here somewhere. Service is starting in five minutes. If you'd like to go in, I'll be sure to let Big Mama know you asked to see her."

Joel had come to church with the intent of meeting the Lord and getting a revelation before the service ended. But Mother Walker was a strong backup, as Joel was convinced that the church mother had a direct line to

God. Waiting to see her after church meant fidgeting through a two-hour service. He needed only ten minutes with her. Somebody had to find her.

"I'd prefer to see her now, if possible, unless she's already gone inside."

The greeter peered around the lobby. "Have you seen Big Mama?" he asked a fellow wearing a name badge.

"We just finished praying with the pastor in his office. She's on her way out."

Joel's face lit up. He struggled to contain his excitement. In the blink of a moment, there she was, in the flesh. He froze, much like a groupie at a concert, until Mother Walker approached him.

"My, my, my," she chanted. "Look what's done blown our way." She stretched her torso upward, and he got the hint and bent down and gave the church mother a hug. "It sho' is good seeing you in church. Praise the Lord. He is worthy."

"Can I talk to you for a minute?" he asked.

"Sure you can. What's on your mind?"

Joel took the mother's hand and led her off to the side. The greeters cleared the lobby, as service was beginning.

"I'm sorry to make you late, but I really need your advice."

"Don't you worry about me. Missing a few minutes of the Sunday service ain't going to put my relationship with God at risk. Me and Him on real good terms," she said, laughing and crossing her fingers on both hands.

He longed to have an ounce of her faith, the kind that didn't waver. He longed to be able to trust God in both the good and the bad times. Joel couldn't help but to think about how solid his relationship with God had been. In those days Joel hadn't worried about tomorrow, because he'd relied on God to direct him when he was making big and little decisions. Once he began relying less on the

Lord and more on his own abilities, Joel's world slowly fell apart. His shook off despair. The past was at rest. This was a new day. Change was in the air.

He realized it wasn't necessary to drag out the conversation. He boldly explained his situation, eager to get help. "My wife had a miscarriage on Friday."

"Oh my. Did you come for me to pray with you?"

"Not exactly. I came for direction."

"Well, you know I'm not a judge or a counselor. Like I've told you many times before, my leading comes from the Lord. I can give you only what He gives me—when He gives it."

Joel had heard her say that before, but if there was only a slight possibility of a word coming through with his name on it, he would be grateful. He didn't care if her message was labeled a *word, advice, insight, inspiration,* or whatever.

"I've been praying, but God hasn't answered me. You know my wife is foreign," he explained.

Mother Walker nodded.

"And she is not a Christian."

She nodded again.

"We were going to divorce a few months ago, until we found out she was pregnant. I decided to stay and raise the baby with her, even though we couldn't agree on whether the child was going to be baptized in my faith or presented in the temple to her gods." Joel spoke quickly to avoid losing the church mother's attention. When Joel realized she was captivated, he maximized their time together. He kept talking. "I'm in a mess and don't know how to get out of it. I want to honor my vows, because marriage is sacred. I get it." Mother Walker didn't interrupt. He continued. "But how can I stay with her and be right before God?"

Joel believed his shot at the CEO post was in jeopardy and outside of God's will until he cleaned up his act. *Nah, this has to end,* he thought. He went on. "I feel badly about divorcing Zarah now that she's lost the baby, but how can we stay together, with our beliefs being so dramatically different? I have to get myself right before God, and staying with my wife isn't going to get me there." His gaze dipped momentarily. "I hate to say this. Maybe the miscarriage was a blessing. No baby, no marriage. What do you think?"

"About what?"

Hadn't she heard him pour out the details of his predicament? Hadn't she been listening? Didn't she understand how dire this situation was?

"What do you think God wants me to do about my awkward marriage?" he asked.

"Why are you asking God what to do? Did He marry you?"

"What do you mean?"

"When you got married, was the marriage blessed by her gods or your God?"

Good question. "I don't know. I guess I never thought about it. We got married in her tradition."

"Did you pray and ask the Lord to cover your marriage?"

"No, we didn't."

"Then, I ask you again, why are you asking God about a marriage that He wasn't included in?"

She definitely had Joel thinking. "But even if I didn't pray for Him to bless my marriage, I have to treat it like any other marriage before God, right?"

"There are all kinds of marriages and unions around the world. Do you think God approves of them all? Just 'cause you got married doesn't mean you were married before your God. The papers say you're legally married, but what about spiritually? That piece counts in the church."

Joel was perplexed. "Are you saying that my marriage isn't a legitimate Christian marriage because we exchanged vows before her gods in a temple?"

"God has a mate for us. If we choose to marry somebody else, then God can bless it because of His faithfulness. Now I can tell you, even when you're with the person God intended, times can get hard," she said, shaking her index finger at him. "You got to expect to have a tougher row to hoe when you pick somebody outside God's anointing."

Joel didn't understand everything she was saying. If history was any indication, Mother Walker's words would make sense in a few days. "I still don't know what to do. Does God expect me to honor the marriage regardless, or am I to make a clean slate and let her go?"

"Are you equally yoked, serving the same God and hearing the same voice?"

Joel shook his head no.

"A wagon can't have two drivers. One wants to steer the mule this way with his faith, and the other another way. Down the road that wagon gone crash or rip clean in two."

"So, just make it plain for me to understand. What should I do about the marriage?" With every passing minute Joel's anxiety level rose, because he knew Mother Walker would be going inside the sanctuary at any moment and might not be able to finish his counseling session.

"Young man, if you want God in the marriage, you have to invite Him. He has to be the only God in your house."

Joel winced.

"But don't you worry none. Know that He is merciful. No matter how you done got yourself into a situation and found yourself drowning, our God is able to get you to dry land. He can cover your household, but you got to put Him in charge. He's not sharing the throne with no other gods. You gone have to decide who the spiritual head of your house is. Do you hear me?"

"Yes."

Joel's mind was buzzing, but she made sense, more than he'd heard anyone make in a very long time. The two chatted a bit longer before entering the sanctuary. Joel was finally getting the answers he wanted. More importantly, he was keen on spending meaningful time with God. Relying on his own limited wisdom had clearly caused him to fall short many times, and he'd learned that wasn't the way to go. Joel felt good getting back to his roots and being able to rely on a source that was greater, wiser, and more powerful than his limited strength.

Chapter 36

Tamara had no place to go on a Sunday morning. Church definitely wasn't for her. God had permeated their household through her father when she was growing up. When he left and married Sherry, God went too. Madeline hadn't pressured her kids to seek religion. As a matter of fact, Madeline had seemed to loathe the concept of relying on an invisible being for guidance and assistance. It was the one area in which Tamara and her mother agreed. If God existed, He obviously didn't have her on His "like" list.

During her late teens, she had dwelled on the distress resulting from her parents constantly arguing and then divorcing, followed by getting raped, and finally her older brother's suicide. She'd felt forced to flee Detroit for her sanity. A pile of bad luck was what she saw when she gazed over her life. After she had suffered more than her share, now, fifteen years later, her mother and brother were kicking her aside to let Joel have what rightfully belonged to her. Somewhere along the way, a God that cared about her would have stepped in to save her from at least one of her devastating tragedies. He hadn't, which was why she wasn't stuck on praying to something or someone who didn't care about what happened to her.

Morning slipped away, and the afternoon rolled in. Tamara wanted to see Zarah. But the thought of running into Joel again at the hospital kept her away. She might have to wait until Zarah went home. Then Tamara could sneak in for a visit when Joel left the house for a few hours. The walls of her studio apartment were closing in. Normally, the small space gave her solace. She could see every inch of the room in one swoop, which allowed her to sleep soundly. On this rare occasion, the limited space was depressing. Tamara was reminded of how alone she was in the world and gloom overtook her. She grabbed her tiny purse and scurried from the apartment. She'd go for a walk and probably end up taking a bus ride to her favorite coffee shop downtown.

When Tamara emerged from the building, the filtered sunlight warmed her face, and she felt better. Her phone rang, and she quickly plucked it from her pocket. She didn't recognize the number but figured it was Zarah calling from the hospital. She was excited to answer.

"Zarah . . ."

Nobody responded.

"Zarah, is this you?"

"It's me, darling. Remo."

Tamara halted when she heard the Italian accent. She felt a burst of adrenaline, and her heart raced so fast. It felt like her chest was going to explode. "How did you get this number?" She wobbled on her feet and found the nearest bus bench to gather herself.

"I told you that you will never be far from me. We belong together. You are my love," he said rattling off the Italian translation. "Ti amo."

Tamara couldn't figure out what to do. Remo had chased her from a remote town in England earlier in the year. Madeline had stepped in and gotten Uncle Frank to handle the problem. Her uncle hadn't provided any guarantees, but Tamara had hoped their solution was extreme and permanent. Given Uncle Frank's track record of pushing the legal limits when it came to handling a problem, she had good reason to feel pretty safe.

Apparently her assumption was wrong as the sound of Remo's voice rang in her ears.

The grip of fear was so tight that she couldn't think properly.

"Where are you?"

"I'm very close to you, darling."

It was hard for her to believe that this was a man who had once held her heart so delicately that she'd found happiness. His melodious voice used to usher her into a tranquil place filled with love and safety. After his doting attention transformed into malicious control, she had run from Italy to Scotland, to Spain, to the South of France, and to England. She had also spent a few months in Dublin but couldn't remember where it fit on her list of moves. After Remo found her in England, she'd fled to Detroit because it was the last city he'd expect her to be, given her family history.

She tensed, terrified that he was within arm's reach. Tamara had to find out how much time she had. "When can I see you?" she asked.

"Tomorrow I shall be with you."

There was a slim possibility he was being honest. Remo might be even closer than he was admitting. She couldn't take a chance. Recalling her routine in the past, Tamara realized she had to take action. Running was no longer a choice; it was a requirement if she wanted to stay alive. She ran to her apartment building and climbed the stairs two at a time. She snatched the key from her purse and fumbled to get the door open. She didn't have a second to waste. She grabbed several items of clothing.

Tamara was angry for letting her guard down. For years she'd run from Madeline and her mother's band of private detectives. Generally, she'd been able to outrun them and Remo too. During her time in Detroit, she had relaxed and had settled into a fictitious life of comfort and safety. But because of her lapse in judgment, she was now in extreme danger and couldn't abandon her apartment quickly enough. She was frazzled as she searched intensely for her passport and other important papers.

Terror began to get the best of Tamara, and she forced her legs to move, instead of standing there, paralyzed. Every sound in the apartment was magnified. She was tired of running, but nothing else had worked. Tamara was tempted to call Madeline but decided there wasn't time. She was getting out of there and getting back to the world of obscurity and being alone. It was the world she knew and belonged in.

Chapter 37

Joel had gotten exactly what he'd sought—wisdom. Big Mama hadn't laid his steps out as clearly as one, two, three, but she'd given him sufficient advice to get him inspired and moving in the right direction. He understood that she wasn't God. However, her lines of communication with Him were intact, while Joel's were undergoing repairs. He rested in the belief that there was a reason that God had placed Mother Walker in his life several years ago. God knew Joel would need someone to lead him back to the Lord after he strayed away from his faith. His spirit leapt for joy as he drove out of the church's parking lot. What had seemed dire two and a half hours ago was now manageable. He felt lighter than ever.

Joel cruised along I-75 and merged onto the Jeffries Freeway. The hospital was calling him, and he responded. When he got there, instead of parking in the garage, Joel maneuvered his vehicle to the valet in front of the hospital. When he was at home, typically, he'd sit in his car for ten to fifteen minutes before going inside. He used the solitude to ponder and prepare for his duty as a supportive husband. Some occasions were easier than others in terms of honoring his role. Not today. He hopped from the Range Rover, drenched in vitality.

Not all his questions had been answered, but he had clarity. Faith was a belief in the unknown. He didn't know how God would work out his relationship with Zarah, but

Joel was confident that the Lord was able. Joel just had to figure out what he wanted first. He acknowledged that his indecisiveness wasn't helping. He had to make a decision about going or staying, but knowing he wasn't alone in this mess worked for him. Joel entered the lobby and didn't stop until he was standing in front of his wife. She was alone and was staring out the window from her bed across the room.

"Good. You're awake," he said, going to her side and pulling up a chair. He couldn't contain his desire to grin. "How are you feeling?"

"Not very well."

"Why not? Are you in pain?" he asked, drawing closer to the bed and taking her hand. She turned her head to the side, away from him. He reached for her chin and gently turned it in his direction. He wasn't letting her retreat before they dealt with the issue at hand. "Are you hurting?"

"Not in my body. Only in my heart," she said, choked up.

Joel didn't rush her. He was willing to let Zarah sort through her feelings and speak when she was ready.

"I am sad that our marriage will soon be over, but I won't return to Jaipur," she mumbled. "I cannot go there without a husband or a child. I will be a mark of great shame to my family." A failed marriage was too much for her to bear. She became increasingly upset as she continued to talk, and Joel tried to calm her with his words and touch.

He let his emotions get the best of him. "Zarah, don't worry about the marriage. I'm not leaving you."

"But the baby is gone. You don't have to stay with me. I don't want to be a burden to you."

"I married you of my own free will. You didn't twist my arm. Your father asked me to marry you, but he didn't twist my arm, either. At the end of the day, it was my choice." Joel placed his hand on his chest.

Admittedly, she wasn't the woman he would have picked on his own. He was drawn to feisty, independent women who had a bold streak in them. That wasn't Zarah, although her grace, devotion, and beauty were undeniable. Surprisingly, though, he'd seen hints of boldness in her when she was planning to take over Harmonious Energy last month. He liked that side of Zarah and had found himself attracted to her on several occasions. In a strange way, he had to credit Tamara for Zarah's temporary transformation. She was the one who'd encouraged Zarah to become more independent. He wasn't happy with Tamara's tactics, but watching Zarah shed her passive disposition was a plus. Kudos to his sister, but he'd never tell her that. Too much Tamara wasn't a good thing.

Joel directed his attention back to Zarah, who was peering at him closely. "I want to do right by you. The fact that we lost the baby doesn't change my commitment. I married you, and I'm honoring my vows."

Zarah was stunned and didn't know what to say.

"But our marriage has to be set in order for me to stay," Joel told her.

"I don't understand."

"I realize that your religion is important to you, but we can't have a house divided."

She still wasn't understanding but didn't interrupt. She hoped his words would get clearer the more he spoke. She listened intently, as her future hung on his every word.

"I will support your career aspirations and will actually help you do whatever it is you want to do professionally," he said.

That she understood, and she was pleased.

He continued. "I think we can make a dynamic team in the corporate arena. Maybe we could even start a company together."

Zarah was overwhelmed. Joel had never shown this much passion and interest in her. She lapped up his kindness like a thirsty pup, craving more and more, unable to quench her thirst.

"However, in order for our marriage to work, we have to be on one accord."

"What do you mean?"

"We have to serve the same God, sell Harmonious Energy, and get married in the church with the blessings of my God, the one of Abraham, Isaac, and Jacob."

Zarah wasn't prepared to respond. Her heart and body wanted Joel. Yet her spirit belonged to the gods. In a dead heat, her soul, the essence of who she was as a person, would have to be the tiebreaker.

"Zarah, I realize that what I'm asking is huge. It's a life-changing request."

"Yes, it most certainly is."

"And I get it if you say no. I get it." He squeezed her hand, and she felt a form of love. "I'm hoping you say yes, but I'll understand either way."

Zarah was most pleased. With her baby dying, she didn't believe there was to be a future for her as Mrs. Mitchell. To have her husband speak to her with adoration was more than she had dreamed. She couldn't pass this opportunity to have a family in the States with her husband. She clung to him as affection and gratitude consumed her.

"My faith and my family's honor have always been the most important elements in my life, until I met you. You are my love. My future is with you, and so I shall honor your requests."

Joel hadn't expected her to agree so easily. Actually, the quick respond made him doubtful that she was fully aware of what was being proposed. He couldn't help but to think that she would agree to just about any terms that kept them together even if it wasn't sustainable. Did she get that her gods would have to be abandoned in order for her to follow his God? He wanted her to know for sure what was being asked of her, because the marriage depended on both of them entering into the union for a second time with full knowledge and a desire to be together. He wasn't convinced that she understood.

"Do you understand that you can't make this life-changing decision for me? Accepting Christ is a forever decision."

"I do understand, and I'm willing to learn about your God."

"Are you sure?" he asked, still not confident.

"Yes, with all my heart. If you follow Him, I shall follow Him."

"It might not be that simple, with you coming from a culture that believes in something else."

"I believe in you and this marriage. As a wife, I must follow my husband. My parents are gone, and they cannot help me now. They lived with their gods. My journey has taken me on a different path and I am me here, with you. This is where I want to be. This is where I must be." She squeezed his hand this time. "I want to live with you in a true marriage, and I willingly accept your God."

"Okay," he uttered. "But God has to come first in your heart, and not me, because honestly, I might fail you again and again. Not intentionally, but I'm not perfect. I will try my best to work at the marriage, but your trust must be in God and not in me. He is our only hope."

Zarah assured Joel that she wanted to know his God.

He wasn't sure how realistic their plan was, but Joel was willing to go forward by faith. He'd have to trust that she was committed to the religious change, and that six months or a year down the road he wouldn't find candles or figurines of gods or shrines hidden around the house. She seemed sincere, and so was he. Therefore, Joel let his doubt subside. He'd give the marriage a real shot. Exactly what that meant was to be determined, but he was thinking along the lines of dating and ultimately renewing their vows in a few months if everything worked out. He was cautious but open.

They embraced, and Zarah was filled with hope.

Chapter 38

Tamara burst into the hospital room, carrying a duffel bag. She entered so abruptly that Joel didn't have a chance to become defensive. Tamara darted to Zarah's bedside and hugged her.

"I came to say goodbye," she said, juggling the duffel bag, which was partially hanging off her shoulder. "Take care of yourself and don't worry. I'm sure you'll have many babies someday."

To Joel, it seemed that she was talking fast and acting very odd, much more than usual.

"I'll see you later," Tamara said and gave Zarah another hug. She turned to leave.

"Where are you going in such a rush?" Zarah asked.

"I'm going to the airport." Tamara cleared her throat and let her gaze drop.

"I didn't know you were traveling?"

"I—I have s-somewhere to be," she told Zarah, stumbling over her words and her feet.

She was frantic, and Joel was curious. "What's up with you? You seem hyped up today," he said.

"I don't know what you're talking about. I have to catch my flight. I'm out of here," Tamara responded, like a person in major distress. Her eyes blinked repeatedly, and she jumped every time somebody walked past the door.

Since Joel didn't believe she was involved with drugs, his curiosity was piqued, which made him very inquisitive. What if she was suicidal? It might be a stretch for some, but tragedy lived in his family. Although he hoped he was wrong, the real possibility that this was the case forced him to take action. He asked again, "What's up with you?"

"Nothing. I'm out of here. I have to go," Tamara shouted, and this seemed to startle Zarah.

"You are too upset to go. Stay with us until you are better," Zarah said.

Tamara seemed to calm down slightly when speaking to her friend. "I'm sorry, but I have to go. There's someone coming to see me that I don't want to see. So, I have to get out of here." She bolted toward the door with her duffel bag in tow.

Without considering the ramifications, Joel grabbed her arm as she tried to get past him.

She stopped. "Let me go."

"Who's coming to see you?" he asked.

"Nobody. Forget I said that. Something has come up, and I have to get away."

Joel wasn't convinced. "Here." He nodded in the direction of the door. "Can you step into the hallway for a minute?" he asked, maintaining a gentle grip on her arm.

"I—I have to go right now. Seriously," she said as they stepped into the hallway. Joel felt the tremor in her body, which gave him even more incentive to figure out who had her acting so frightened.

"I know. I get that you have to go, but just give me a minute. I need to ask you something."

"No, I have to go," she insisted, wiggling from his grip.

He didn't know what her problem was, but it was serious and he was concerned. Regardless of their strained relationship, he could tell she was troubled, and Joel wanted to help if he could. He had to act quickly.

"Fine. But can I get your help? I need to take care of something. Can you stay with Zarah for a few minutes? I'll be quick."

Tamara appeared uncertain. Joel had to keep her in sight. He had to take a delicate approach and capitalize on Tamara's affection for Zarah. It was the last resort. He poked his head into the room and called out to Zarah, "Wouldn't you feel better if Tamara stayed a bit longer?"

"Oh, yes. I would," Zarah agreed.

Joel could tell Tamara was caving. "Hurry up, because I can't stay long. I mean it," she said and reentered the room.

"Thanks," Joel said and bolted down the hallway. There wasn't much time. He went five doors down the hallway, which allowed him to see the entrance to Zarah's room clearly. He dialed Don's phone. It rang and rang before the call bounced to his voice mail. He didn't waste a second dialing Madeline. He should have called her first. The phone rang as his anxiety escalated. A few rings and Madeline was on the line.

"Thank goodness you answered. It's Joel."

"Yep, I caught your voice. What can I do for you?"

"Thought you might want to know that Tamara is here at the hospital and is acting strange."

"What do you mean?"

"She said that someone is coming to see her, and whoever it is has her scared and in a huge hurry to get out of town."

"Oh my goodness! It can't be!"

"What?"

"Earlier this year her crazy boyfriend chased her from Europe to Detroit. He had her worked up in a similar way. I paid Frank to take care of him, and I assumed he was gone for good."

"You think this is about him?"

"I don't know, but I pray it's not."

"Let me go back to the room and talk to her. I'll see if I can get anything out of her. I better go. She is very antsy and isn't going to hang around for long."

"Where are you?"

"We're at Henry Ford Hospital, the main one on West Grand Boulevard."

"I'm on my way. I'll call Don too since he's closer to the hospital than I am. Joel, please don't let her out of your sight."

Joel hustled back to the room. Tamara was there but was ready to bolt. "Can I talk to you outside?" he asked.

She followed him as he gently pulled her arm toward the door and then stepped into the hallway. Her shaking continued to unnerve him. Tamara had never shown signs of weakness or fear. Seeing her so vulnerable drew out his protective nature. First, he had to get her to talk.

"What's going on? And don't tell me, 'Nothing.' I know you well enough to see you're scared to death. As tough as you are with me every single day, I know this isn't you. What's going on? Let me help you."

"You can't help me. It's best for me to get out of town and go back to the life I had before moving to Detroit."

"You don't mean that."

"How can you tell me that? I need to go. I'm not safe here."

"Oh, yes you are. You're here with me. I'm not going to let anything happen to you."

"Yeah, right. Like you care about me."

"Believe it or not, I do. I haven't always shown you the best of me, but then, you never gave me the chance."

She looked away but didn't interrupt.

"Let's face it. We're family. That's not going to change. Plus, we share a common interest, and that's Zarah. She wants both of us in her life. So, we might as well figure out how to respect one another. Who knows? Maybe one day we'll grow to like each other," he said and laughed. "Seriously, what's going on? Does this have anything to do with that Remo guy?"

She jerked her arm from his grip. "How do you know his name?"

"Madeline told me."

Tamara looked confused.

"I called and told her you were leaving town."

"Why did you do that? Now she's going to be rushing over here and try to save the day. I don't need all this drama. I have to go." She turned to leave.

He reached for her arm again, but she pulled away. "Tamara, wait."

"I can't." And with that she took off down the hallway.

Joel opened the door and yelled into Zarah's room, "I'll be right back." Then he chased Tamara down the hallway, down the stairs, and into the lobby. Out of nowhere, Joel saw a guy approach Tamara. He was about five-ten with olive-colored skin and long black hair. The guy grabbed her arm. Joel ran up to them.

Joel couldn't understand everything the guy was saying to Tamara. His accent was quite heavy, and Joel couldn't tell if it was French or Italian. "Are you Remo?"

"Yes!" Tamara screamed before the guy could respond.

Joel didn't wait for any more questions and answers. He caught the eye of a guard standing nearby. "Call the police! This guy is assaulting my sister. Hurry!" he yelled to the guard and then pushed Tamara away. Joel wrestled with Remo, who had initially attempted to flee, but he wasn't getting away without a fight. After a brief tussle, Joel and the guard successfully subdued Remo, and the guard held him until the police arrived.

Joel was wired. His adrenaline was pumping fast. Tamara leapt at Joel and cried without speaking. Ten minutes or so passed before the police arrived. Joel did most of the talking, as Tamara was very withdrawn.

Don ran into the hospital's lobby ten minutes after the police arrived, which wasn't surprising, since he lived downtown. "Tamara, are you okay?"

She shook her head no.

Don went to speak with the police officers, who had placed handcuffs on Remo. Another twenty minutes later, as the police were taking Remo away, Madeline ran into the lobby. She rushed toward Tamara and pulled her from Joel and Don's circle of protection. "Are you all right?"

Tamara nodded. "I'm okay."

"What happened?"

"I don't want to talk about this," she said, pulling away from Madeline's embrace. "I have a flight to catch."

"No, you don't. You don't have to run away. That nutcase will be locked up," Madeline told her daughter.

"For how long?"

"Don't you worry. I'll take care of it," Madeline stated.

"No, Mother, you won't. You can't. You tried to take care of him before, and it didn't work. Don't you see? You can't fix our lives or our problems. As much as you want, you just can't."

Madeline was silent. Tamara was right. Her daughter's words were hurtful, but she got it. "Okay. Then, what can I do? How can I help you? How can any of us help you?"

"By giving me some space to figure this out myself."

"Fine, but can you at least wait forty-eight hours before flying off. We'll all feel safer if you're here with us."

"All right. I'll stay a few days, but if Remo gets out before then, I'm gone, without a word to anyone."

"Agreed," Madeline said.

"You can stay with me," Don offered.

Tamara reluctantly accepted.

"Do you want me to take you by your apartment to pick up a few things?" Don asked.

"No need. I already have everything that I want," she said, patting her duffel bag.

"Get her out of here and take her to your place," Madeline said. "Hire a legion of off-duty police officers with guns to guard your condo if you need to. I'll cover the cost."

"Mother, I just told you to let me figure this out. Don't crowd me with cops or guards or your rules. I won't take it," Tamara stated.

"I got it," Madeline said, throwing up her hands. "I'm zipping my lips."

"Let me know if there's anything I can do for you," Joel told Tamara.

Tamara reached for his hand and squeezed it. "Thank you."

Don and Tamara left without further incident.

Chapter 39

The activity in the hospital lobby returned to normal. Madeline and Joel chatted for a bit after finding a quiet corner.

"What a mess, huh?" she said with her arms folded.

"I'm just glad this turned out the way it did," Joel replied.

"Thanks to you. I don't know what would have happened if he'd caught her at the airport, alone."

"Well, we don't have to worry about that."

"Seriously, thank you," she said, extending her hand to him. Instead of taking it, he wrapped his arms around her shoulders and held her tightly. Madeline didn't resist. The hug wasn't so bad, after all. "All right. Don't get too mushy on me. We need a strong CEO."

"What do you mean?" Joel asked, giving her a little space.

"With Tamara all messed up from this Remo thing, I can't in good conscience remotely consider putting her in the top spot. I wasn't comfortable from the beginning." She gasped. "I'll admit that I let my emotions cloud my judgment. One day, when you become a parent, you'll understand." Immediately after the words left her lips, Madeline was mortified. "I'm sorry. That was an insensitive comment, given what you and your wife have just experienced. Forgive me."

Joel shook his head. "Don't worry about it."

Madeline wasn't accustomed to apologizing. And the phrase "Forgive me" was especially foreign to her. Good or bad, she had always been willing to live with her successes and mistakes. To a fault, she held others to the same high standard. According to her, there wasn't a reason to apologize and seek forgiveness if everyone owned up to their decisions and choices. When she was younger and the world seemed manageable, Madeline had routinely clung to that view of the world. Somehow it was changing. She reflected on the tragedy her daughter could have suffered at the hands of Remo. Regrettably, she had to face her limitations. She couldn't stop bad things from happening to any of them, not really. Invincibility was not possible. Madeline felt small in a big world that she didn't have the ability to control.

It dawned on her that changes were required at the top of DMI, and in the Mitchell family, if there was to be a legacy worth protecting. Madeline courageously set her pride aside and opted to assess situations from that point on through the lens of an accomplished businesswoman instead of a wounded mother bent on protecting her children.

"I have my head on straight now. You're our best option for CEO." Madeline peered directly into Joel's eyes, refusing to let him look away. "Please say yes. I'll even throw in another hug."

"Nah, the CEO position isn't for me, Madeline, but thanks for the offer. I've done some soul-searching of my own, and it's time for me to settle down and do as you've done, get my head on straight. I've played this back-and-forth game far too long."

"So that's it? You're out of the corporate scene?"

"Yep. I want to start fresh with Zarah—everything new and build from scratch."

"That's a shock. I figured with the baby dying, your marriage was over. It's an easy out. There's nothing tying you to the arranged marriage now."

"Only her love for me and my commitment to her."

"Didn't you hear that love is overrated?" Madeline said.

"Maybe, but she loves me, and I care deeply for her."

"But you don't love her. Why stay in a loveless marriage?"

"Like you said, love is overrated. I'm staying with her out of respect, admiration, and a need to honor my commitment to her father." Joel wasn't going to tell Madeline about his budding physical attraction for Zarah. That would be sharing too much personal information outside the confines of his marriage. To tell the truth, he hadn't made such a declaration to Zarah. He resolved that many things were better left unsaid.

"Doesn't sound good enough for me."

"Once we get God into this marriage, we will be fine. I'm sure of it."

"With divorce rates so high, how can you be so sure? Church folks do get divorced too."

"I can't worry about what-if. As long as I hold on to God's hand and she does too, we'll be okay."

"Excuse me for being so direct, but I recall that Zarah has an entirely different belief system. You're not getting her into a baptismal pool or a Bible study class anytime soon. When people are deeply rooted in a religion, they don't just change overnight. You might be seeing through rose-colored glasses on this one."

"I can't speak for Zarah and how much she'll change." Joel laid his hand across his chest. "I can only speak for myself. I know the life I lived when God was in charge. It's a lot different than the drama I've dealt with when He was out of the picture. I'm like a kid who was told not to touch the hot stove and did it, anyway. Once you get burned, only a fool returns for more, and I'm not a fool."

Talk about changes, Madeline thought. There was a time not very long ago when Joel was deemed the biggest fool she knew. This Joel was much better to be around.

"Sounds well and good, but I don't know. A so-called relationship with God didn't get any stronger than what your dad had, and we ended up divorced."

"That's true, and it happens, particularly if a person is unforgiving."

Madeline was quiet briefly. "Well, I hope it works for you, the marriage and all. But stop messing around and come back to DMI. Don is leaving soon. I need you in the company," she told him, definitively.

"I can't. In order to make the marriage work, I have to step away from DMI, and Zarah has to release her father's company."

"I don't get it. Why so extreme?"

"I can't ask her to do more than I'm willing to do. It's unfair for her to give up Harmonious Energy if I stick with DMI."

Why did Joel have to be selfless and present a rational rebuttal at the very instant when Madeline needed him to be his old self—selfish and reckless? She wasn't giving up. It wasn't her style to quit until the deal was done. He was forcing her to take extraordinary measures. There was one button she hadn't pushed. Backed into a corner, Madeline had to come out swinging, using every trick at her disposal.

"Your father put his heart and soul into building DMI. He felt called by God to build this company in order to help struggling ministers and churches. Your father is gone, but the call is still alive and well. He always said there is much work to do, and that's true. Churches need our help if they are to have leadership and sound financial management skills."

Joel slid his hands into his pockets.

She figured he was processing her appeal. Madeline didn't let up. "You father established the Mitchell and DMI legacy. It's up to his children to carry the legacy forward, to future generations. It is your turn to carry the torch. Don't walk away when the church needs you the most."

"I'll admit, you have me thinking."

"Great. That's all I can ask of you. Tell you what. Take a few days and think it over. Talk to your wife and see what she says. I bet she'll want you to take the job."

"You think so, huh?"

"Absolutely. A good wife supports her husband." The sacrifices Madeline had made while she was married to Dave were enormous. As a wife and a partner, she had made it her goal to hold the family together, while encouraging her husband to be the most that he could be. She suspected Zarah had a similar mentality.

"I'm not changing my mind. However, I will take a few days to consider your proposal."

Madeline had something to say that she'd been holding in. "Joel, I can't change the past. None of us can. Although I don't like many of things you've done, I do admire your passion and gutsiness. Somehow, in a different place and time, the two of us could have been friends."

Joel grinned. "Thanks, Madeline."

"Seriously, I've always respected your business aptitude—except when you were plunging into the deep end with your craziness." She hadn't appreciated his tactics, but he was a formidable opponent, one who had given her exciting challenges over the years.

"Touché." He laughed. "I think that's a compliment."

"Certainly is. You are a strong businessman who hasn't begun to realize his full potential. I'd love to see you resume the top spot and take this company into the stratosphere," she said, flinging one arm high into the air. "You can do it. I know you can."

Joel thanked her again. "The world must be ending if you're giving me two compliments in the same meeting. I don't know what to say."

"Don't say anything. That way, you won't mess this up." She giggled.

"I better get upstairs to Zarah."

"Sure. And give her my regards. I have to go take care of some business, anyway. Your uncle Frank owes me a refund, because he didn't get the Remo job done. You know I'm going to call him on this."

"I have no doubt," he echoed as they parted on a positive note, even though nothing was settled.

Chapter 40

Monday morning was filled with worry for Madeline. The sting from Tamara's encounter yesterday was too fresh. She had agreed to back off, but that promise was proving to be more difficult to keep than she'd imagined. She'd keep trying, without making any more promises to Tamara or herself. As a distraction, she diverted her attention to DMI, her other troubled child who was in dire need of a miracle.

She hadn't expected Joel to turn her offer down. He was too driven to morph into a househusband when there was a corporate carrot the size of the CEO position dangling in front of him. Madeline believed he'd eventually change his mind. Yet there wasn't any guarantee. She was forced to pursue plan B, with Don's departure looming. Appointing a leader was paramount, and none seemed to be falling from the sky.

She emerged from her car with her phone pressed against her ear. "How is Tamara doing?" Madeline asked Don as she spun through the revolving door leading into the DMI building.

"She's in the guest bedroom, resting."

"I'm sure you're taking care of her."

"Don't you worry. She's safe."

"Just don't let her leave. Until this Remo guy is locked up for good or deported, with 'Do not fly' stamped on his passport, I don't want her running around alone."

"You know how Tamara is. When she gets something in her head, it's hard to change her mind. She's a lot like you."

"Humph. Well, lock her inside the guest room if you have to. Do whatever it takes to protect my child." Madeline hit the elevator button. "I'm at the office. I hope you aren't planning on coming in today."

"No. I think it's best to hang around here with her."

"Just what I wanted to hear." Madeline breathed a sigh of relief. "I'm getting into the elevator. Call me if Tamara needs anything. Otherwise, I'll call you later," she said as the elevator doors opened and employees filed into the lobby.

Madeline didn't go to her office. She made a beeline to Abigail. Madeline didn't knock on the door or ask the assistant who was sitting out front for clearance. She burst in, closed the door, and took a seat in front of Abigail's desk. If Don and Tamara and Joel were out, Abigail was the only choice left.

"You know why I'm here. I'm not going to blow smoke up your leg. We need you to take the CEO post."

"Me? What about Joel?"

"He's out due to some personal issues," Madeline said, tugging on the corners of her short jacket and then pretending to knock off a piece of lint. "He's out, and that leaves you. I'm here to ask you personally to take the position. You weren't my first choice, but I will back you one hundred percent."

"First! I wasn't your second or third, either," Abigail said.

Madeline tipped her head. "True, but that's not important at this juncture. You are my best option given a series of factors."

"In other words, I'm your last choice."

"Come on, Abigail. You're a smart woman. CEO positions don't come around very often. You've worked hard from the day Dave recruited you. Don't let this rare opportunity slip through your fingers just because you weren't my first choice. Set your pride aside and be smart about this." What was the corporate world coming to? She had three hotshot executives between Joel, Don, and Abigail, and each one was emphatically walking away from the prize position, a seat at the top of the DMI food chain. She had to believe that such foolishness occurred only in the halls of DMI. Anywhere else, people with far fewer qualifications than her three would kill to get the opportunity.

Abigail tapped her fingers on the top of her laptop before responding. *"Pride!"* She cackled. "Are you kidding me? Staying here and putting up with everybody's garbage confirms that I have no pride." She cackled again and folded her arms. "Seriously, I expect a self-righteous statement like that from Joel, but not from you."

"Hold on, missy. Who are you talking to?"

"I'm sorry, Madeline, but I've already told you and Don that my mind is made up. I'm not getting suckered back into this place. I should have stuck to my guns from the beginning and stayed out of the CEO race, but silly me. I let Don and this place lure me right back into the DMI shark-infested waters. Anyway, I've had enough. I'm done, and it's time to go."

"You're making a mistake," Madeline said, crossing her legs.

"Maybe, but it's my mistake to make. That much I have earned."

"I'm surprised to see you running from a challenge."

"Madeline, I understand the position you're in. I wish you'd extend the same courtesy and appreciate my position. The bottom line is that I'm at peace with my resignation."

"Are you trying to convince me or yourself?" Madeline asked. She'd approached Abigail from various angles without success, but she wasn't close to giving up.

"With all due respect, I don't have to convince you or anyone else. I feel like God has released me. For me to stay where I'm not supposed to be is an automatic recipe for problems. And trust me. We've endured enough problems to last a lifetime. I want something new."

"Here you go with the religious factor. My goodness, maybe you and Don should have gotten together. It seems to be the only argument the two of you have." Madeline twisted in the chair, annoyed. However, she was in begging mode and didn't have the luxury of harping on Abigail. Yet her natural reaction was to be up front, even if it meant that she was jeopardizing her chances of Abigail accepting the CEO position. "Let me give you a piece of advice," Madeline said, pulling closer to the desk. "Be bold enough to say what you want and make no excuses. You don't have to hide behind God or anyone. It makes you look weak."

"Okay. Then my resignation stands. I'm out of here, and nobody is changing my mind. Not even the persuasive Madeline Mitchell is going to win this discussion."

Madeline left the office in a funk. Every option had been a bust today. She fretted for a little while and decided to do the unthinkable. Finally coming to terms with reality, she shuffled to her office and stopped at the desk of her administrative assistant. "Pull up Sherry Mitchell's home phone number." Madeline walked to her office door and stood there. "Let me know when you have her on the line."

As directed, Madeline's assistant made the call. "Mrs. Mitchell, I have Mrs. Sherry Mitchell on the line."

There were numerous occasions when hearing "Mrs. Mitchell" uttered in reference to Sherry sent Madeline into a fit. As far as she was concerned, Dave Mitchell had one legitimate wife and that was her. Sherry was at best a lackluster sideshow. How Madeline felt about Sherry was immaterial at this juncture. Business and legacy had to take precedence in this surreal predicament.

"Good. Forward the call to my phone," Madeline said, then entered her office and closed the door.

Madeline strolled to her chair and exhaled before taking the call. There were a thousand reasons why she didn't want to speak with Sherry. However, one in particular spurred her to pick up the phone. She grabbed the receiver and let her words flow without thinking about the implications. "Sherry, this is Madeline. I need your help."

There was no response.

"Hello? Are you there? Sherry, this is Madeline."

"I heard you. I just wasn't expecting a call from you asking me for help."

Madeline suppressed her dignity and continued. "I'm sure you weren't. To tell the truth, I didn't expect to be calling you, but here I am."

"What do you want, Madeline?" Sherry asked, coming across as defensive.

"It's about your son. I need your help in convincing him that DMI is where he needs to be. I'm not sure if you know that I made him a second offer to take on the CEO role. He's declined for reasons that don't make sense."

"And what makes you think I can change his mind?"

"Because you're his mother and you can appreciate what this means for him." Madeline knew Sherry had lived on the fringes of DMI and the Mitchell family, never having full access to the building or enjoying any other rights and privileges. Madeline had made sure that

Sherry stayed on the outside. Perhaps that would work in her favor now. Maybe Sherry's desire to feel validated by the Mitchell family would compel her to push Joel into the CEO post. Madeline could only hope. "Can I stop by and go over the details of the offer with you?"

"Don't you think you should be talking to Joel, not me?"

"You're exactly the person I need to speak with. Can I stop by?"

Sherry gulped softly. "I guess you can drop by."

"Good. I'll see you within the hour."

Madeline was pleased that she had survived one of the toughest calls she'd ever made. It was humbling to ask her husband's former mistress for help in saving the family business that Madeline had helped build. It was insane. Yet that was what she had to do.

Chapter 41

Madeline cruised down the Chrysler Freeway, headed to the house she'd moved out of after divorcing Dave. She hadn't stepped on the grounds of the Mitchell estate in West Bloomfield since his funeral. Thousands of memories, not all pleasant, rushed in as she drove up the driveway. Madeline smirked, remembering how often she'd dropped in without notice to see Dave during his illness. Sherry had often complained to Dave, but it had been pointless. Madeline had designed every inch of the house on Mayweather Lane, down to the twelve-foot-tall double doors, which she had had shipped in from Spain.

She parked her car and meandered toward the front door. Her purpose for seeing Sherry should have sparked more urgency, but Madeline didn't pick up her speed. She had to accept the gravity of this "full circle" moment. Madeline stopped several feet from the door. Not in a million years could someone have convinced her that this would be her fate. She was coming to her old home, the one she had shared with her ex-husband, to ask his former mistress for help. Technically, Sherry was Dave's widow, but that title would never cross Madeline's lips, regardless of how civil they became with one another. Some titles had staying power, and from Madeline's perspective, *mistress* was it for Sherry.

What a twist of fate, Madeline thought. She should have erupted in laughter as she reflected on the quirky pieces of the Mitchell puzzle. Her situation was too funny not to laugh. It was laugh or cry. She agonized for several minutes and finally knocked on the door, intending not to let her history with Sherry derail their impending conversation.

Sherry opened the door and asked Madeline to come in.

Madeline entered graciously, which was in stark contrast to her prior entrances. She had typically pushed past Sherry on prior visits to the house. Madeline had intentionally not shown Sherry any respect, taking the stance that she didn't have to.

When Dave asked Madeline to stay in the mansion with their children and let him find another house, she turned him down flat. He went on to marry Sherry several years later, after it was clear that Madeline didn't want him back. His second marriage actually infuriated Madeline and caused her to show even greater disdain. Truth was, she had discarded Dave and the mansion, but that hadn't tempered her fury. As a result, she'd vowed to make Sherry's life a living hell through intimidation and entitlement. Madeline knew the trauma she'd inflicted on Joel's mother. She didn't feel badly about it, but Madeline wasn't proud of her actions, either. She exhaled. Regardless of what had transpired, Madeline needed Sherry.

"I appreciate you letting me drop by on such short notice." She sensed that Sherry had her guard up.

"I had to, once you told me this was about Joel."

The house was familiar yet strange. Madeline stood in the foyer, as Sherry hadn't asked her to step any farther. In the past, Madeline would have wandered throughout the house, with Sherry on her heels, begging her to stop. Looking back wasn't very gratifying. It had been much easier to view Sherry as the culprit on all accounts. It had been easier to blame Sherry than to accept Dave's second family. But today Madeline stood respectfully in the foyer of the house belonging to her ex-husband's wife, prepared to plead for help. Life was twisted, and Madeline didn't have the power to straighten it out on her own.

"Can I get you a cup of coffee or tea?"

"Tea would be nice," Madeline said, following Sherry into the kitchen.

Sherry poured two cups of tea from a pot sitting on the stove. She handed a cup and saucer to Madeline. They took seats across from one another at the table.

Madeline let her gaze roam and her thoughts wander. "In all these years, I guess I never paid attention to the changes you've made in the kitchen," she finally said, sipping the tea. "You've done a nice job in here. Looks nice."

"Thank you, but I doubt that you came here to discuss interior decorating."

Madeline gently slid the teacup and saucer away. "You're right. I came because I need your help."

"Mine?"

"I know. Can you believe it? But I'm counting on you to help me save DMI."

"How?"

"I need Joel to take the CEO position before Don relocates to South Africa."

"When is he leaving?"

"I don't think he has an exact date, but it's within the month."

"Good for him."

"Perhaps, but that creates a problem for DMI. We don't have a CEO to replace him."

"Joel told me you asked him. He was very excited."

"That's exactly why I'm here. Joel agreed to take the position a few weeks ago, and then some things happened, and a bunch of stuff got in the way. Anyhow, I need him to reconsider my offer."

"I'm surprised he turned you down, given how much he's wanted to come back. You gave him so much hope when you backed his candidacy. Why would he turn you down?"

"Out of some misguided loyalty and fairness to his wife." Before Sherry could get defensive, Madeline qualified her statement. "I appreciate him being willing to give up his position at DMI because Zarah is selling her family business, but it doesn't have to be that way. He loves DMI. He belongs in the top post. He was created for the job. If his wife loves him as much as she confesses, she wouldn't want him to be deprived of his passion. That could set him up for resentment later."

Sherry related to the scenario very well. Her marriage to Dave had been built on sacrifice, mostly hers. She'd given up her self-respect and her desire to be accepted in the Mitchell-DMI world. Not only had Madeline tormented her for nearly three decades, but outsiders had also labeled Sherry as a home wrecker. The label had driven her to stay at home more than she should have. The terrible memory of her extreme isolation and inadequacy wanted to wash over her. But Sherry wasn't going to let Madeline see her vulnerability and judge her. She toughened up and continued with the discussion. Besides, this was about Joel, her heir to the Mitchell dynasty. It was better for her little family if Joel was on the inside of DMI, as CEO. When he was in that position before, she'd been lavished with respect. She wanted her higher status back.

"Joel is a grown man. He makes his own decisions."

"I know all that," Madeline said, her curt tone indicating that she was slightly agitated. Sherry wasn't afraid. "Then you know I can't tell a grown man what to do."

"He might be grown, but you're his mother. I imagine that you have some influence on him."

"I'm not sure." Sherry covered her face with her hands briefly.

"Excellent," Madeline replied. "You have to convince Joel that taking the CEO role is the best decision for the entire Mitchell family. His dad worked incredibly hard to get DMI to this point. We can't let his legacy die with him."

Sherry listened intently. She'd never felt so empowered and meaningful. The entire family's legacy was depending on her. She eagerly took on the personal challenge. "If you think I can help, then I'll give it a try. I'll have to remind Joel of what DMI means to the family and to his father."

"Good. That's what I want to hear." Madeline took several sips of the tea.

"I'll do my best."

Madeline stood. "I need to get back to the office. I can't thank you enough for reaching out to Joel."

"No problem. Like you said, I'm his mother. I want him to get everything that he's entitled to receive."

"Hopefully, your encouragement will sway him our way. Please let me know when you've spoken to him." Madeline began walking out the kitchen.

"Do you want me to call you at the office?" Sherry asked, since she didn't have another number for Madeline.

"That's fine. I'll look forward to hearing from you," Madeline said, reaching the front door.

"Maybe we can have tea again."

"I think I'd like that." Madeline turned the doorknob. "By the way, how's the dating going?" Sherry had a bewildered look. "Remember you told me about Joel setting you up for online dating?"

"Oh, that," she said as Madeline snickered. Sherry snickered too. "I haven't started yet, but I am seriously considering it."

Madeline laughed out loud. "Let me know how that goes."

Chapter 42

Madeline drove slowly down the driveway. She wasn't desperate to get off the property. Yet she wasn't hanging around for an extended visit, either. Once she'd cleared the driveway, Madeline pulled off to the side of the road and called Don. She'd have to use every means available to fulfill her plan of appointing Joel CEO and retiring shortly. She was getting close and felt a small amount of relief.

"Don, you'll never guess where I am."

"Should I be afraid to ask?"

"Oh, silly, don't be so dramatic. I'm not causing any trouble, if that's what you're thinking. As a matter of fact, I'm doing just the opposite. I'm making amends, if you can believe it." In the rearview mirror Madeline saw a car pull behind her. She rolled her window down and waved at them to drive around her. At first they didn't move, but they eventually took her direction.

"Okay. You have me interested. Where are you?"

"Sitting on Mayweather Lane."

"What in the world are you doing there? Looking for Joel?"

Madeline grinned. "I came to see Sherry."

"Yeah, right."

"Seriously, I met with her, and it was pleasant."

"Oh, my goodness, what did you do?" he asked, sounding concerned.

"Pipe down. I didn't hurt little Miss Sherry. She was alive and well when I left," Madeline said good-humoredly. "I can't be responsible for what happens to her afterward."

"Mother, please tell me you didn't get into an argument with Sherry. The constant bickering has gotten old, and I'm tired of the trouble between you. You have to give this a rest."

Madeline had to diffuse the tension that was building in what was intended to be a lighthearted conversation. "I told you the visit was quite pleasant. We had a nice chat."

"About what?" he asked, his tone softening.

"Joel and her dating."

"Dating?"

"Ah, don't worry about that. I really went to see if Sherry could talk Joel into taking the CEO position." Another car slowly drove past Madeline. There wasn't much traffic on the secluded road. It was a key selling point for Madeline when she'd originally purchased the house so many years ago with Dave. "I figure that if anyone can convince Joel to reconsider my offer and accept the job, it would be his mother."

"I guess, but I can't believe you went to see her."

"Well, she has been known to take advantage of an opportunity."

"Come on, Mother. Don't go there."

"Wait. I'm not saying she's an opportunist, but there was a time when Sherry was more than willing to take whatever her hands could grab."

Madeline didn't have to go any further. They both knew she was referring to Sherry's interest in pursuing a married man.

"I thought you said the meeting was pleasant? Sure doesn't sound like it."

"Don't mind me. I didn't bring up your father or any of our history."

"Good—"

"I went with a purpose, and nothing was going to distract me, not even my justifiable anger toward Sherry."

"Good for you."

She paused. "Revenge doesn't trump my mission to get what I want."

"I really don't care why you went. I'm just glad you reached out to Sherry."

"Don't read more into this than it is. I admit the visit was nice, but we're not best friends. Let's not go too far." Madeline had to admit that Sherry wasn't so bad. Previously, she hadn't viewed Sherry as a woman filled with emotions, fears, and hopes for her child. All she'd seen clearly was the woman who'd brought hurt and shame to Madeline's family. Every other aspect of Sherry's character had been a blur.

"You think she'll get through to Joel?" Don asked.

"I hope so. I need your help too. We have to convince Joel before you leave me high and dry. You have to speak with him and sell Joel on the plan. We have no other choice. I spoke with Abigail earlier, and she's definitely not interested in pursuing the job."

"Really?" Don said. "Joel and Tamara finally got to her. She's tired of the Mitchell infighting. But then, who isn't?"

"I'm sorry, son. I know you wanted her to get her day in front of the board."

"Ah, don't worry about me. We need to get a replacement so I can get out of here as soon as possible. So I will talk to Joel for you if it will help."

Madeline thanked him. "I can always count on you."

"I'll meet with him. However, as you said earlier, don't read more into this than it is."

Madeline accepted the gesture as a positive step for the family. She let her Bentley glide onto the road, both calm and hopeful.

Chapter 43

The night had been a restless one for Don. Each noise had him jumping up to check on his sister.

"Tamara," Don called out as he approached the rear wing of his condo. He'd allowed that section to be his sister's private sanctum. Don wanted to strangle this Remo guy for sending Tamara spiraling into a severe state of fear. As tough and ostentatious as his sister appeared, she was a wilting lily who had endured one devastating event after another. "Are you awake?" Don asked when he reached the guest suite.

"I guess," she responded.

"Are you decent?"

"Yeah," she said, sounding weak.

Don turned the knob and stood in the doorway. He refrained from entering the room. Too much crowding from anyone was bound to drive her into the streets and out of the country. He agreed with Madeline that they couldn't let Tamara get away. If she left town, this time he feared it would be for good. He couldn't bear the thought of losing a third sibling.

"I'm just checking in," he said.

She was balled up on the bed. "You don't have to babysit me. Don't worry. I'm not going to jump off the roof or blow my head off."

Don had to believe she wasn't seeking a response. He concealed his reaction.

"Oh, don't look so serious," she told him, her words punctuated by a thin trace of humor. "I'm not losing my mind. You can tell Mother that I'm doing just fine."

"Are you?"

"Doesn't it look like I'm doing fine?" she asked eerily.

"Depends on who you're asking." Don wanted to keep Tamara engaged without agitating her. "Why don't I get out of here and let you rest?"

"I *am* tired, actually."

"I'm not surprised. You should be worn out after your ordeal."

She pulled the pillow underneath her head and shrieked, "When will I ever get a break! Every time I turn around, there's another problem or controlling person waiting for me. I don't get it. What did I do so wrong in my childhood that has God punishing me like this?"

"You can't blame God for what happened Sunday."

"Then *who* can I blame?"

"You can begin with Remo and go from there. God was the one who protected you."

"No, that was Joel."

"Who do you think put Joel in that lobby at the exact second when you needed help? Hmm. Have you considered that? Nothing is random." Tamara seemed to be processing what he had said, but he couldn't tell for sure. "Even when you don't want to be bothered with God, He's with you."

"He clearly doesn't care about me."

Don pressed his hands against the door frame. "You are so wrong. You're covered by my prayers and the ones Dad sent up for you before he died. There are people who love you. I love you, and God does too."

"Whatever," she said, turning her back to Don. "Let me take a nap and get my head clear."

"Cool. I'm running out. Will you be all right for a few hours?"

"Go. I'm good. I told you, I don't need a babysitter." She flung her hand in the air. "Go," she repeated until he honored her plea.

Don thought about staying at the condo and catching Joel later, but Madeline's appeal was echoing loudly in his head. It wouldn't be silenced. He'd better run on over to Joel's house and hustle back home. On his way out he'd tell the guards to enforce tight security around his unit. No one in or out. Tamara would be safe, particularly after Don prayed for her. If Tamara ever needed a circle of protection around her, it was now.

Chapter 44

Don had to get moving. Joel had agreed to meet with him by three o'clock. It was already 2:30 p.m. Don whipped his BMI out of the garage and weaved into traffic. He zoomed from downtown Detroit to Joel's house in the far western suburbs. Fortunately, traffic was light, and with an extra nudge on the gas pedal here and there, he cut his thirty-minute ride down handsomely. Arriving at Joel's house, Don barreled up the driveway as his digital clock on the console flipped to 3:00 p.m. He had Tamara fresh on his mind. The visit would be short and direct. He rang the bell, and Joel came to the door right away.

"Thanks for letting me drop by," Don said, entering his brother's house.

"No problem. Sunday was weird, right? How's Tamara doing?" Joel led the way toward his office.

"She's as good as can be expected." Joel sat at his desk and gestured for Don to take a seat too.

"Yeah, well, I'm hoping she'll get past this."

"Me too. How's Zarah?" Don asked reluctantly. With so much going on at DMI, Don hadn't been able to check on Zarah and Joel since the baby died.

"Ah, she's upstairs. I brought her home from the hospital this morning. Let's just say this hasn't been fun for her." They finally reached Joel's office down the back hallway.

"How are you doing with all of this?" Don asked. He couldn't imagine the feelings associated with losing a child. His compassion went out to Joel.

"I'm better than I've been in a long time."

"Really?" Don said, nodding. "Is that the voice of contentment I'm hearing?"

"Maybe."

"What? Coming from you, this is nothing short of a miracle. You've seemed anxious over the past couple of months. What changed?"

Joel chuckled, then appeared serious. "You know, big brother, I've decided to slow it down and live one day at a time, instead of constantly being on the hunt for the next big thing."

"I hear you." Don couldn't recall when he'd last heard Joel speak with such promise.

"I had to get back to the basics and appreciate my blessings."

Upon hearing that, Don wanted to look around the room to see if he was in the right house. Seven or eight months ago an arrogant, self-servicing young business-man sat at that very same desk, threatening to reclaim the CEO post at DMI any way he could. This wasn't the same man in front of him. This guy spoke with wisdom, humility, and sincerity. Don settled in his chair, glad to be there. He wanted to absorb fully the atmosphere and the pleasantries with his brother. Knowing the Mitchell family as he did, there was no telling when the old Joel would rear his head. Don concentrated on remaining positive. It made his request simpler, because there was more sincerity.

"You seem to be in a good place. I'm happy for you," Don said, relieved that Joel was in a mature state of mind. It was good to see someone in the family making changes.

"I'm trying," Joel said, tossing a miniature ball up in the air and then snatching it in midair.

"That's how I know you're ready to assume the CEO position again."

Joel abruptly stopped tossing the ball and sandwiched it in between both hands. "No, let's not get into that discussion. I've already turned Madeline down. Zarah needs me here, and I'm not going to abandon her."

"Come on, Joel. You need a better answer than that one. Zarah is going to recover by faith."

"Who's faith? Mine or hers?"

"Yours. She'll work through her grief. Can you work through your fears?" Don asked.

"Fear of what?" Joel asked, seeming quite irritated.

"Fear of failing again."

Joel began tossing the ball again and laughed aloud. "That's ridiculous. I'm not afraid of anything."

"Really—"

"Yes, really,"

Don didn't mind Joel getting upset. It meant that his strategy of psychoanalyzing Joel was working. Joel was many things, but he was not a quitter. Don would draw on his passion and on prayers to get a yes out of Joel. He was close and would keep chipping away. "We each have a purpose on this earth, a divine calling to do whatever we have been equipped and anointed to do."

"I get all of that, but being CEO isn't it for me," Joel said, still tossing the ball. "Once upon a time, I thought running DMI was my calling. Dad said so. I believed him, and look at what a disaster that turned out to be."

"Okay, so you messed up. You got cocky and lost your way. So what?"

"It's quite a bit more than just getting cocky. I nearly bankrupted the company," Joel stated.

"So?" Don replied.

"You weren't so calm about it last year."

"You're right. I was angry last year, when my mother and Abigail summoned me from South Africa to help clean up your mess."

"That wasn't the only time you were mad. You were angry when Dad chose me to run DMI four years ago."

"You're right. I was the oldest and most experienced. It should have been my job."

"Don't I remember. You and Madeline made that very clear."

Both of them laughed.

"Seriously, I hated Dad and God. I figured if they were going to reject me, then I had no use for a father or faith," Don stated, wishing to be fully transparent with Joel.

"I know. That's when you ran away."

"Best decision I've made. Cape Town was my refuge." Don became choked up a little. "Going to Robben Island and hearing about Nelson Mandela's willingness to forgive those who persecuted him changed me forever."

"That's heavy," Joel commented.

"Tell me about it. Forgiveness changed my life. I was a wealthy young man who didn't have any health challenges or other major issues, other than not getting hired to run my father's company. I know it sounds like a spoiled rich kid who didn't get his way, and honestly, it was. What a disgrace it was for me to act that entitled."

"Jeez, when you put it like that, we all sound silly, fighting the way we do."

"I'm glad you said that. It's precisely why we can't waste energy passing our bitterness from one generation in this family to the next. This has to stop. Life is too short to waste on nonsense and bickering over every little thing. Let's get over ourselves, for goodness' sake. We both have a purpose to fulfill. Yours is running DMI."

"Then what's yours?" Joel asked.

Don was filled with contentment. "God used me to help bring the family together. Like you said, this fighting is silly. There are people out there battling cancer. There are people without enough money to take care of their families, people with real problems who find a way to get along with their loved ones."

"It's true," Joel said, leaning his chin against his closed fist. "Our family is very unforgiving."

"We can do better, and we will as soon as you accept the CEO post."

"I thought you wanted Abigail?"

"I did, but she withdrew her candidacy. Regardless, this is your season, and you have my vote."

"I don't know what to say."

"Don't get me wrong. You squandered two key DMI divisions, but those poor decisions can't keep you strapped to the past. It's your time to accept forgiveness and move on. There's work to be done at DMI. This is your destiny."

Joel fumbled with the ball for a while longer. Don prayed silently as he patiently waited for Joel to accept the invitation.

"Are you sure no animosity will come from you if I run the company your mother helped Dad build?"

"None. Besides I can't worry about what you're doing if I'm submerged in my next assignment."

"Which is what?" Joel asked. He stopped tossing the ball.

"Not quite sure yet, but I know it's in South Africa."

"You're definitely leaving?"

"How many ways do I have to say yes before you believe me? I'm out of here this month. I have my own company to run."

"And a lady friend to help you," Joel said, grinning and resuming his ball tossing.

"We each have our incentives," Don answered, upbeat. This was one of the best chats he'd ever had with Joel. There was maturity and wisdom in their conversation, which hadn't existed between them previously. Whatever was causing them to connect so well, he'd take in triplicate. "So, what's it going to be? Are you going to do the right thing and come back to DMI as the CEO-elect?"

Joel stared directly at Don. Neither of them blinked.

"Yes. What the heck? I'll come back," Joel said finally.

Don stood, and then Joel followed suit. They shook hands. Elation overtook Don, and he hugged Joel tightly.

"Welcome back, little brother. This is a great day for the Mitchell family," Don told him.

"Careful or I might think you actually consider me your brother," Joel said as they stepped apart.

"You are. That's a fact." Don patted Joel on the back. "I have to get home and check on Tamara."

"Sure. Go on. I'll catch up with you later," Joel said with a dose of excitement.

"Oh, and please give Zarah my regards."

"And you do the same with Tamara for me."

"Will do," Don said, hustling down the hallway.

Before he reached the foyer, Joel stopped him. "Thanks."

"No need to thank me. I did what had to be done."

"You've done more than that."

Don was pleased. "I have to go. Take care and stay strong in the Lord, little brother."

"I'll do my best," Joel said as Don walked out the front door.

Don hurried to his car and called Madeline, eager to give her the good news. "Mother, it's done."

"He accepted?"

"Uh-huh," Don said, feeling both smug and relieved.

"This is great. We have to move quickly," she said, talking extra fast. "Let's meet in my office tomorrow morning at eight. We have to put together a stellar presentation for the board. Choosing Joel over a qualified candidate outside of DMI will be a hard sell, but I'm not worried."

Cool, Don thought. "If you're not worried, I'm not, either."

He ended the call and coasted down the driveway. Good things were finally happening for DMI and the Mitchell family. He prayed they'd be able to maintain this unfamiliar state of euphoria. It would take a miracle for them to keep working together, but then, he did know a miracle worker. Don careened into traffic with the wind at his back and the Mitchell worries in his rearview mirror. He'd focus only on today. Tomorrow would have enough troubles of its own.

Chapter 45

Late last night Joel had gotten a call from Madeline, instructing him to be at DMI by 8:00 a.m. It was 6:15 a.m., and he was dressed and ready to go.

"Must you go so soon? The office is only thirty minutes away," Zarah told Joel.

"I know, but this is important. I can't be late, not today," he said, clearly oozing with joy.

She was pleased that Joel had something to be happy about, but her soul wasn't as content. Many days and nights would have to pass before her heart could mend from the loss of their child.

"I can see how important this is to you," she said, reaching for his hand. "Then you must go and do well."

He gave her a quick peck on the cheek and darted to the door. "I'll be gone most of the morning. Call me if you need anything."

"Don't worry about me."

"But I do," he said.

His concern melted her. "Please don't worry."

"I'll call your assistant on my way into the office and see if she can sit with you."

"No, please, no. She hasn't been over here since I went to the hospital . . . the first trip. I don't want to bother her with this. I will be very well. The cook is here, and the housekeeper will be in later. I am not afraid to be alone. It is good for me."

Joel peered at her adoringly before saying goodbye.

Zarah lounged around the bedroom after he left, wishing her self-imposed fifteen-minute grace period would fly by. That eliminated the chance of Joel running back in the house for something he'd forgotten and finding her on the phone. She rubbed her moist hands together, longing to see Tamara after having her friend rush from the hospital. They hadn't spoken since, and Zarah couldn't wait a single minute longer. She dialed the phone frantically. Her greeting erupted when Tamara answered.

"Zarah, I didn't expect to hear from you this soon. Are you at home or still in the hospital?" Tamara had wanted to call several times over the past couple of days. She'd decided to show Joel some consideration for a change and not bother his wife. She owed him that much for protecting her from Remo. Staying away from Zarah had been hard. She desperately needed her friend.

"Joel has gone for the morning. Can you please come for a visit?"

"I don't know about that. Joel might not like me dropping by."

"I was most worried for you. Joel told me why you had to rush from the hospital. I must see you. Please, come for a visit."

Tamara considered the request and weighed the many reasons why it was a bad idea. In the end she said, "Okay. I'm on my way, but I hope this doesn't cause a problem for you."

"No problem. I will look forward to seeing you soon."

Tamara dressed and made her way to the lobby.

"Excuse me, Ms. Mitchell, but we've been instructed not to let you leave the building," a security guard told her.

"What? I have somewhere to go."

"I'm sorry, but we were given strict orders by Mr. Mitchell." The guard wasn't budging, and Tamara wasn't interested in waging a fight. She was exhausted. "Then how do you suggest that I get to my appointment?"

"There are only two options."

"I'm listening," she said, tense.

"We can call your brother to get a release,"

Unless Tamara had missed the processing center, this wasn't a prison. He didn't have the right to detain her. Remo had tried, and look where it had gotten him. Yet Tamara didn't make a scene. She acquiesced and actually appreciated the spirit behind this effort to protect her. Don meant her no harm, and the guard didn't, either. She opted to be gracious and let him finish. The sooner she found a way to get out those doors, the quicker she could see Zarah.

"I don't like that option. What else can you do?"

"We can escort you to your destination."

"*Without* calling my brother," she stated ardently. Tamara was willing to go along with the program, but the guard had to give her some decision-making ability. She wasn't a child.

"As you wish."

"Fine. Let's go," she said, eager to get rolling.

Tamara sat quietly in the backseat of the private car as the security guard pulled up Zarah's driveway. "I'll be in there for maybe an hour," she told the guard.

"Take your time. There's no hurry. I'll wait as long as you need."

"Okay," Tamara said with reluctance. Although he didn't appear to be rushed, she'd be conscious of the fact that he was waiting outside. It was awkward, but she didn't contest the arrangement.

Zarah came to the door immediately. Jubilation glowed on her face. "I am most happy to see you. Would you like a bit of breakfast?"

Tamara had too much on her mind. Food hadn't been a priority over the past three days. "I'm not hungry, but I'd like some of that tea you drink with milk."

"Yes, indeed." Zarah conveyed her request to the cook. "We have so much to share. Let's sit in the library. It will be quiet in there," she told Tamara.

Tamara followed Zarah to the library, and they sat next to each other on the wide sofa.

"You look and sound much better than you did at the hospital. How are you feeling?" Tamara asked.

"I'm better."

"I'm very sorry about the baby. I know you would have made a great mother."

Zarah blushed. "It is my dream," she said as her voice dipped. "But it must wait. This was not our time."

Tamara patted the back of Zarah's hand. "Good for you. That's a great attitude. I'm sure that one day you and Joel will have a beautiful baby."

Teardrops formed on Zarah's eyelids. "If he stays married to me."

"Why wouldn't he? You're an amazing, beautiful woman with a kind heart."

"Thank you," Zarah squeaked.

"I mean it. You've been an incredible friend to me. Joel is blessed to have you in his life. I hope he knows it."

"In the hospital he said we would stay together."

Tamara stroked her hand across Zarah's cheek to catch the falling teardrops. "Then why are you crying?"

"I was most pleased to hear his commitment to me. Then I began to think about his words. Now I feel like a burden to him. He is bound to me out of obligation. It is not fitting. I desire to have a husband who loves me and sees my worth."

Tamara was kind of confused. From the day she'd met Zarah, her sister-in-laws goal seemed to be to win

Joel's affection and his dedication to the marriage. Zarah had clearly done that if Joel was talking about staying married even when there wasn't a baby to force his hand. She figured if Joel was staying with Zarah, it had to be because he wanted to.

"Joel hasn't been my favorite person, but I can tell he cares about you."

"But I do not have his love. What if he cannot bear me in a few years?"

"Does love really matter as long as you're together? And who knows? In time he could grow to love you in the way you want." Tamara had to pinch herself. "I'm shocked to be saying this, but people can change, including Joel. Give him a chance."

The cook interrupted with their tea. She set the cups on the table and slipped out the library. The ladies continued their chat.

"I will take your advice. This is a good day for my marriage," Zarah said.

The two hugged briefly as Tamara had learned that embracing wasn't natural for Zarah. Her displays of affection were different, but her love and friendship seemed to be the same. No language translator was required to figure that one out. Tamara and Zarah were more alike than different, and that was what made their relationship work.

"Now it's time for me to share my news," Tamara said, briefly shifting her gaze toward the ceiling.

Zarah sat up tall, with anticipation glistening in her eyes.

"I wanted you to be the first to know that I'm leaving town as soon as the proceedings are over with Remo. Hopefully, it won't take much longer for his trial or deportation. Either way I have to stick around, since I'm his victim. Ugh. I hate that term," she bellowed.

Sadness overcame Zarah, and Tamara was touched. "You mustn't go away. You are my only friend. I would not want to be here without you."

"You'll be fine. You'll have Joel. You'll have plenty of babies running around. Plus, you'll have Harmonious Energy to run. Trust me; you'll be very busy once you fully recover. You'll forget that I exist."

"Never will I forget you." She squeezed Tamara's hands tightly in her typical way. "Where will you go?"

"I'm honestly not sure. I'll go to the airport and just pick a flight to somewhere in the world that doesn't require a travel visa." The same sadness that Zarah had expressed fell on Tamara. "It's better that way. Nobody can follow me and try to lure me back to Detroit."

"It's not good for you to be in the world alone."

She had a point, but what alternatives were there? Oddly, a longing for familiarity gripped Tamara. Her five months in Detroit were the most she'd spent with family in fifteen years. The time hadn't been all bad. The extended stay had brought a boatload of trouble, but also some much-needed rest and reflection too. The longing drew stronger, making it tougher to walk away.

Tamara grappled with her feelings, hoping to avoid making an irrational decision. If she stayed, there would be a ton of emotional and relationship repairs that had to be done. Tamara wasn't sure she was up for the challenge. Being vulnerable might lead to pain, and she didn't like the thought of suffering. Running was simpler. It was what she'd become good at doing. Besides, after a few months the Mitchells would settle into a state of normalcy, and no one would miss her. She had no choice. Taking flight was right.

Chapter 46

Madeline basked in her victory. She bopped through the DMI lobby as if there wasn't a single concern weighing her down. She hummed while waiting for an elevator. Minutes clicked by as she stood there. Normally, she'd grow impatient, but Madeline was too happy to get upset. Several minutes later the elevator arrived, and the doors opened. She sashayed into the elevator without shedding an ounce of bliss. There was no guarantee that her mood would last, but she'd savor the moment.

At 7:15 a.m., the executive floor was silent. Madeline approached her office and paused. Accustomed to getting what she wanted, Madeline shouldn't have been surprised to see Joel standing outside her office. Having him waiting for her direction was a sweet reminder she'd savor. She fumbled with the keys on her ring, searching for the DMI ones. "I see you're here early. How long have you been waiting?"

Joel reached for her leather bag, and she let him hold it. A few seconds later she found the key and opened the door.

"Ten or fifteen minutes. No big deal." He handed her the bag. "I would have gladly waited another four or five hours."

"Now, that's the right attitude." Madeline opened her laptop and set it on the conference table. She took off her suit jacket and placed it on a chair, then beckoned for Joel to join her at the conference table. "Nothing worth having is going to fall in your lap. Sometimes you have to roll up your sleeves and put in backbreaking work. This, Mr. Joel, is one of those situations," she said, glancing at him and refraining from smiling. Somehow it didn't seem appropriate. Instead, she ended up with what felt like a silly grin. "Have a seat and let's get to work on our presentation."

"Just the two of us?" he asked, taking a seat.

"Don should be here by eight, but we can get started without him. The more we get done now, the longer we'll have to plug the holes in our proposal." Madeline pulled a bottle of water from her bag, followed by a pair of reading glasses. "Would you like a bottle of water?"

"No thanks, but I'm eager to get going."

Madeline was glad to see Joel's enthusiasm. She could push his candidacy, but ultimately, he had to deliver the knockout punch by coming across as a strong and personable leader who was receptive to change. She plucked a stack of folders from her bag and slid several papers over to Joel. "Take a look at these sales reports. Our selling point is going to be a presentation of the facts. For two years, you were a success as CEO. I looked over the reports and realized I was mistaken. Revenue didn't double while you were in charge. It tripled. That's a compelling case."

"Think it will be enough?"

"Hope so. At the end of the day, DMI is in business to provide leadership support and make money doing it." She adjusted the glasses on her nose.

"You think the board will put sales above my indiscretions?"

Since Madeline didn't read tea leaves or believe in magic wands, she didn't have an answer for Joel. Realistically, getting the board to approve him as head of DMI would require every contact and favor Madeline could tap. She'd have to cash in all her chips and go for broke to get Joel appointed.

"I wouldn't have asked you to consider the position if I doubted our ability to win." She peered at him. "You should know me by now. I don't take on battles with the intent of losing."

Joel smirked. "Yes, I do know that."

"But we agree that you have to get rid of Harmonious Energy. That is an albatross around your neck. There is zero chance in hell that you're getting the appointment if you're juggling a conflicting company. We have to sell it and fast. Did you talk to Zarah about this, like I suggested a few weeks ago?"

"I did, but then she had the miscarriage."

"Right. I get that the timing is pretty lousy to ask her to give up something else, given that she recently lost the baby, but there's no other choice. Either Harmonious Energy goes or your CEO post is out the window. I'll let you choose."

"I'll take care of it. You have my word."

Madeline desperately wanted to believe him. He was her last hope for filling the CEO position from within the family. "We'll put a strong case on the table and let the chips fall as they may."

"All right. Let's go for it."

Madeline stopped what she was doing and stared directly at Joel. "I understand that you don't completely trust my abilities on your behalf, but believe me when I tell you that I intend to win this. With Don flying off any day and Abigail resigning, I want you in the corner office. I've worked too hard and sacrificed too much to let a stranger off the street traipse in here and even think about giving me orders. That day will come only after I'm dead and buried, and maybe not even then," she said, maintaining a serious demeanor. Then she winked, and

Madeline could tell that Joel lightened up. "I'll do my part, and it wouldn't hurt for you to say a few of those prayers."

"That's an automatic. I prayed from the minute you called last night until this morning."

"Who said something about prayer?" Don asked, sticking his head in Madeline's office.

"Hey, you. Come in and get comfortable. We have a full day of strategizing and building a case for Joel's redemption. If we can magnify his successes, I'm hoping the board will overlook his failures."

"None of us are perfect. I'm sure they'd agree," Don said as Joel stood. They locked hands and drew close for a brotherly hug. Both sat at the conference table with Madeline. "Joel made mistakes like the rest of us. He's repented, and I believe God will restore him."

Joel gave Don a nod of appreciation.

"You stay positive, son. We need all the positivity we can get," Madeline told Don, taking a sip of water that she'd poured into one of the glasses in the center of the table. "A few of your prayers wouldn't hurt, either."

Don peeled off his suit jacket and swung it across the back of the empty chair next to him. "Mother, you can always send up a prayer to the Lord too."

Madeline laughed. "I just might take you up on it. Sure can't hurt to have the extra assurance." She was joking, but she was serious at the same time. Madeline let her gaze glide around the table feeling satisfied. All three of them were operating together for a common goal. She hadn't experienced such unity in the Mitchell family since the years before her children were born, when she, Dave, and Frank were an unstoppable team.

Around 8:40 a.m. Abigail poked her head in the office. "I'm sorry. I didn't realize you were in a meeting." She had turned to walk away before Madeline stopped her.

"Come on in and join the party. The more the merrier," Madeline said.

"Yeah, have a seat," Don told her as he pulled his jacket off the back of the chair next to him.

Abigail seemed reluctant until Madeline gently urged her to join them. "This is history in the making, and you can't miss out."

"What history?" Abigail asked, wearing a perplexed expression.

"Can't you tell? This is a miracle in the making. Don and I are drafting a knockout presentation to get Joel appointed as CEO of DMI . . . of my company, my baby. Did you think such a day would ever come?"

"Definitely not," Abigail said, giving a giddy chuckle.

"Me either," Madeline stated. "They must be handing out ice chips in hell."

It took a few seconds for the group to catch Madeline's humor. Once they did, there was a laugh fest at the table.

"Oh, what the heck; I might as well help. What do you need me to do?" Abigail asked and sat between Don and Joel.

The morning flowed, with several breaks sprinkled in.

"So, Don, when is the big day?" Abigail asked.

"I'll fly out sometime soon, if that's what you mean by 'the big day.'"

Madeline was tickled but gave no indication. Even she knew exactly what Abigail meant by the question. She was certain Don did too, and she had to intervene quickly to avert disaster. Some topics were bound to create problems, and this wasn't the time for distractions and petty, jealous rivalries.

"Abigail, you're last day is coming up quickly," Madeline said, steering the conversation in a different direction.

"We have to throw you a huge going away party," Joel said.

"That's a great idea," Don added. "All the bells and whistles. You deserve it."

"What about you, Madeline?" Joel asked.

"What about me?"

"Don is heading to South Africa. Hopefully, I'll be CEO. Abigail is leaving, and Tamara too. What are you going to do?"

She'd have thought Joel had asked the million-dollar question gauging by the stares coming from those seated at the table. She would have gladly answered the question if there was something to say. The truth was that getting Joel appointed and looking out for Tamara had been her primary priorities recently. There hadn't been room for much else.

"Maybe I'll create an online dating profile for you, like I'm doing for my mother. Who knows? Maybe you'll both meet guys and go on a double date," Joel said.

The room erupted in laughter.

He was funny, but Madeline didn't give him the satisfaction of making her laugh too. She peered over her glasses, which had slid down to the tip of her nose. "Why don't you save the jokes for comedy night, after your behind has finished this proposal?"

The laughter didn't subside.

"All right, enough. Is anyone here going to get serious? We have two days of work to complete in one." Madeline sounded irritated. In actuality she wasn't close to being upset. She was gratified to see those at the table working together and better than they'd been in months, maybe years, maybe ever.

Her euphoria would have lasted well into the day if Tamara had been at the table too. But she wasn't. Madeline wept within. "Excuse me for a few minutes. I need to make a call," she said, grabbing her cell phone from her bag and taking it into the hallway. Madeline had resigned herself to the notion that her happiness would never be complete unless both of her children were thriving. Don was set. Now it was Tamara's turn, and Madeline aimed to help her.

Chapter 47

Madeline's confidence wavered. She could run a DMI meeting packed with clients, board members, and senior managers without breaking a sweat. She had proven that the business arena was her playground, and she thrived on the constant rush. She would give anything to possess an iota of that boldness when handling her single area of weakness. She'd reluctantly reach out to her daughter, hoping for the best, while preparing for far less. She wasn't big on prayer, but this might be the ideal opportunity to give it a try. Her breathing intensified.

"Mrs. Mitchell, do you want to use my desk?" her assistant asked with a weird expression on her face.

"No," Madeline whispered, not wanting to draw any more attention than she already had by standing outside her office and toying with a phone.

She felt foolish but quickly acknowledged that love for her child was the justification needed to do just about anything. She slid down to the next door, which was closed, and turned her back to the administrative assistant. She still felt uncomfortable being out in the open. Madeline strutted to the break room near the elevators and was pleased to find the room empty. She retreated to a corner and made her call.

After several attempts and multiple mistakes made in dialing the right series of numbers, Madeline temporarily halted her effort and took a deep breath. She ran her hand across her brow and then rested her fist against her waist. She allowed her heart rate to slow down and prayed silently. The concept was so foreign that she didn't know what to say. So she recited the Lord's Prayer, which she'd learned from her grandmother during her childhood. Madeline was absolutely certain that she hadn't got all the words right, but that was the best she could do. Focusing on the prayer took her mind off the pressure she was feeling about calling Tamara. Once she'd settled down, Madeline got the number right on the next try.

Once the phone rang, her heart rate threatened to fire up again. Madeline had spent so much energy on making the call that she hadn't thought about what she'd say when Tamara answered. After three rings, it was show time. Her daughter was on the line, and Madeline had to say something.

"Tamara, I, well . . . I'm, uh . . . ," she stammered.

"Mother, are you all right?"

"Yes," she replied. "I am, but I would be much better if Remo was extradited to a remote prison thousands of miles away from you."

"That would be nice, but I doubt that you called about Remo's travel plans."

"You're right. I didn't. I called because I need to know that you're getting past this ordeal."

"I wouldn't call it getting past. It's more like surviving."

Madeline wasn't about to disagree. She was happy to get any time with Tamara. She wouldn't squander the morsel of time under any circumstance. "We all deal with situations in our own way. Do whatever you need to do."

"I'm glad you said that, because I really must get out of town. I'm not even sure I can wait until this legal business is over."

"When I said 'whatever you need to do,' I didn't mean leave in a hurry." Madeline wanted to cry out. Having her personal business exposed for all her subordinates to see wasn't a remote possibility. "You at least have to stay long enough to finish this situation with Remo and the courts."

"That's what I'm telling you, I don't know if I can."

Madeline had to hold her feelings together in case someone walked in the room. "Tamara," Madeline said, staring at the floor and enunciating each word, "you don't have to run away. We can protect you. Remo is not going to get away this time."

"This isn't about Remo. I'm leaving because there's no purpose for me here. I need to move on and, quite honestly, get a life."

"Sweetheart, Detroit is home. You have a life here. You'll always have one here."

"No, I don't. You and Don are businesspeople. Joel is too, for that matter. I guess that Mitchell gene skipped me."

Madeline traced circles on the floor with the tip of one of her high heel shoes. "You belong at DMI as much as the rest of us. With the proper mentoring and assignments, you'll be ready to assume a senior management position in no time. I'll make sure of it."

"Mother, face it. I'm not cut out for a senior position at DMI."

Madeline listened but refused to hear what Tamara was saying.

"And don't worry. I'm not upset about it anymore," Tamara added.

Don stuck his head into the break room. "Oh, there you are. Joel's ready to walk through the presentation."

Madeline covered the phone. "Give me a few minutes."

"Hurry up. We're waiting," Don said and ducked back out.

"Where will you go?" Madeline asked.

"Don't know."

Madeline swallowed hard. "When will you return?"

"I won't. This is it. Once I leave, I don't plan on coming back." There was an extended pause followed by, "Isn't that good news for you, Mother? You don't have to worry about me anymore."

Madeline clutched her chest as if she could reach her heartache. "Don't you know how much I love you?" she said, pressing her back firmly against the wall and refusing to sit down and fall apart. She had to keep standing. "I don't care whether you're in Detroit or Timbuktu. I will always worry about you and Don. You're my most important reason for living."

"Mother, I have to go."

It sounded like Tamara was crying, but Madeline wasn't sure. She wanted to keep her daughter on the phone, afraid that when the call ended, that might be the end of their relationship. Madeline couldn't bear the notion. She consciously chose to be in denial. Tamara wasn't really going to disappear. She'd fly away and drift back in a few months. If not, she'd disappear and then show up on the radar of the private investigator that Madeline would be hiring later today. That was the routine they'd established over the course of fifteen years. It wasn't pretty, but the process worked for Madeline. Some awareness of Tamara's whereabouts was better than none.

"Mother, I have to go. Take care of yourself. Bye," Tamara said and disconnected the call as Madeline stood frozen. She batted her eyelashes repeatedly until they were completely dry. She cleared her throat quietly and patted down her hair. Madeline held her head high and returned to the office, clutching her phone like it was a piece of Tamara.

"It's about time," Don said. "We better get through this walk-through and get back to work. We are still running a company here."

Madeline waved her hand at him and gently set the phone on the table. "Let's get it done."

Joel queued up the presentation on his laptop and projected it onto the whiteboard. "I'll skip the intros and go directly to the selling points," he said.

Madeline watched him flip through several slides and didn't utter a word. Joel must have noticed her distraction.

"Madeline, do you have a question?" he asked.

"Uh-uh," she muttered.

"You seem distracted, or is my pace too slow? Heaven knows I don't want anyone to fall asleep during my presentation."

Don and Abigail laughed briefly.

"Do we need to make changes?" Joel asked.

"I'm not sure," Madeline responded, not wanting to elaborate. It wasn't Joel. She just didn't want to be there.

Don interjected, "Mother, are you all right?"

"No, I'm not. I just got off the phone with Tamara." Madeline was broken. Yet she still wasn't going to crack publicly. There would be ample opportunities to deal with her anguish alone at home later. "She's leaving town for good. She might not even wait for Remo's court date. She wants to go now. That's what she told me. So, please forgive me if the presentation doesn't have my full attention. This isn't exactly my finest hour."

"I understand," Joel said and shut off the laptop.

"I'm sure Tamara didn't mean that she's leaving for good," Abigail remarked. "She'll probably take an extended vacation. She'll be back. I'm sure of it."

"Well, I'm not. You didn't hear the tone in her voice. She's serious. When she leaves, this is it. I know it," Madeline said.

"Mother, you can't believe any of that. Tamara was traumatized a few days ago. She needs time to recover.

Actually, I think it's a good idea for her to get away. She should stay away until Remo goes to court and gets sentenced to some real jail time. The farther away she is from Detroit, the better for all of us," Don said.

"Speak for yourself," Madeline lashed out at him.

"I'm not sure that Tamara leaving the area is best," Joel said.

Joel instantly had Madeline's attention, since he was articulating her sentiments. "Me either. She's much safer here with us than traipsing around some foreign country and constantly living in fear," Madeline stated.

"Agree. I have a suggestion," Joel stated.

"What is it?" Madeline was open to any suggestion, even a bad one. Nothing could be totally ignored, except for Don's ridiculous idea of letting Tamara go off on her own.

"I want to help. It's the least I can do, given that you're the reason I'm sitting here. You and God, of course," Joel said. "You've put your reputation on the line to support me and to give me a chance to prove myself when no one else would. I'm grateful to you."

"You know I don't like this mushy stuff. Let's get on with the presentation," Madeline told him.

"It can wait," Joel said. "God has used you to change my life. Please let me return the favor. I want to help Tamara for you."

"What do you have in mind?" Don asked.

Desperation strangled her pride and freed Madeline to accept the offer.

"I don't have a plan yet, but I will try to change Tamara's mind."

"Joel, that's a noble offer, and I thank you. But Tamara is very strong-willed," Madeline told him.

"Wonder where she got that characteristic?" Don echoed.

Madeline rolled her eyes in his direction and kept talking to Joel. "Like I said, I appreciate your offer. And I won't turn you down. However, I have to be honest. I don't expect anything you do to work. Tamara has made up her mind, and dissuading a stubborn person can be impossible."

"Maybe not," Joel replied. "Look at us."

Chapter 48

Joel meditated on the drive home. His mind was as clear as he could get it in light of the promise he'd made to Madeline. Joel didn't have any idea of how to reach Tamara. Yet he had to give it his best shot. As the past and the present paraded among his thoughts, he couldn't avoid harsh introspection.

The old Joel would have done anything to get what he wanted. He wouldn't have given a second thought to making a promise that he couldn't fulfill legally, morally, or ethically. What Joel Mitchell wanted, he got. It wasn't that long ago when he had the top spot at DMI, a hand on the Bengalis' wealth, a special friend in Chicago to boost his ego, and a doting wife at home. He'd once savored local stardom and international acclaim—and a very long list of women who'd tackle any obstacle to spend a single evening with him. Admittedly, he'd enjoyed more of life than most could even begin to dream about experiencing.

The memories came hard and fast. Some poked at his sound state of mind. He resisted as he sped down the street leading to his house. Joel wasn't sure if the flood of memories was God allowing him to see from whence he'd come or the devil reminding him of who he was. He honestly couldn't tell, but then he suddenly realized the source didn't matter. The end result was the most important aspect. Without some type of divine intervention, he could very well be in that same place, chasing women and craving notoriety with no regard for the role God and faith had played in his life from birth. Dave Mitchell might have done some things wrong, but he'd been a real father to Joel. His father was the one who'd taught him to put God first and let Him do the heavy lifting when it came to challenges in life.

Joel had strayed away from his spiritual truths for close to two years. *But thank God for His mercies,* Joel thought as he turned into his driveway. He could see clearly. The blinders of self-righteousness and thinking that he could accomplish anything on his own had been shredded. God seemed to be much better at putting plans together than he'd been. Regardless of who he was or what he'd done, this was a new day. Joel wholeheartedly believed that repenting and relying on God for direction had given him a clean slate. Madeline had given him a second chance, but the one coming from God was untouchable. He was determined not to stray away ever again from the only true peace he'd known, and that peace came from trusting God in all things, big and small. Some lessons were learned in classrooms. His had played out in the real world, in front of a highly judgmental and unforgiving audience.

He parked near the garage. Before he left the car, Joel sealed his revelation with a chat. "Lord, I'm grateful." He let his head rest on the steering wheel. "I'm not worthy, but your purpose for my life is bigger than my shortcomings. I can see that now." He shut his eyes tightly and let the Holy Spirit bring comfort. Joel hadn't realized just how exhausted he'd become from groveling for success and redemption on his terms. "I'm not sure how to help Tamara, but, Lord, I ask that your mighty hand move in this situation. Not my will, but yours be done, in Jesus's name." Joel lingered a bit in the car, wanting to gobble up the tranquility.

Eventually, he went inside the house, where he found Zarah watching TV in the den. "You don't come in here much," he said.

"This is true. Thought I'd watch a show, but there's nothing of interest for me."

"Maybe we should check into getting a Bollywood channel," Joel suggested.

"That would be nice," Zarah said, lighting up.

Her expression was a reminder that his wife had sacrificed a great deal to be in the United States with him. Zarah had given up her family, her traditions, many foods, and even little things, like places to shop for the clothing she was accustomed to wearing. He felt awkward asking for more.

"Would you mind turning off the TV? I have something important to discuss." She obliged, and he sat near her. "I had a very productive meeting at DMI."

"Very good. I am most pleased that you will be in charge of DMI again. It was your father's desire. You will do well."

"I plan to do my best, but the job isn't going to happen without your help."

"How do you mean?" she asked.

"Harmonious Energy has to go. I know we talked about this before you went to the hospital, and you weren't sure—"

Zarah cut him off. "And I've decided it is best to sell as well."

"Wait. When did you decide this?" Joel asked, shocked. He tried to come up with the proper response to her news. He was excited, but he also recognized that she was selling her family's legacy. He had to tread softly.

"I have given much thought to our marriage, to my family's business, and to my faith. Every time I think of a scenario where you are not present, my heart weeps. My destiny is with you. I am your wife in my soul. This means I must be the wife you need and must support you at this most critical time." Her voice dipped, followed by her gaze.

"Are you sure?" he asked, placing his index finger under her chin and gently lifting her head. Their gazes met. "I can understand if you don't want to part with your family's business."

She peered deeply into his eyes and said, "*You* are my family. There is nothing on earth more important to me than being your wife and friend."

Something washed over Joel. For a split second, she was simply divine. It wasn't what she said that melted him to the core. It was how she looked at him. Her inner being stood naked before him, and he didn't see any blemishes. He couldn't recall experiencing such pure and profound devotion. Abigail had loved him. Samantha had lusted after him. Sheba had supported him. But Zarah was different than the rest. She honored him. Maybe that wasn't the right word to describe how he felt in her presence, because it was so hard to describe. Yet the feeling was one he intended to hang on to.

"Then, it's a done deal. I'll give Don a call later and let him know. The DMI financial team will need to work out the details with Kumar." Joel could see Zarah's tears swelling. "We can deal with the details later. Let's focus on us," he said, scooting within several inches of her. A year ago she would have shied away. Zarah held her ground, which drew him an inch closer to her. "About the marriage . . ." He could see her tensing. "I meant what I said last week. I want our marriage to work."

"I don't want you to stay out of obligation."

"Trust me; there is more in this for me than obligation. I sincerely care about you and want to make this work." He desperately wanted to convince her. She deserved his devotion in return.

"Yes, and I as well. Tamara helped me to see that it is good for me to be happy about the marriage. Love will come from you in time. There is no shame for me if I stay. There is shame only if I go."

"Tamara, huh? That's great. I'm glad she's been a good friend to you. It's going to take some work with our different backgrounds. And you'll have to give me time to develop the kind of love that you deserve. I'm not there yet, but I'm willing to get try if you'll accept me on those terms."

Zarah was beaming. "Yes, yes," she said, squeezing his hand. "I am."

"Cool," Joel said and embraced her with as much passion as he could earnestly muster. "Then we have to rewind this relationship and start over. We have to date and get to know one another."

"That would be very nice," she said, with a smile that lit up the room.

"I know we're doing this whole marriage thing backward by getting married and then dating, but what the heck? We have to do what works for us," he said, laughing. "What do you think?"

"I am most pleased."

He was touched. "This weekend I'll take you shopping. Shoot, we might as well make a day of it, with lunch and maybe a movie."

She nodded profusely as her tears flowed. He wasn't delusional enough to think this chain of events would erase the devastation she'd endured with the miscarriage. However, he was thrilled to see the happiness bubbling in her. She deserved a break, and finally, Zarah was getting it.

"I have to run out," he told her.

"Where are you going?"

"To call Don and take care of a few things." He was inclined to be evasive, but then he decided against the temptation. "I want to stop by the Westin to close my account and officially move out of there and back in here."

He knew Zarah was pleased without her having to utter the words. He'd already spent a month in the guest room. So the move wasn't going to change much, except he would no longer have a hotel bill. He was going home, but he didn't plan on sharing the same bed with Zarah. That would happen if and when they got remarried. He didn't bother sharing that tidbit with her and potentially dampening the mood. She was elated, and he was too. The rest would fall into place naturally. Why not? Everything else had, thanks be to God.

Chapter 49

Solemn, Madeline stood in her office, peering out the window. She wasn't a stranger to grief. Being married to Dave Mitchell had served as the basis for her greatest joys and her most crushing sorrows. She let the memories marinate. If Madeline had to live the past thirty years over, there wasn't much she'd change. The good outweighed the bad, with the exception of one vital element of her life, and that was her relationship with Tamara.

"Excuse me, Mother. The meeting starts in half an hour," Don said. "Are you ready?"

She continued peering out the window. "I'm as ready as I'll ever be."

"You don't sound too confident. Are you concerned that the board won't vote Joel in?"

She turned in his direction. "I'm not worried about Joel. He'll get appointed one way or another. At the end of the day, this is my company. If I want Joel to be CEO, there's not enough resistance on the board to stop me."

"Okay. Then if it's not Joel, what is bothering you?"

"What else? Tamara."

"Have you spoken with her?"

"I haven't, and that's what worries me. At least she's still staying with you," Madeline told Don.

"She is, but if you ask me, Tamara could be out of here any day. As a matter of fact, I'm surprised Tamara's still here after telling you that she was ready to go, regardless of the pending legal case against Remo."

"You don't seem too alarmed," Madeline told Don, crossing her arms.

"Because worrying isn't going to change her mind."

"We can't stand by and do nothing."

"I understand, but she's a grown woman who's fully capable of making her own decisions," Don said. "She knows I want her to be happy. How she chooses to get there is on her. We have to trust her and not impose our will on her."

"You're probably right, but it's hard to let go. Maybe Joel can convince her to stay. Remember, he was going to try." Madeline unfolded her arms and rested both hands on her hips. "Ah, in my gut, I know you're right. What can Joel or any of us do? I appreciate his effort, but I highly doubt that he can make a difference. She's through with us. I just know it. I've lost my child for good." Madeline became very sullen.

"I don't know what Joel can do, but there's something *we* can do," Don stated.

"What?" she asked, cheering up slightly.

"We can always pray."

"Prayer, prayer, prayer; that's always your same canned answer. It has never done much for me."

Don approached his mother and placed his hand on her shoulder. "The way I see it, you don't have anything to lose. If you do nothing, she's gone. Prayer and God's involvement are not your last option. They're your only option."

Madeline prided herself on being a wise businesswoman who made rational decisions. She couldn't ignore Don's argument, and actually, Madeline wasn't completely opposed. She'd recited the Lord's Prayer a few days ago. She wasn't convinced that it had helped, but for sure the prayer hadn't hurt, either. "I guess you have a point."

"Excuse me, Mrs. Mitchell. The board members have arrived," Madeline's assistant said after poking her head in the office.

"Is my daughter here?"

"No, every other member except her."

"Fine. Can you close the door? Don and I will be there shortly."

The assistant did as she was told.

"I was hoping Tamara might show up for the board meeting, but it doesn't look like she's coming," Madeline told Don.

"The offer to pray is still out there."

"Sure. Let's pray. Like you said, what do I have to lose?"

The two joined hands as Don prayed. "Father, I thank you for my family. We know that you have a plan for Tamara's life, a purpose, and a calling. We ask you, Lord, to allow her to fulfill her destiny in you. No matter where she goes, Father, I ask that you allow her to see, feel, and touch true love. I pray that the trauma she has suffered in the past will not hold her future hostage."

Madeline began sobbing softly. Don clutched her hand tighter, and then went on. "I pray that she will no longer feel a need to run from her problems. I ask that you plant her in a place where she can come to know you as her Savior and protector and provider. I pray that she no longer lives under the shadow of fear. Neither Remo nor anyone in this family can cause her to feel unsafe. Deliver her, Lord. Teach her to have a forgiving heart. Wherever she goes, I know that you will be with her. Thank you, Lord, and in Jesus's name, we pray. Amen."

Don sealed the prayer with a hug, which his mother gladly received. Madeline's sobbing remained mild, although her spirit was severely wounded.

"Thank you. That was a very nice prayer. Maybe it will work. I hope so," she said, seeking a tissue in her desk.

"We better get to this meeting," she added, then cleared her throat and grabbed a tube of lipstick from the top desk drawer. There was a place for tears, but it wasn't in the boardroom. She adjusted her suit jacket, patted down her hair, and led the way. Business was calling, and she fully intended to answer.

Chapter 50

Joel sat quietly at the oversize conference table, patiently waiting for Madeline and Don to arrive. There was another ten minutes left before the meeting was scheduled to begin, and it seemed like an eternity. He couldn't possibly survive another five minutes, let alone ten.

"Good morning, everyone," Madeline said, entering the room with Don and her assistant, who was following closely behind with a stack of presentations.

Shew. Joel was relieved.

"We can get started in a few minutes. We'll give our ninth member a chance to get here," Madeline stated, letting her gaze circle the table.

"Do we expect her to arrive on time?" one member asked.

"I guess we'll have to wait and see, won't we?" Madeline snapped. They all were going to give Tamara the courtesy of waiting. Madeline would see to it.

Minutes passed, but Tamara remained a no-show. Before some pushy board member reminded her of the time, Madeline took charge. "My assistant is handing out copies of the presentation. As soon as she's finished, I'll have you turn to page one and we'll get started."

"This may be a technicality, but Joel is no longer a board member. It seems a bit unorthodox to have him attend a session where we're evaluating his candidacy," stated the same outspoken board member who'd made the comment about Tamara.

"Come on. This is DMI. We don't have to be so formal," Don responded.

"That's the beauty of being privately held. We can extend a few privileges that might be frowned on elsewhere," Madeline added.

"But—" the member uttered before Madeline cut him off.

"But we don't have anything to hide. We're offering full transparency. Joel is sitting right here. As we walk through the proposal, you'll have a chance to ask him questions directly. Are there any objections?" Madeline said, seeming to stare each member down. No one objected.

Joel appreciated Madeline's take-charge approach and relaxed a tad bit. He'd been in the seat where the ill-advised board member was. Several years ago, he'd been the one grilling Madeline, only to have her unleash a whirlwind of fury, which was not readily contained. Round one was over, and Madeline had won handily. They were in good shape, but a silent prayer for extra reinforcement couldn't hurt.

"Seeing that there are no objections, please turn to page one. Don and I are recommending that the DMI board of directors appoint Joel Mitchell as the new CEO upon Don's departure. We understand this will be a tough sell given some of the challenges we endured during Joel's past tenure. However, we have a compelling case as to why he should assume the role."

"I'm curious to see what you have to say," a second board member said.

"Joel, why don't you kick off the proposal we've laid out," Madeline suggested.

"Sure," he responded and stood after sliding a paper from his portfolio. He had a better command of the audience on his feet. "Let's deal with the elephant in the room upfront, which is Harmonious Energy." At the mention of that company, some of the board members began whispering among themselves, and Joel allowed them to quiet down before proceeding. "My first assignment as head of DMI will be to complete the sale of Harmonious Energy."

"That's quite a task, seeing that DMI owns only half," a board member stated.

"True, but I have a signed letter of intent to sell from Zarah Bengali Mitchell. As you know she owns the other half of Harmonious Energy."

"Can I see that?" someone asked.

"Sure," Joel said, gladly passing the letter around. "My top priority will be to sell the company jointly or divest our holdings. We'll pursue whichever option will create a win-win for both companies."

"Looks good," said one of the board members who hadn't spoken previously.

"This appears legitimate on the surface, but you've presented proposals in the past that didn't turn out to be as ironclad as you thought. Why should we believe you?" the outspoken board member asked.

"As current CEO, I find the plan to sell Harmonious Energy a sound proposition," Don said.

Joel chimed in as the tension in the room intensified. "In addition to selling Harmonious Energy, there may be an opportunity to regain the West Coast division in this deal."

Several eyebrows rose, and there were nods of affirmation.

"That sounds intriguing," one board member stated.

"Oh, come on," the outspoken board member interjected. "Don't waste our time with folly. Unless you have a second letter of intent, let's stick to the facts about your proposal. Keep the fuzzy deals off the table. We've already experienced our share of that with you."

Don jumped in. "No one else in this room can get Zarah Mitchell to sign off except Joel. So if we want to divest the company and have a shot at getting the West Coast division back under the DMI umbrella, Joel is our best means of getting this done—plain and simple," Don said and sliced his hands in the air like an umpire calling a runner out.

"But this is his wife. How do we know it's solid?" one of the board members asked.

"Did you read the document for Harmonious Energy?" Madeline retorted. "It has bonded signatures from Zarah, her father's estate executor, their chief financial officer, and their chief counsel. That seems pretty official to me. If you want, I can have my assistant get our chief counsel in here to authenticate the document," she said, waving the paper in the air.

"It won't be necessary," the board member replied, acquiescing.

"Great. Then let's move on, shall we?" Madeline said curtly. No one else would dare protest.

Chapter 51

The heated board meeting drew on as noon approached. After several hours of being grilled, Joel wrapped up his presentation.

"Thanks, Joel. If there aren't any other meaningful questions," Madeline said, staring each member into submission, "we'll call for the verbal vote."

"I'd prefer to cast private ballots," the outspoken board member said.

"Me too," someone else agreed.

"How odd, coming from a group that preaches about the need for transparency. If you need to hide behind a ballot box, then maybe we should be seeking more than a new CEO. Perhaps we need to look at our list of board members too," Madeline stated in such a harsh tone that Joel grimaced.

"Joel, you can stay for the vote, or we can come and get you afterward," Don said.

"If it's all the same to you, I'll stay here," Joel answered. Facing down those he'd wronged and publicly seeking their redemption required him to be present, and not cowering down the hall in some remote corner. He had to face down his doubters and stand with his supporters.

"Please get some makeshift ballots for the group," Madeline told her assistant. "We're looking for a yes or no on the sheet. That's it. Since Tamara didn't show up, we'll have to base this on eight votes."

"What if there's a tie?" her assistant asked.

"Unless Tamara shows up, Joel will serve as the tie-breaker," Madeline replied.

"How did you reach that determination?" the outspoken board member asked.

"Easily. He's a Mitchell, which counts in a company where DMI stands for Dave Mitchell International. If you need more explanation, accept the fact that he held the board seat before we appointed Tamara. He was on the board for years after Dave died. It's not much of a stretch to recommend him," Madeline said, almost daring someone else to respond.

"That violates the company's charter. The process of selecting a CEO is clearly defined. Madeline, you can't make up rules as you go along and maintain a sense of integrity."

"Watch me," she fired back at the outspoken board member.

"If you proceed in this fashion, we'll be forced to challenge the results in the event of a tie."

"Then I guess you better make sure we don't end up with a tie," Madeline asserted.

Joel enjoyed being on Madeline's team. He knew firsthand how she could be incredibly supportive or absolutely destructive. Avoiding the hot seat was refreshing.

The assistant passed out small rectangular pieces of paper upon Madeline's request, and a few minutes later she collected them for the tally.

"That's everyone," the assistant told Madeline as she handed her the ballots.

Joel cringed before allowing his faith to wash over him and drive out his anxiety.

"Here goes. One yes, two yes," Madeline said, revealing the count.

Joel's heart was racing.

"One no," she said, sending a fiery glare to the out-spoken board member, even though the votes were anonymous. Madeline resumed tallying. "Two noes, three noes." Madeline sighed aloud. "This is ridiculous. My son is leaving DMI soon, and you're going to tell me that we can't agree on the best DMI candidate available?"

Joel had allowed his hopes to rise far beyond the ceiling, into the stratosphere. He hadn't considered being turned down. His spirit said that returning to DMI was God's will. Redemption was to be realized during his next term. Resting in the confirmation that was residing in his spirit, Joel kept from panicking. "Keep counting, Madeline. We're fine."

She obliged. "Another yes, which makes three," she said, stacking the yes votes together. "And another yes. Four yeses." Madeline paused before opening the last ballot. "That's it. Regardless of what's on this final ballot, Joel is our new CEO," she shouted.

"How?" Don asked.

"If it's a no, we would have a tie at four each. Then Joel would vote yes, and we'd be done."

"Ah, right," Don said, grinning. "And a yes vote would give us five, a clear win."

"Exactly," Madeline said. She opened the ballot and showed it to the crowd. "It's a yes. Congratulations, Joel. You'll be the next CEO when Don leaves." Not everyone at the table was thrilled about the outcome, and Madeline didn't care. Good business wasn't personal.

Joel wasn't able to move. Her words enveloped around him. He was overcome. God had delivered him from the bondage of his past mistakes. Together with Don and Madeline, he'd wrestled a giant and achieved a decisive victory.

"Let's set his effective date in ten days," Don said.

Nods around the table affirmed the plan, including a nod from the outspoken board member.

"Thank you for the vote of confidence. I will work tirelessly to restore your trust in my leadership abilities," Joel said.

Shortly after the vote, several handshakes, and well-wishes, the board members filed out the room. Only Madeline, Don, and Joel remained, and then Abigail joined them. Joel eagerly shared the good news with her.

"We did it," Joel said. "I owe all of you."

"You don't owe me anything," Abigail said.

"You can repay me by letting God lead you this time. Stay on track and you'll be all right," Don stated as he and Joel locked fists and shared a quick brotherly hug.

For Joel, having his older brother's approval meant a great deal. He was touched.

"How about celebrating with Zarah and me at my house? We have several blessings to celebrate."

"What else?" Madeline asked.

"There's Don's going away party," Joel replied.

Don shook his head. "I appreciate the offer, but no party for me unless it's going to be in South Africa."

"Yeah, right," Madeline mocked.

"I was joking, but actually, that's not a bad idea. I'm inviting everyone to join me on my flight to South Africa. I can show you my home away from home. Naledi will be excited to meet my entire family."

"I'm in," Joel said.

"I guess I am too," Madeline said.

"What about you?" Don asked Abigail.

"Not this time."

Joel understood why she refused to go. He was certain Don did too.

"Joel, you think your mother would be interested in joining us?" Madeline asked.

He was floored by the comment. "I can ask."

"Good. Ask."

"Are you feeling all right, Mother?"

"I'm fine. Don't act so weird. Why not let Sherry come along? We're not best friends, but we both love our kids. We will always have that in common."

"That's fantastic," Don said.

Joel couldn't thank God enough for the flood of miracles rushing through DMI and the Mitchell family. He'd never known a family circle larger than his father, mother, and Uncle Frank. Having a few more people who actually wanted to be around him was amazing. He was blessed, and he knew it.

"We can all go together," Don said.

"The corporate DMI jet might not be suitable for such a long trip," Madeline stated.

"It's not a problem. We'll book a bunch of first-class seats together on a commercial flight, Mother. It is how most of the world flies, you know."

"Yes, I do know, smarty. However, we're not taking a commercial flight. I'll treat the group to a private plane. Let me know when you're ready to go, and I'll make the reservations."

"As one big happy family?" Don asked, beaming.

"God help us," Madeline said, trying to retain her stern disposition, which didn't work. She was pleased, and it showed.

Joel recognized the look. Forgiveness had a way of doing that to people. If there was hope for Madeline, then there was hope for Tamara.

Chapter 52

Joel was wired and struggled to contain his euphoria. His dash through the lobby was a blur. He recalled speaking to a few people, but the details were hazy. He bopped to the second row of the parking lot and opened his car door. He didn't get in until he glanced up a row at the CEO parking spot. Don's BMW was tucked in the spot today. Soon his Rover would be nestled in the spot reserved for the top dog, and that would be him. He was filled with glee, vindication, and grace for the entire Mitchell family. Joel couldn't be more hopeful. "Thank you, Lord," he whispered and got in his car.

He dialed Sherry, unable to contain his delight. "Mom, it's done. I'm the new CEO."

"Oh my goodness!" she shouted. "Oh my . . ."

He could tell she was crying, and allowed her a few seconds to digest the gravity of this victory. "It's a miracle."

"I can't believe it," she uttered through the soft sobs.

"Me, either." Joel turned on the car in order to let the windows down.

"I'm so happy for you. You deserve this job. Your father would be so proud."

"I think so. I know I'm eternally grateful. God has been so good to me, and Madeline too. She really came through for me in the meeting. Don too."

"That's quite a shock after everything we've suffered over the years. You couldn't have told me this would happen in a million years."

"Make that two million," Joel joked. "Madeline can be a handful."

"Who are you telling?"

"But when she's on your side, Madeline is a great ally."

"Sounds like I owe her a big thank-you."

"I think she'd like that," Joel said, finding it hard to believe the words were flying from his mouth. "As a matter of fact, she's asked you to join the rest of us on a trip to South Africa. Don invited the entire family, and you're included."

"I doubt that Madeline wants to sit on a plane with me. I might as well walk into oncoming traffic blindfolded. Think I'll pass on that trip."

Joel recognized why his mother was reluctant. How could she not be? She and Madeline had been enemies for three decades. Had Joel not worked closely with Madeline and Don over the past few weeks and witnessed their sincerity, he would have taken the same guarded position as Sherry. "Mom, Madeline was serious about the offer. I can't tell you what to do, but this is good for our family. I'm going, and I hope you come along too."

"Maybe you're right. Madeline and I did have a few good chats here lately. Many years ago, before your father and I got married, I idolized her. You know, maybe a family vacation is exactly what we need."

"That's what I want to hear. If God is giving us a chance to reconcile and come together as a family, we have to take it. South Africa, here we come."

"Joel, I'm willing to go, but keep the God references to yourself. Let's keep this entire conversation very positive."

"All right," Joel said, but little did she know that he had no intention of keeping God to himself. With the DMI matter settled and Zarah doing better, Sherry's well-being was a key project on his list. He couldn't convince her of

God's role in their lives, but what Joel could do was pray constantly for her salvation. He felt very encouraged. If Madeline could change, then anyone could, especially his mother. "I'll call you later, Mom. I have a few more calls to make."

They exchanged loving goodbyes, and Joel was on to the next family member who could benefit from a dose of reconciliation. He dialed the phone number, eager to share his good news.

"Frank Mitchell here," the voice belted on the line.

"It's Joel."

"Well, if it isn't my wayward nephew. To what do I owe the pleasure of this call? Or do I have to ask?"

Joel had undertaken several ventures with his uncle. None of them had worked. Reflecting on this, Joel had realized that he shouldn't have expected any of his proposals to work. Each had been conceived in sheer desperation. When the DMI board had rejected the purchase of Harmonious Energy a year ago, Joel had refused to accept the decision. He had partnered with his uncle to secure untraceable funds and had made the purchase on his own. Despite having to put up a DMI division as collateral, Joel had proceeded with the undercover deal. He hated remembering just how badly the deal had failed. He ended up getting Harmonious Energy but lost the Southern division to a group of Uncle Frank's shady investors. Joel didn't reflect for long. Those days and those deals were behind him. This was a new day, and by God's grace, he didn't plan on squandering his opportunity again.

"I'm calling to share some good news," Joel said.

"Oh yeah? What's that?"

"Don is resigning, and I'm going to be CEO of DMI again."

"Oh, boy. Madeline must be spitting fire."

"Actually, she's the one who recommended me to the board."

"What! Pigs must be flying somewhere. I can't imagine the old girl getting soft." Uncle Frank let out a gigantic chuckle. Joel wasn't bothered. That was who his uncle was. Mostly, he was family.

"When do you step into the corner office?" Uncle Frank asked.

"In just over a week, right before I go to South Africa with Don. What are you doing this month?"

"Depends on who's asking."

"I'm asking you to jump on the plane and join the rest of us in South Africa for a Mitchell family vacation."

"Have you lost your mind? Isn't that about twenty or thirty hours in the air?"

"Around twenty."

"Shoot, there's no way in the world I'd be in the air for that many hours, especially with a bunch of folks sporting the last name Mitchell."

"Come on. Don't tell me you're scared of a little flight," Joel teased.

"The flight doesn't scare me. It's the thought of being stuck in the air with Madeline and your mother. That would drive a man to drink or to the grave, and I'm not in a hurry to do either. Nope, nephew. You can't pay me to get on that plane," he said, chuckling loudly. "Go on your trip, and tell that good-looking stepmother of yours I said hello."

"Ugh, Uncle Frank. Aren't you married?"

"For forty years, but I'm not blind. Madeline is a good-looking woman. That's the truth. She always has been. Dave hit the jackpot with her."

"Uncle, I have to go."

"All right. Well, give me a call once you move into the corner office. I'm sure you'll want to get a deal going."

"Nope. Those days are over. Never again."

"Never say never."

Uncle Frank didn't have to believe him. Joel would just have to show him.

"I like you, nephew. You got something special in you. For what it's worth, I wish you the best."

Joel thanked his uncle and sat in the car, in good spirits. His uncle hadn't changed. But God was moving in the family. Joel had witnessed Madeline's change of heart toward him, and his own toward Zarah. Uncle Frank might seem unreachable, but he hadn't wrestled with the Lord yet. Like his uncle had said, "Never say never."

The next call was much more difficult to make. To maintain his fresh outlook, certain doors had to be closed. That meant Sheba had to be removed from her pedestal, which he'd labeled SPECIAL FRIEND AND CONFIDANTE. Doing what was right wasn't simple. His relationship with her had a reserved place in his soul, and it was not easily removed. Yet there wasn't a choice. He couldn't genuinely get to know Zarah and tackle his personal problems head-on if there remained a secret escape door leading to Sheba. In an idyllic universe, his undefined relationship with a woman in Chicago could coexist with his marriage to a doting wife in Detroit. Reality quickly reminded him that he wasn't in an idyllic universe. He was on earth and couldn't split his affection fairly between the two women. He was torn up from actually thinking about letting Sheba go.

Joel didn't know what words would materialize when he actually made the call sometime over the next week. He knew only that he unpleasant task had to be done, just like many other tough decisions that would undoubtedly have to be made. With that in mind, he had to reach one more person in order to make his day of celebration complete. Instead of placing the call, he'd see Tamara in person.

Chapter 53

When Joel arrived at Don's building, he had a tough time getting past the guards. Instead of being irritated, he was pleased with the level of security Don had placed around Tamara. The truth was that she was safer in town. Home was Detroit. That was where the Mitchells' saga had begun and where it would most likely end. He patiently waited for the guards to let him go upstairs.

Finally, a gentleman in a suit and security patch on his left jacket pocket approached Joel. "I just got off the phone with Mr. Mitchell, and he's given his permission for you to go up."

Joel thanked the guy and took the elevator to the thirty-fourth floor. Before ringing the bell, Joel stood and soaked in the gravity of this moment. The last and only time he'd been to Don's place was memorable. He'd come here to hand the CEO position over to Don. That seemed like a hundred years ago. Joel also remembered the regret he'd experienced the day after. Giving up the CEO post had been the hardest, selfless, and dumbest decision he'd ever made. It had been a sobering reminder of his failure.

Standing in the same space, as a changed man, refreshed his spirit and bolstered his resolve. He rang the bell, excited about reaching out to Tamara. She needed a champion. He had one in the least likely person, Madeline. If God could use Madeline to bless him, He could certainly use Joel to help Tamara. He rang the bell again, confident that the Holy Spirit was standing there with him, ready to soften a heart that was ready to be touched.

Tamara opened the door after a short while. "Wasn't expecting to see you," she said, bracing her hand and her head against the door and gesturing for him to come in.

"I guess you've heard by now that I was appointed CEO," Joel said as he entered the condo.

"I hadn't, but I guess congratulations are in order," she said in a way that might be construed as a backhanded compliment.

Joel decided to take her well-wishes at face value and not read more into her comment. He was on a mission, and minor misunderstandings wouldn't derail him.

"I guess the best man won, huh?" She shut the door and leaned her back against it.

"I'm grateful for the opportunity. I know I have a lot to prove, and I'm willing to dig in and get the job done." Joel kept standing near the door, since she hadn't asked him to sit.

"Good for you. I hope it works out for you."

"So what's up with you? Last I heard, you were leaving town."

"I am."

"When and where?"

"I decided to stay until Remo goes to court, which should be soon. The prosecutor is pushing for a date in the next few weeks, and I can't wait to get out of here. Don't ask me where I'm going, because I don't know."

Joel grasped how critical it was for him to speak up. He didn't know what to say, so he prayed silently for the right words. "You know why I'm here?"

"Not really, unless it's to rub your victory in my face," she said, bending her knee and pressing her foot backward against the door.

"I'm definitely not here to gloat. Why would I? You're my sister. I came to make peace, not stir up trouble. Plus, I thought we'd made a connection after the Remo incident."

Tamara slid to the floor and sat with her legs outstretched. Joel didn't wait for an invitation. He plopped on the floor next her. For a second he thought fondly of Sheba. There had been countless occasions when she'd plopped down on the floor next to him in her Chicago penthouse to encourage Joel during his lowest points. He was honored to be in a position to pay the kindness forward.

Tamara shrugged. "I guess you're right. By the way, I didn't get a chance to thank you for helping me get away from that nutcase."

"No thanks needed. Like I said, you're my sister. I'm just happy it ended as well as it did."

"I have no idea how far he would have gone that day."

"Good thing we'll never have to know. You're safe here in Detroit, with us."

"Ah, not you too? Please don't tell me they have you singing the 'Best to stay with us' tune?"

Joel hunched his shoulders and grinned as he tried to find a more comfortable position on the floor. He stretched his arms out behind him and pressed his palms against the floor. "That's what family does. We look out for one another." The word *family* warmed his soul. He'd longed to have siblings who cared about him his entire life. He found the notion of acceptance almost dizzying. Tamara would benefit from the same sense of belonging. He wasn't giving up. He'd made Madeline a promise, and keeping her daughter in town would be repayment in full.

"You use the word *family* like it means something to the Mitchells," Tamara said.

"It does, which is why I'm asking you to come and work with me at DMI."

Tamara appeared startled. "What? You want me to be your flunky?"

"I specifically said to work *with* me, not *for* me."

"*Please.* You're the CEO. Everyone at DMI will be working for you."

"Not everyone," he said, laughing. "Madeline never will be called an employee."

"You have a point there." She joined him in his laughter and then abruptly stopped. "I'm glad you came by, but tell Mother that I'm still leaving. It's best for everyone. There have been a lot of problems since I came home. So let me get out of everyone's hair and start over somewhere."

"Tamara, you're not the source of all our problems. We had plenty of issues in the years before you returned. Every single person in this family has contributed equally. Sorry, but you can't get all the credit for this chaos we've constructed. Get in line if you want a slice of the blame."

"But it feels like I'm the problem. I honestly believe everyone will be better without me."

Joel's compassion kicked in. "That's not true. I want you to stay, and Zarah certainly wants you here. She needs you now more than ever due to the miscarriage. She loves you as a dear friend, and I get that."

Hearing his sincerity, Tamara was moved. Zarah had been the calm in the midst of a long and arduous storm. Maybe Joel had a valid point. She thought about her relationship with Zarah and how lonely it was on the run. True friends didn't leave in the middle of a crisis. They hung around and supported each other.

"I might consider staying a little longer than planned, just until Zarah recovers." She couldn't make any plans beyond a short extended stay.

"I'll take it. What about working with me at DMI? Are you up for it?"

She appeared doubtful, which meant he had to sweeten the offer.

"This request is as much personal as it is professional," he told her.

"How?"

"Because we can do this. We can work together for a common purpose and take Dad's company to the next level."

"Why should I trust you?"

"You shouldn't, not at first. But if we're willing to take a risk, this could be a happy ending for our family. Let's face it. Neither of us had a say about how we came into this world, but we can certainly take ownership of how we live going forward." Joel stood and shook his legs, which had been falling asleep on the floor.

"You sound serious."

"I *am* serious. I'm not wasting time any longer. I have a purpose to fulfill, and I'd love for you to join me on this mission," he said.

"I don't think so."

"All right. If you won't work with me, then what if I offer you the West Coast division?" Joel asked her and extended a hand to help her up, which she grabbed.

"Why would you do that?"

"It would keep you in the States. If I can't talk you out of leaving Detroit, I'd at least like to keep you in the United States." He was very much aware of how much she wanted the West Coast division. She'd clawed and scratched to buy the division from Zarah behind his back. Today he was offering it to her on a silver platter lined with fine linen. All Tamara had to do was say the word, and it was hers, with no questions asked. "Owning the West Coast division will keep you close enough."

She mulled over the idea and eventually responded, "Selling the division to me would be a bad move so early in your tenure. Remember, that's what got you ousted the last time."

He agreed. "But you're entitled to a relevant portion of DMI. It's your birthright, and I'll honor it. The board would have to give up on the notion of reuniting the division with DMI. It's yours if you want it."

She gritted her teeth and told him no. "I'll find another business opportunity."

"If you come to DMI with me, I promise to create a significant and highly visible role for you."

Tamara wasn't ready to trust, but it felt good that someone was approaching her about a legitimate role in the company. "I appreciate you making me this offer." It was nice being treated like an adult. That was what she'd wanted from Madeline all along. "I'm not going to say yes, but I'm not saying no, either." She wasn't going to make a hasty decision. Keeping her options open felt right.

"At least it's not a no. That will have to do for now."

"Give me a few weeks, until after this Remo stuff is over, and then I'll look at my options." Tamara allowed a smile to cross her face. "At least I'm staying a few extra weeks. And who knows? Weeks might turn into months."

"Or into years," Joel said jokingly.

"Let's not go that far," she said, letting a full grin shine through this time.

Joel lifted Tamara up and twirled her around. Shockingly, she didn't resist.

"Your mother and Don are going to be overjoyed." Joel was too. Don was leaving DMI in Joel's hands. Don was also leaving Joel with a love for the family and a desire to facilitate reconciliation. "Since you're in somewhat of a receptive mode, I'm going to strike while the iron is hot, or so they say. What about joining the family for Don's trip back to South Africa?"

"Uh-uh. That's going way too far. I need to take baby steps before leaping into a family soiree. Besides, I don't think my sanity would last on a flight with my mother. No way. Be happy with me hanging around here for a while. That's the most I can do right now."

"Done," he said. But he was already envisioning her on the plane.

Chapter 54

As Madeline's limo approached the Detroit Metropolitan Airport, she was submerged in mixed emotions. The past few weeks had been a roller-coaster ride. Joel had been appointed as CEO. They'd had a going away party for Abigail. Don had packed up, and shockingly, Tamara had returned to her marketing post at DMI. Of all the good things that had occurred recently, the best was having Tamara stay put. Joel had done the impossible: he'd convinced her daughter to stay and work with him at DMI. Miracles did happen.

Madeline sat in the backseat, reflecting on what today meant. She was thrilled to see Don so happy about returning to South Africa. He'd served DMI well. The company had been restored to a solid footing under his administration. Sales were up, and their restoration was intact. As much as she hated to see him go, Don had professed that this was his time to move on. She wholeheartedly believed that a mother's job was to support her children, even when it hurt. Her heart ached. Yet she was determined not to succumb to her desires and stand in his way.

Besides, she had other worries. Just because Tamara had agreed to stay in Detroit didn't lessen Madeline's concern. If history was an indication, her daughter could bolt at any minute. Despite the nagging need to worry about what Tamara was going to do, Madeline and the family were better off having her in town. Tamara was complicated, but Madeline wouldn't let that overshadow the love she had for her daughter. She desperately wanted her daughter to be happy.

Having Tamara close by was like being on a diet and eyeing a large slice of cake within arm's reach. So many times Madeline had wanted to grab her in the hallway and hug the pain from her. But she knew it was a dream. If nothing else, she'd learned not to push. When people were ready to make changes in their life, they'd make it happen. Nobody had the power to push them before the appointed time and get meaningful, sustainable results. She'd learned the hard way with Don and Joel, and even with herself. Most importantly, she'd learned. She guessed the saying was wrong. Turned out that an old dog could learn new tricks.

Her limo came to a stop. She mustered a smile, which wasn't too difficult to do given that her heartache kept giving way to elation. "Let's get this show on the road," she shouted as the driver assisted her from the car.

Don had been awaiting her arrival and eagerly kissed her on the cheek. "You can't possibly know how much this trip means to me. Having you come along is icing on the cake."

"Honestly, you didn't have to twist my arm too much. I was smitten with Cape Town when I visited you there a few years ago. Who knows? I might decide to spend a few extra months there and help you with LTI."

"You have an open invitation," he said, directing Madeline's driver to take her bags to the plane.

"On the other hand, maybe I'll hang around to support Joel in his transition phase. The board members approved him by a narrow margin, but they might not play nice if I'm out of town for an extended stay," Madeline said.

"You might have a point."

"Given what he's done for Tamara, I will do whatever it takes to support him. I owe him."

"He's owes you too; seems to me the support is mutual."

Madeline agreed. "This day would be perfect if we had Tamara with us, but I can't worry about what isn't." She grabbed Don's hand. "We're going to stay upbeat." Madeline shoved her disappointment to the recesses of her mind. This was Don's day, and she wasn't going to express sadness. He deserved her positive vibes and would have them.

Another vehicle pulled onto the tarmac. Shortly afterwards, Sherry and Zarah got out.

"Are we late?" Sherry asked.

"No, you're right on time," Don replied.

Madeline let her gaze wash over Sherry and was pleased. Normally, a mere look at Joel's mother sent her into fits. She would rather be dropped into a wasp's nest for twenty days than sit on a plane with Sherry for twenty seconds. But that was yesterday. This was a new day.

Madeline peered at the group of Mitchells gathering on the tarmac and breathed the fresh air. Maybe Don had been correct all along. Both hers and Sherry's children were grown. Both women had watched their children endure ups and downs. Dave was dead. There was no point in hating Sherry. The past was done. She felt light and reveled in the moment. She was only sixty-six. There was more life to be lived. She wasn't going to waste it by dwelling on infractions incurred thirty years ago.

"So, are you ready to sit on the plane for twenty some hours?" Madeline asked Sherry.

"I am, and thank you for inviting me."

"You should be thanking Don. This was his idea."

"Yeah, maybe, but we both know that if you didn't want me on this trip, I wouldn't be here," Sherry said.

Madeline blinked at her and grinned softly.

Sherry was pleased that she and Madeline were forging some kind of positive rapport. They'd fought for so many years, and she'd come to accept that there would always be tension between them until recently. Sherry had envied Madeline's relationship with Dave as far back as she could remember. She'd envied Madeline's strength. She'd envied her business aptitude. Madeline possessed what Sherry had longed to have before Dave died. Now that he was gone, she had to let go of her bitterness and be there for Joel. He needed a strong mother who didn't flinch in the face of fear.

"Look at you," Madeline said to Zarah, who was dressed in a bright red Indian outfit adorned with gold trim. She had at least twenty thin gold bracelets on each arm, and her exquisite veil matched her outfit. Her rich dark hair cascaded underneath the veil, which covered her head but not her olive-colored face. She was simply breathtaking. "I see why Joel is staying married to you. Smart man."

Zarah blushed.

"Where is that son of yours?" Madeline asked Sherry, glancing at her watch.

"We better get this show on the road if we're going to make the five o'clock departure," Don told everyone.

"Joel asked me to pick up Zarah. I guess he had to make another stop." Sherry peered at her watch too. "He should have been here by now," she said, not wanting to worry. "I'm sure he's on his way, but I'll give him a call."

"While we're waiting, let's get the bags on board, and I'll check in with the crew to make sure everything's set," Don said. He turned to walk away, and all of a sudden the bellowing sound of a horn came from around the corner.

Sherry was relieved to see the yellow Lamborghini buzzing toward the other cars.

Joel parked the car and got out. He went around to the passenger side and opened the door. Nobody got out until he extended his hand. Then Tamara appeared. Don's mouth flew open, along with everyone else's.

"Look who I found," Joel said.

After the initial shock, Zarah and Don ran to Tamara. They each hugged her in rapid succession. Madeline stood still. She wanted to grab her daughter and hold her tight. Fear said not to crowd her. It was unbelievable that Tamara was there. Madeline didn't want to be responsible for frightening her off. She'd restrain her tongue and let the events play out as they would.

Don sensed his mother's hesitation and went to her. He draped his arm over her shoulder. "Can't believe it's happening. The Mitchell family is in the same place at the same time, and there's no arguing. Only God could have orchestrated all the pieces that have plopped us here together."

Madeline nodded. "Hmm. You might have a point. Only God could bring this bunch together."

Zarah and Tamara were talking. Sherry and Joel were chatting. Madeline and Don strolled toward the plane.

"Mother," Tamara called out and approached Madeline.

Don tensed, not knowing what she was going to do. Then he relaxed and thanked God silently as Tamara embraced her mother quickly and then walked toward the plane.

Madeline wept. Sherry handed her a tissue as they hung back. Madeline grabbed it, and they both held the same tissue briefly for a few seconds, gently nodding in affirmation.

"This might be a bad sign if we're getting along. The world must be coming to an end," Madeline stated.

Don was pleased and grateful that God had allowed him to see the fruits of his labor. His sacrifice had been worth it. Reconciliation was in the air, and the aroma was sweet. He looked on as Madeline and Sherry followed their children toward the plane.

"I still can't believe we're all here," Sherry said, climbing the stairs.

Madeline and Sherry giggled. Don was right behind them and overheard the comment. He laughed too.

"It's unimaginable having this many Mitchells on board the same plane. Oh my goodness. With our luck, I hope it doesn't crash," Madeline said jovially and squeezed Sherry's hand as they boarded the plane together.

Don stood at the plane's entryway and absorbed the sweet scent of harmony. Armed with a newfound dose of forgiveness, the Mitchells were embarking on a fresh start. Don was excited about the possibilities. As long as God was in the picture, victory was theirs. As the plane's engine hummed, Don was reminded that victories came only from battles. He was certain there would be more to the Mitchell story, more disagreements, more heartache, and more challenges, but none that could destroy their ties. They were healthy and happy. He stepped onto the plane, peered into the majestic sky and whispered, "Thank you," to the God that he and his father served, the one of Abraham, Isaac, and Jacob.

"I think we're good to go," he told the captain.

"Looks like it's going to be smooth sailing," the captain stated.

"Good. It's well overdue for this family," Don said and took his seat. All was well, just as God intended.

Reading Guide

MAKES YOU GO "HMMM!"

Now that you have read *Unforgiving,* consider the following discussion questions.

1. Although he didn't love her, Joel initially decided to stay with Zarah because she was pregnant. Do you think that was the right decision? Why or why not?
2. Joel has established quite a track record, one lined with an abundance of successes and failures. He seems to be serious about restoring his relationship with God and turning away from his pursuit of power and fame. Do you believe his commitment to change is sincere?
3. At times, members of the Mitchell family are out of control. Based only on *Unforgiving,* which Mitchell would benefit the most from psychological therapy? Tamara, Madeline, Zarah, Sherry, or Joel?
4. Is Joel and Sheba's relationship finally over, or will he find a way to maintain their "unconventional friendship"? If you believe they're truly platonic friends, is it okay for them to stay in contact? Throughout the series, did you ever think that Joel and Sheba's relationship would get serious? Why or why not?

5. Who do you think will get married (in the church) first? Don or Joel? Why?

6. Is it realistic for Joel to believe that Zarah's love for him is so strong that she will truly be able to walk away from her religion and accept Christianity? How long will her conversion last?

7. Although intent on getting Joel appointed as CEO, Madeline actually had five options for filling the CEO position: herself, Abigail, Joel, Tamara, and outside candidates. Who was your choice to replace Don and why?

8. Who's your favorite character and why? (Note: base your answer on any title in the series.)

9. As the Mitchell family drama series winds down (or so we think), what do you believe is going to happen to each character? You probably have your own list of scenarios to ponder. If not, here are some questions to consider. Do you see Don actually getting married? Will the hold that the Mitchells have on Abigail draw her back to DMI? Will the company fall apart again under Joel's watch, and will Don be forced to come back yet again? Will Joel get involved with Uncle Frank's shady dealings when financial decisions don't go his way at DMI?

10. It's quite a feat to have the Mitchell clan on a twenty-hour flight together. Do you think they will still be thrilled and happy when they arrive in South Africa, or will old wounds cause someone to act out on the plane and plunge the trip into disaster?

11. Will Madeline or Sherry remarry? If so, to what kind of guy(s)?

12. Let's say the Mitchell family drama series is being made into a movie, and you are the casting director. Who would you select to play Madeline, Sherry, Don, Joel, Abigail, Zarah, and Tamara?

13. At the core of the Mitchell family's discord is an unwillingness to forgive. Regardless of how much money, power, and influence they possess, it doesn't help them fix their family issues. Don understands the freedom that comes from forgiveness early in the series. It looks like others have finally come around too. How about you? Is there anyone you are estranged from or have been unwilling to forgive? Forgiveness doesn't mean that you endorse their betrayal, hurtfulness, or violation. Forgiveness means that you are no longer willing to let that infraction provoke a negative reaction from you. Forgiveness is liberating, and it's the best gift you can give to yourself, as well as to someone else.

Note: The Mitchell family drama is loosely based on the story of a mighty biblical warrior, King David, who had God's unprecedented favor and a profound purpose. However, King David was also plagued with family problems, personal failures, and sinful mistakes. Because he was able to forgive himself and those who had wronged him as well as go the extra step of forgetting (letting go of) the pain, the anguish, and the bitterness associated with mistakes of the past, he was at peace regardless of what was going on around him.

Acknowledgments

God is good, and His mercy endures forever. I thank Him for the opportunity to write and touch the lives of so many wonderful readers. I sincerely hope you found *Unforgiving* and the entire Mitchell family drama series entertaining, funny, insightful, and thought provoking.

In addition to my readers, I must thank my beautiful, comical, and incredibly talented daughter, T.J.; Deacon Earl Rome, Jeraldine Glass, Bethany Tenner, Gracie Hill, Mom Dottie Fisher, and Frances Walker. Many thanks and much love to my dear friends, spiritual parents, church family, god sisters/brothers, goddaughters, and the rest of my loving family (Haley, Glass, Tennin, and Moorman). I also take this opportunity to honor the memories of my beloved Aunt Lela Haley Dockery, Uncle Jim Haley, Uncle Bill Walker, and Aunt Vera Ford in their recent passing. Love never dies.

Thank you to my Delta Sigma Theta Sorority sisters, especially my chapter, Schaumburg-Hoffman Estates (Illinois), Valley Forge alumnae (Pennsylvania), and my home church, World Overcomers-Encounters (Illinois) with Pastors Jim & Joni DePalma. Special thanks to my editor, Joylynn Ross; the Urban Christian team, Andrew Stuart, Shirley Brockenborough, Dale-Lee Shape; the ladies of Circle of Hope-Jones Memorial (Pennsylvania) and First African–Sharon Hill (Pennsylvania). I'm grateful to all readers. However, I must acknowledge my 90+ year old supporters who got caught up in the series and had very distinctive opinions about the characters: Dear Washington (IL), Ellen Wilson (OH), Ms. Christine Vailes (Mischelle's grandmother in D.C.), and Minnie Hamilton (IL). Much love to my prayer warriors, a long list of book clubs, media venues, booksellers, ministries, and Sirius Web Solutions.

There's no way I could list all my supporters by name. So, I will simply say thank you to everyone else who has helped me in this incredible literary journey. I pray that the Lord blesses each of you for your kindness and generosity.

P.S. Congratulations to my very special niece, Azhalaun Haley, on her high school graduation in Illinois. Enjoy your college years. May God's blessings and favor always be with you. Congrats to my oldest nephew, Fredrick Haley II on his graduation in Arkansas. Happy Birthday to my many loved ones in the 80 years old and over club: John (Emma) Foots, Sr., Don and Mary Bartel, Lorena Skelton, Uncle Charlie (Mary) Beasley, and Aunt Vernell Tennin. Much love and many blessings to Will, and my girl, Kimberla Lawson Roby, as they celebrate their 25th wedding anniversary. May you enjoy many more happy and healthy years together.

Author's Note

Dear Readers:

Thank you for reading *Unforgiving*. I hope you found this addition to the Mitchell family drama series as entertaining as *Anointed, Betrayed, Chosen, Destined, Broken,* and *Humbled*. Look for *Relentless,* the first installment in Redeemed, my exciting new faith-based drama series, and coauthored with the dynamic Gracie Hill.

I look forward to you joining my mailing list, dropping me a note, or posting a message on my Web site. You can also friend me on Facebook, at Patricia Haley-Glass, or *like* my Author Patricia Haley fan page.

As always, thank you for the support. Keep reading, and be blessed.

www.patriciahaley.com

UC HIS GLORY BOOK CLUB!

www.uchisglorybookclub.net

UC His Glory Book Club is the spirit-inspired brain-child of Joylynn Ross, an author and the acquisitions editor at Urban Christian, and Kendra Norman-Bellamy, an author for Urban Christian. It is an online book club that hosts authors of Urban Christian. We welcome as members all men and women who have a passion for reading Christian-based fiction.

UC His Glory Book Club pledges its commitment to providing support, positive feedback, encouragement, and a forum whereby members can openly discuss and review the literary works of Urban Christian authors.

There is no membership fee associated with UC His Glory Book Club; however, we do ask that you support the authors by purchasing their works, encouraging them, providing book reviews, and, of course, offering your prayers. We also ask that you respect our beliefs and follow the guidelines of the book club. We hope to receive your valuable input, your opinions, and reviews that build up, rather than tear down, our authors.

What We Believe:

—We believe that Jesus is the Christ, Son of the Living God.

—We believe that the Bible is the true, living Word of God.

—We believe that all Urban Christian authors should use their God-given writing ability to honor God and to share the message of the written word God has given to each of them uniquely.

—We believe in supporting Urban Christian authors in their literary endeavors by reading their titles, purchasing them, and sharing them with our online community.

—We believe that everything we do in our literary arena should be done in a manner that will lead to God being glorified and honored.

We look forward to online fellowship with you.

Please visit us often at www.uchisglorybookclub.net.

Many Blessings to You!

Shelia E. Lipsey,
President, UC His Glory Book Club

ORDER FORM
URBAN BOOKS, LLC
97 N18th Street
Wyandanch, NY 11798

Name (please print):_____

Address: _____

City/State: _____

Zip: _____

QTY	TITLES	PRICE

Shipping and handling: add $3.50 for 1st book, then $1.75 for each additional book.
Please send a check payable to:
        Urban Books, LLC
Please allow 4-6 weeks for delivery

ORDER FORM
URBAN BOOKS, LLC
97 N18th Street
Wyandanch, NY 11798

Name (please print):_____

Address: _____

City/State: _____

Zip: _____

QTY	TITLES	PRICE
	3:57 A.M Timing Is Everything	$14.95
	A Man's Worth	$14.95
	A Woman's Worth	$14.95
	Abundant Rain	$14.95
	After The Feeling	$14.95
	Amaryllis	$14.95
	Anointed	$14.95
	Battle of Jericho	$14.95
	Be Careful What You Pray For	$14.95
	Beautiful Ugly	$14.95
	Been There Prayed That:	$14.95
	Betrayed	$14.95

Shipping and handling-add $3.50 for 1st book, then $1.75 for each additional book.
Please send a check payable to:
Urban Books, LLC
Please allow 4-6 weeks for delivery

ORDER FORM
URBAN BOOKS, LLC
97 N18th Street
Wyandanch, NY 11798

Name(please print):_____

Address: _____

City/State: _____

Zip: _____

QTY	TITLES	PRICE
	By the Grace of God	$14.95
	Confessions Of A Preachers Wife	$14.95
	Dance Into Destiny	$14.95
	Deliver Me From My Enemies	$14.95
	Desperate Decisions	$14.95
	Divorcing the Devil	$14.95
	Faith	$14.95
	First Comes Love	$14.95
	Flaws and All	$14.95
	Forgiven	$14.95
	Former Rain	$14.95
	Humbled	$14.95

Shipping and handling-add $3.50 for 1st book, then $1.75 for each additional book.
Please send a check payable to:
Urban Books, LLC
Please allow 4-6 weeks for delivery

ORDER FORM
URBAN BOOKS, LLC
97 N18th Street
Wyandanch, NY 11798

Name (please print):_____

Address: _____

City/State: _____

Zip: _____

QTY	TITLES	PRICE
	From Sinner To Saint	$14.95
	From The Extreme	$14.95
	God Is In Love With You	$14.95
	God Speaks To Me	$14.95
	Grace And Mercy	$14.95
	Guilty Of Love	$14.95
	Happily Ever Now	$14.95
	Heaven Bound	$14.95
	His Grace His Mercy	$14.95
	His Woman His Wife His Widow	$14.95
	Illusions	$14.95
	In Green Pastures	$14.95

Shipping and handling-add $3.50 for 1st book, then $1.75 for each additional book.
Please send a check payable to:
    Urban Books, LLC
Please allow 4-6 weeks for delivery

ORDER FORM
URBAN BOOKS, LLC
97 N18th Street
Wyandanch, NY 11798

Name: (please print):_____

Address: _____

City/State: _____

Zip: _____

QTY	TITLES	PRICE
	Into Each Life	$14.95
	Keep Your enemies Closer	$14.95
	Keeping Misery Company	$14.95
	Latter Rain	$14.95
	Living Consequences	$14.95
	Living Right On Wrong Street	$14.95
	Losing It	$14.95
	Love Honor Stray	$14.95
	Marriage Mayhem	$14.95
	Me, Myself and Him	$14.95
	Murder Through The Grapevine	$14.95
	My Father's House	$14.95

Shipping and handling-add $3.50 for 1st book, then $1.75 for each additional book.

Please send a check payable to:

Urban Books, LLC

Please allow 4-6 weeks for delivery

ORDER FORM
URBAN BOOKS, LLC
97 N18th Street
Wyandanch, NY 11798

Name: (please print): _____

Address: _____

City/State: _____

Zip: _____

QTY	TITLES	PRICE
	My Mother's Child	$14.95
	My Son's Ex Wife	$14.95
	My Son's Wife	$14.95
	My Soul Cries Out	$14.95
	Not Guilty Of Love	$14.95
	Prodigal	$14.95
	Rain Storm	$14.95
	Relentless	$14.95
	Right Package, Wrong Baggage	$14.95
	Sacrifices of Joy	$14.95
	Secret Place	$14.95
	Without Faith	$14.95

Shipping and handling-add $3.50 for 1st book, then $1.75 for each additional book.

Please send a check payable to:

Urban Books, LLC

Please allow 4-6 weeks for delivery